STAIN

J.M. WALKER

ISBN: 978-1-989782-57-6

DEDICATION

To you.

ACKNOWLEDGEMENTS

I find acknowledgements are the hardest thing to write. Almost as hard as writing the blurb. I'm always afraid that I'll forget someone or a blog or an author…So many people have touched my heart through these past couple of years since I've been in this industry, I'll never be able to thank you enough. Whether you have read my books, liked my posts, shared my release…everything you have done for me means more than I can ever say. Don't think I don't notice. I see every like. Every comment. I read all of the reviews, good and bad. I pay attention. I try with everything in me to let you know that I am here and I do pay attention.

I know I'm still working my way through the book world, trying to figure out what's best for me and my books but I couldn't do it without any of you. I have the best team a girl could ask for and all I can do is thank you over and over.

I'm not an outgoing person, I am who I am and you take me accept me that way. THAT is all I can ask for. Even if you don't read my books, you support me in some way. You tell people about my writing, recommend my books maybe at a book club or a girl's night out. If you are reading this still, know that you have touched my heart in some way.

Everyone knows that I of course thank my family, friend, authors and bloggers. My husband who is my rock and has supported me immensely throughout this journey. But I know my hubby wouldn't want recognition. He's a behind the scene's kind of guy. He would want me to thank you.

Yes YOU.

Because of you, this book was born. Yes, I wrote it. I cried, bled and poured words onto the pages so you could be entertained. But if I didn't have you, the reader, soaking up these words, my characters wouldn't be able to tell their story. They don't just want to tell it to me. They want the whole world to know what they have gone through, what they are currently going through and how they are going to get out of it.

So with that being said and you have read this far, my dear sweet reader, I thank you. From the *very* bottom of my heart.

I would also like to throw some names out there who have helped make Stain so much better and have helped me grow as an author:

Jen Lum and Tammi Plummer

Angie Stanton

Wendi Lynn

I love you girls!! And I honestly couldn't have done this without your help and expertise.

Christine Stanley.

My poopy, my publicist and one of my favourite people in the whole entire world. Thank you for all that you do for me. I love your beautiful face!

J.M.

CHAPTER ONE

Asher

DEATH. IT WAS ALL I could smell. Putrid. Acidic. It took everything in me not to spew my lunch all over my boots. Bodies lined the walls. Guts spilled on the floor from where they hung from the rafters. Blood seeped into the cracks beneath them, disappearing into the ground much like the souls of its victims.

Women—all different shapes and sizes—filled my vision. The predators had started off young but now, they were going after all ages. Young. Old. It didn't fucking matter. Not to these sick fucks. They preyed on the weak. The lesser sex.

STAIN

Voices sounded in my head, urging me to move forward. The women, they needed to be saved. They had no one looking for them. I couldn't leave them behind. There was so much death; I could hardly breathe.

A heavy hand landed hard on my shoulder, forcing me to take a step back. Hot air coated my ear, the stale scent of liquor stinging my eyes.

"This is the result of our true desire," the voice purred in my ear. "Everyone has a dark sadistic side to them. Sometimes people allow it to come out and play; other times, they ignore it. I chose to embrace mine. There is no grey when it comes to our world. It's either black or white. Whether they explore it or not, is up to them."

My body vibrated, my heart echoing in my thoughts. Mustering up the courage to speak, I swallowed hard. Once. Twice. "Anything goes, I take it?" Relief flooded through me that my voice hadn't cracked. I wasn't scared of him but even I was man enough to admit that I was terrified of the situation at hand. If I found someone I knew in this shit, I would react first, think later. There would be no questions asked as to what I would do to him. To these men.

"Anything at all." Charles Brian walked further into the room of decay. The walls were stained with every form of liquid a body could release. "We leave these bodies in here for extra practice until the smell gets to be too much. And before you jump to conclusions, no, we do not fuck the dead. We're sadistic, but that's a line even we won't cross."

Yeah, because that should have made me feel better. It *should* have helped me undergo this mission with strength and confidence. But it didn't. Nothing did. Until the bastards were caught and put six feet below ground, nothing would ever be the same.

"You're a quiet one," Charles pointed out. "I like that. It leaves more to the imagination. But before I speak with the boss regarding your entry into the organization, you will need to tell me a bit about yourself."

Every time he turned his back to me, my fingers twitched. My palms became itchy with the need to wrap around his neck and squeeze. But instead, I ground out, "What would you like to know?"

"We need to know what you like." He winked. "The usual."

Everything in me said to hit him. To put an end to the meeting, head back to base and be done. "I like whatever you have available," I replied, regretting the words. Knowing that would lead Charles into a whole new territory of questioning, I braced myself for it.

"Ah. An open book," Charles clapped his hands together. "Perfect." He smirked, walking to the back of the large room. He didn't look over his shoulder to see if I was following—he knew I would.

My feet moved of their own accord, not giving me a chance to hesitate.

Charles Brian wasn't your typical bad guy. He was young. I would give him thirty, tops. The guy was Hollywood good looking. Blond and blue eyed. Well built. It would be easy for him to get his prey. Show them some attention from someone who wouldn't normally approach them and they went willingly. It wasn't their fault. These bastards preyed on the insecure. Charles was the epitome of evil. He played the good boy perfectly until he got you in his clutches. Then the true darkness would shine through.

STAIN

His eyes showed the truth. They were dark—soulless. I knew Charles was chosen to run the house because of his lack of remorse. But, he didn't know me. He didn't know that Vice-One had been watching him for months. Or that we knew how he worked. We could have caught him in the beginning, as soon as he had a girl at his side, kneeling on the ground with her head lowered. Blood and dirt marred her pale skin.

The image of her burned in my mind, seared there to remain forever.

Even though we had done everything to make sure Charles would never know that we were on to him, there was always that thought of *what if.* Maybe he did know. It was all a game. Cat vs. Mouse. Predator vs. Prey. But who was the captor, and who was the victim?

"How many girls do you have here?" I made sure not to seem nosy. Charles would become suspicious if I asked too many questions, but I needed to know how many females we had a chance of saving. If any at all.

"Why do you ask?"

He didn't answer right away. Why would he? "I need to know how many whores I have a chance of destroying." As soon as the words left my mouth, my stomach tightened. I might have had a poor excuse for a male role model growing up, but there was no way I could ever mistreat a woman. Now if they were into name calling in the bedroom, I would let the insults fly, but that was all on them. Consent at its finest.

"Good man." Charles pushed open the door. "Twenty-eight. But, of course, that number can change at any point." He winked.

"Of course." The man, if I could even call him that, disgusted me. I understood everyone had their own vice, their own kink, but Charles Brian was the worst kind. He got off on the weak. Forcing submission before the victims even had a chance to decipher between the two. Did they want to be submissive? Maybe they would grow up to be Dominant. Lawyers. Doctors. They could rule at work and submit in the bedroom. But it was ruined for them. Their right to choose was taken from them before they even had a chance to decide. The BDSM lifestyle would forever be engrained in their minds as something abusive and horrific when in reality it was a beautiful thing.

We walked into a second large room, and I never expected to see what I saw next. Women. All different ages. Bound and gagged. Blindfolded and chained. All of them were naked. Nothing was left to the imagination as their legs were spread apart for anyone's view. My heart thumped hard, my blood pounding in my ears until all I could focus on was killing the man standing a few feet away from me. But I didn't. For fear of ruining the whole operation, I stayed calm and silent. *Emotionless.*

"Ah, my favorite room." Charles walked up to a cage and banged on the metal bars. The girl didn't move. She kept her head down, remaining perfectly still. She was trained. Or, she was so far gone, she just didn't care anymore. Why fight against the devil knowing you would lose anyway? Most would be better off giving in. It would mean less pain for them. But scars would lay on them internally for the rest of their lives no matter how short lived it may be.

"These females are trained," I said, pointing out the obvious.

"Some of them." Charles grinned. "But most are so fucked up on drugs, you wouldn't know the difference."

"And the customers enjoy that? It would be like fucking a dead body." I held back the urge to console a small girl who was curled into a fetal position, tears streaming down her face. I stepped in front of the tiny cage she had been placed in, for fear Charles would see the utter defeat written all over her. Not sure what he would do, I shielded her from him for as long as possible.

"As long as their heart beats, it doesn't matter how coherent they are." Charles clapped his hands together. "Do you know why this room is connected to the other one?"

"No." *But I could take a guess.*

"So they know what happens to them if they step out of line." A dark shadow passed over his face. "We take them from their cage, lead them through the death, and they instantly submit. It's the perfect mind fuck."

I didn't say anything. I couldn't. No response could leave my lips that wouldn't get me into trouble and fuck up the whole operation. I had been undercover for a month, earning my way into Charles' house. I hated that part of my job, but I refused to sit behind a desk day in and day out. It wasn't how I was wired. I needed to be out in the field. Although Vice-One was military operated, I ventured out into the human trafficking field. SEALs had nothing to do with that shit, but when Angel approached me with the job offer, I couldn't say no.

"Anything here you like?" Charles asked, interrupting my thoughts.

Anything. Like those girls were fucking objects and not living human beings. I wanted to say no. The word was on the tip of my tongue, but it would throw

Charles off. It would make him second guess my intentions, and I didn't need that.

I made a point of glancing around the room, walking back and forth between the cages. They were looking down at their hands folded in their laps. Aside from being drugged, they were kept in good shape. Hair clean. Skin washed. Unless the men specifically asked for them to be dirty, they were otherwise well taken care of. If you could get past the idea of them being kidnapped.

"You look like you're searching for something," Charles sauntered from cage to cage before stopping at one holding a tiny frail body. The female was curled into a fetal position, her form still and unmoving. "Ah. I think we lost one." He tapped on the bar, a sly grin spreading on his face. "It's about time, you little—"

"No."

Charles gaze slid to mine, his eyebrow raising.

Clearing my throat, I tried again, "What I'm looking for isn't here. I'm not into fucking the dead." And I refused to allow him to speak ill of them as well. The poor thing was better off. My fingers tingled, itching to rip out his eyes so he never had to look at another innocent victim again. To tear him limb from limb, feeding his entrails to the pigs. The worthless piece of shit would meet the end of my knife, sooner rather than later.

"We don't like fucking the dead, either," he reminded me.

"But these girls are so far gone, you might as well be."

"Who do you have in mind?"

"I have someone." I was grasping at straws. Name after name bounced around in my head but I would never bring them into this hell. Except for one. She would want these fuckers dead as much as me, if not more. "Give me a week."

"One week." Charles scratched his jaw. "Fine. I'll make it a point to meet the toy of your choosing."

"Of course." I turned on my heel and left the confines of that room. Back through the stench of death and out into the fresh evening air.

I had one week.

Fuck. Me.

CHAPTER TWO

Meeka

"HARDER. THAT'S IT. HARDER!"

With all of the screaming, you would think I was having sex. But nope. Not me. Meeka Cline hadn't had sex in over a year. God, I was as dry as the desert heat.

"Harder, Meeka. Focus. Hit it like you hate it."

I glared at my sparring partner, hitting the punching bag with my closed fists. Brogan Tapp, one of my best friends, winked and continued barking orders.

"Meeka, you wanted to work out. This is your year. Blah blah fucking *blah*. Now, work it, girl."

"I hate you right now," I grumbled, jumping from foot to foot. Sweat dripped down the back of my spine, my muscles burning at the excessive use. It had been so long since I had any sort of workout. Stupid me decided to ask Brogan, the fittest woman I knew, to help me get in shape. I was regretting it at that very moment.

"You don't hate me," she corrected, holding the bag in her small but toned arms. "You hate that you are single and haven't been laid in months. You need a man. A *real* man. Not one that comes with batteries."

"I don't have that, either." Why would I? I lived at the club and the walls were paper thin. My sisters would hear everything and tease me about it. I was more confident than I let on but I didn't need the jokes or the reminders that I was lonely.

"Please. I hear the buzzing late at night and the soft moans." She grinned, shaking out her arms.

"You're fucking lying." I hit the bag hard, making it swing unexpectedly into Brogan's body.

She gasped at the sudden movement, falling back a step.

I laughed. "Never mess with a woman who hasn't seen a man naked in thirteen months, one week and three days."

"Now we're counting?" She hooked an arm around my shoulders, kissing my cheek.

"Yes." I had been counting every damn day since the last man who graced my presence, but having a guy as your best friend made it difficult to date.

"Stop counting and go find a nice fine piece of ass." Brogan opened the door, leading out into the hallway at the back the King's Harlots clubhouse.

"I don't want a one-night stand, bro," I complained, which was something I had done for months. I needed a man to own me. To take what he wanted from me and not give me what I craved until I begged for it. I had been so tired, I wanted to submit to that one person I could trust. Not overly into kink, I never embraced that lifestyle. I was ashamed to admit that the girls who disappeared had sparked something inside of me. It was sick and disgusting what those people did to them but the part that intrigued me was the ownership. I had often wondered if they were given to men or even women who took care of them. Maybe they didn't know what they were getting themselves into. Maybe they thought they would get someone who would submit or take control. Someone they could trust. I bit back a scoff. *Yeah. Right.* Those people were just as bad as the bastards who kidnapped their victims.

"You need to get out of your head." Brogan hugged me against her. "And a one night filled with hot sweaty sex won't hurt you."

But that was it. I wanted to hurt. I wanted to ache. Not the, *oh I need you* ache but the, *I can feel you for days* ache. I craved it. I needed it.

"I don't want just hot sweaty sex," I muttered.

Brogan started barking orders to the staff at the clubhouse of King's Harlots. With the president, Jay Gold, being away, she left Brogan in charge. She took that to heart. Good thing because then she didn't hear my complaining. Again. For what felt like the hundredth time.

I sighed, grabbed a bottle of water, and sat in one of the large booths.

"Hey, Hummingbird."

I looked up at my best friend approaching me. Asher Donovan was a tank of a man. Being 6'5" and over two-hundred-and-thirty pounds, no wonder I had been single for so long.

"Hey." I smiled at the childhood nickname he had given me. "What's up?"

He sat down beside me and handed me an envelope. "Before you read the letter, know that it isn't what I wanted."

"Cutting straight to the point, are we?" I teased, not liking the sound of hesitation in his voice. Asher had always been the go-getter. The one who kept me on my toes and my shit together. My parents may not have liked that I followed him to another town, but they understood. For the longest time, people thought I followed him because I was in love with the guy, but that was not the case. We worked well together. We knew each other better than anyone else. Yes, I loved him, but only as a brother.

"Shit needs to happen fast," he said, his voice lowering. "I don't want to bring you in on this, but you're the only one I can trust."

My heart sped up. "What's going on? I haven't seen you for a week and you're dropping this in my lap now?"

"Just read it, Meeka," he demanded, his words taking on an edge I had never heard directed at me before.

"Fine." I opened the letter, my eyes moving back and forth over the words. After each sentence, my palms became sweatier. A cold shiver raced down my back. Fear gripped my spine. "Did you write this?"

"No. The only person who knows what I'm trying to do, did."

"Who?"

"It doesn't matter." Asher tapped the table. "I need an answer."

"You can't expect me to drop everything and join you, Ash." I shook my head. "After last time, I stopped going undercover. I can't do it anymore. You know that."

"I know. But I trust you. Only you. I need your help." His jaw ticked. "Please."

"You can't throw the trust card at me." Shit. The guy knew how to fight dirty. Asher didn't trust anyone. He let on that he had it so easy growing up but living with a bastard of a step-father, his soul had been shattered more times than I could count.

"I need you, Hummingbird. Please."

He had been the only man ever to tell me he needed me. A man I loved but as a friend. Just my luck. "I can't." My stomach twisted, tying into tangled knots of anxiety.

"Fine." He got up from the table, turning back to face me. "I don't ask you for much."

"I can't do it," I mumbled, gripping the letter tight in my hands.

He nodded once, pausing briefly before making his way outside. The door slammed shut behind him, making my heart jump.

Asher was pissed, but there was nothing I could do about it. What he wanted from me was beyond normal. I would have to go undercover, live with him, and meet with these bastards who kept taking those girls. I didn't know much more than that. The letter gave little information, but I knew it would be a dangerous job. It was one reason why I gave up on becoming a police officer. I could have passed the academy. I was at the top of my class, but when Asher said he was moving because his base was relocating, I didn't even hesitate to go with him. What that meant, I wasn't sure. There had been rumors, but none of them were true.

"What's his problem?" Brogan slid into the booth beside me, handing me another bottle of water.

"Uh … who knows?" I had to try and figure out a way to make him happy. The guy was stubborn.

"Maybe *he* needs to get laid." Brogan waggled her eyebrows.

"Why are you doing that?"

"Because!" she cried. "*You* need to get laid. Asher needs to get laid. Put two and two together, girl."

"What!" I shrieked. "Are you fucking kidding me right now?" A bubble of laughter escaped me. "You think … Me … Him …" I doubled over, holding my stomach.

"Why is it funny? He's hot. You're hot." Brogan smacked me on the shoulder. "Stop laughing. I'm being serious."

And that made me laugh even harder. The thought of Asher and me together—oh, God, even I couldn't think of that without bursting into hysterics.

"What is so damn funny?" She shook me. "I'm being serious. Hasn't the thought ever crossed your mind?"

"No! Are you insane? He's my best friend. He's like a brother to me." Yeah, the guy was good looking, but I had never thought of him that way. He had women coming and going faster than I changed panties. The guy was a user. A player. Even if we weren't as close as we were, I would never think of him that way. He was not my type.

"A man and a woman can't have a platonic relationship." Brogan held up her hand when I went to argue. "I say by the end of the year, you two will be knocking boots and then some."

"Knocking boots? Who says that anymore?" I tried to ignore what she was predicting, but it made me wonder … I shook my head. *No. Not going to happen.*

"*I* say it." She fluffed her hair. "Now, go see what has his panties in a bunch." Brogan left me alone, greeting Maxine Stanton, the Vice-President of King's Harlots, before she made her way to the back. Probably to work out again. Brogan was a little tank, but I often wondered why she worked out so much. She never gave me a reason when I asked. All she ever said was that she wanted to be healthy. But everything in me told me it was something else.

"Checking out?" Max called from behind me.

"Yeah. I have to meet someone."

"Okay. Jay should be here soon," Max warned.

I swallowed hard. The president and I got off on the wrong foot, and I didn't know how to make it better. I joined the club because of Brogan. It showcased powerful and strong women, and I wanted to be a part of it. But when the president didn't trust you, you lived day to day on a very thin wire. Most people didn't think she would do anything to harm any of us—and she wouldn't, as long as we remained on her good side.

"You two need to talk," Max suggested. "Jay can be hard-headed, but she's softening up a bit now that she's with Angel."

"She's done talking to me." I shrugged. "I'm not going to force her to like me or to understand why I did what I did. It involved her sister. I should have told her." It was my fault Jay hated me. I got that. Angel wasn't a huge fan of Asher right at that moment, either.

"Give her time." Max gave me a quick hug, wincing.

"How's that baby of yours?" I leaned back, placing a hand over her small belly.

"Growing." She sighed, her eyes shining.

"Give him time," I said softly, referring to the man who had invaded her life months before.

She nodded, turning away from me but not before I saw her wipe a tear that slipped down her cheek.

My heart panged. The father of her baby, Dale Michaels, wanted nothing to do with them. From what I had heard, he had fallen into a darkness.

Partying. Drinking. Ladies.

It was horrible to see Max's heart break day after day.

Loud laughter sounded as the door swung open, revealing Jay and Angel. The boisterous sound simmered when Jay's gaze locked with mine.

"Hi," I said, my voice soft.

"Hi." Jay walked by me, pulling Angel along behind her. "We have a meeting at five." She turned back to me. "But you and I are meeting beforehand."

I nodded. "Okay."

Angel mumbled something in her ear.

She grinned, smacking him playfully on the arm.

He chuckled, wrapping his arm around her shoulders, and kissed her fully on the mouth.

My cheeks heated. Leaving the club before I intruded even more on their private moment, I headed to Asher's. Knowing he was going to be difficult as shit, I put on my big girl panties and walked the two blocks to his home.

CHAPTER THREE

Asher

MEEKA SAID NO.

I lifted the 250lb weight, shoving the barbell above my head. My muscles trembled. My arms shook. Sweat dripped down my face, droplets falling off of my chin. I should have given up. I should have dropped the weight so long ago but when I was pissed, I fought. It was how I had been trained. How I had been taught.

Charles Brian had called me personally when I left Meeka at the club. He wanted to see how my progress was going. The bastard had the nerve to laugh at me when I told him my *pet* was being difficult.

STAIN

The only way to get through to Meeka, to get her to understand that I needed her with me, would be to guilt her. It was my last resort. I had to play the card I didn't even want to think about.

"*Fuck.*" I dropped the weights, the crash vibrating down my spine.

The phone rang, interrupting my next self-inflicted torture. "What?"

"Status?"

I mentally counted to ten before I answered Angel. "Negative."

"She needs in. It's the only way."

After meeting up with Charles, I drove right over to Angel's and explained the situation. He had convinced Jay to give us some privacy, but with them living together, I didn't know how much was shared between them. "I'm trying."

"Try harder."

"But I—"

"There has been more information leaked on Charles Brian," Angel said, his voice rough. "We meet at King's Harlots Club House at five." And with that, he hung up.

He may have been in on the operation with me, but it still wasn't the same. The only way I could even begin to convince Charles to let me into the main house would be with having Meeka at my side. But I still wasn't sure if that would work. It was worth a shot, and I would die before I gave up.

Continuing with my workout, I tried to think of every possible scenario that would convince Meeka to join me.

A heavy knock sounded on my front door, jarring my thoughts, but I ignored it. Whoever it was could wait or come back later.

The knock sounded again. It became angry and forced. Heavy footsteps bound into my foyer.

"Next time, you should try locking the door if you don't want any company." Charles stood at the entrance way to my home gym with two larger men behind him.

"Most people wouldn't just barge in." I slammed a fist against the punching bag in front of me. "They would get the hint."

"They would. But if you don't already know, I'm not like most people." He smirked, crossing his arms under his chest.

"How did you find my address?" I wasn't surprised he had shown up. He gave me a week but I didn't take him for a patient guy. I knew he had been bluffing.

"You're seriously asking me that? You didn't hide yourself very well."

I wanted to, but Angel wouldn't have any of it. He wanted to make it easy for Charles and for us to get our hands on him. I didn't understand Angel's logic at times, but I knew he was desperate. I would be too if my girlfriend had been taken by those bastards and if those same bastards had taken her sister.

"Have you talked to your pet? I don't see her tied up anywhere. Or is it a male? Is he strapped to your bed maybe?"

My jaw tightened. "No. I appreciate both sexes, but men don't do it for me. My pet is occupied." My skin burned. Meeka was in no way my pet. Even if she agreed, she would fight me every step of the way. She may have been small and shy at times, but she was *not* submissive. Not from what I could make out, anyway. Although, at times I wondered. My dick jumped. Where the hell were these thoughts coming from?

Best friend, Asher. Remember that.

"Make her unoccupied." Charles leaned against the wall. "I want to meet her."

"You will." I went back to hitting and moving around the bag.

"No. I want to meet her now."

Well, that stopped me in my tracks. "She isn't here."

"Really?" Charles looked around the room. "I never would have guessed."

I bit back an eye roll.

"You will call her and get her here. If you have to drag her, tie her up, drug her … I do not fucking care. Just get her ass here."

I should listen to him. I should give in and force Meeka to help me. But she didn't owe me. If anything, I owed *her*. For my life. For my well-being. For my fucking sanity. She was the voice when I couldn't speak. The eyes when I couldn't see. I never told her any of that because I couldn't. Words didn't come easily to me and as much experience as I had being undercover, even I couldn't fake that.

Another knock sounded on the front door, softer this time. My stomach twisted into knots. Every inch of me told me that it was Meeka. Knowing her it was probably because of our earlier argument. She never liked leaving things open-ended with us. We were like brother and sister that way. Fight. Apologize. Move on.

"Ah." Charles clapped his hands together. "Could that be your little toy?"

I prayed it wasn't. *God Almighty, if anyone is listening. Please don't let it be her.*

"Asher?" Meeka's small voice sounded from the doorway.

Shit.

"Is that her?" Charles asked, grinning.

"Let me deal with her first," I ground out.

"Of course." He winked. "I wouldn't have it any other way."

Fucking fucker. I pushed past him and his goons, making my way to the door.

Meeka smiled, closing the distance between us. She wrapped her small arms around my middle, hugging me tight. "I'm sor—"

I gripped her hair, tugging her head back. Crashing my mouth to hers, I acted first.

Meeka gasped. She hesitated for a moment before opening up to me.

A slight shiver ran up my spine at the rough contact. "Trust me," I said against her mouth before deepening the kiss.

She moaned, sliding her tongue between my lips.

My cock twitched unexpectedly. *Best friend. Best friend.* Warnings sounded in my head but my body took over. I had no intentions of kissing her, but I needed Charles to see that I had control. That Meeka was my pet as he liked to call her. That she was in on this even though she hadn't agreed. Even if outside of this operation, she didn't cooperate, I, at least, needed to show him otherwise.

Before I could take the control further, Meeka broke the kiss and took a step back. Her cheeks flushed, her gaze dark and billowing with a lust I never thought I would see from her. Not over me, anyway.

"You need to tell me what that was for before I slap you." Her voice came out breathless, wavering with the uncertainty of whether she should like the kiss or not. I knew because I felt the same way.

I smiled at her sass. Playing into it a little more, I leaned down to her ear and tightened my hold on her hair. "Are you threatening me because you liked the kiss, Hummingbird? I thought for sure you would have pushed me away but your body melted into me."

"You took me by surprise," she said, her voice low.

"You need to trust me." I wanted to tease her but we needed to get Charles and his bastards out of there first.

"Of course I trust you. I just don't know why you kissed me."

"I'll explain later." I turned back to Charles, keeping Meeka safely behind me. I knew she would play along. It was the police training in her blood. Even though she never became an actual cop, she was good at everything she did. She worked hard and played even harder.

"Well, look at this little one." Charles clapped his hands together. "Do you have control on her yet, Ash?"

I gritted my teeth. "She is everything she's supposed to be."

"Vague answer." His brows narrowed. "Your lack of information is starting to piss me off. You come into my house, demand answers, and you won't give me anything in return. You won't even take the toys I have to offer and insist on bringing in your own. We don't work that way, but I have made an exception for you."

I opened my mouth to respond, but he only raised his hand, cutting me off.

"If she's not submitting like she should be by now, bring her ass in, and I'll break her into being nothing like she was before."

"You gave me a week. It hasn't been a week yet." I gripped Meeka's hand tight in mine, knowing she was itching to fight back.

"Maybe so, but I can still check in whenever I want."

"Send me to the person who runs the organization then if you're not happy with how I do things." For whatever reason, Vice-One hadn't been able to get any information except for what we found on Charles, and even then, it wasn't much. We should have brought Charles in, but Angel insisted I go undercover to get the info we needed to bring this system to justice. A part of me felt it wasn't even worth it, knowing they were probably dead.

Charles threw his head back and laughed. "Not going to happen. You know the rules." His gaze zeroed in on Meeka. "What is it, pet? You need a man to show you how to submit? Is Asher not doing it for you?"

Her back stiffened.

"I could break you." He licked his lips, letting his eyes roam down her body. "You're pretty athletic. I bet you'd put up one hell of a fight."

That's it. "What the hell do you want?" I snapped, forcing Meeka further behind me.

"There you are." He glared at me. "I want you and your toy at my place in two days. If she doesn't meet up to my standards, I am taking her off your hands. You got me?"

"Listen—"

"I said, do you got me?" he asked, slowly.

"Yes," I growled.

"Really?" Meeka gasped. "You can't be serious."

"Quiet." The situation could end deadly if she kept up with her outbursts.

"I will not stand here while you two talk about giving me away." She pulled from my grasp and placed her hands on her hips.

In a quick move, I fisted her hair, pulling her head back roughly. "You will do what I say," I growled in her ear. "If you want to make it out alive, you will do exactly what I tell you to do. You got me?"

She pushed me, glaring daggers between Charles and me. A tingle shot up my back. What I wouldn't give to have her over my knee and the feeling of her flesh burning beneath my palm.

"You need to tighten your leash," Charles teased. "Two days." He snapped his fingers and approached the door, his two goons following behind him.

I pulled Meeka out of their way, careful not to let them touch her.

Charles chuckled, his laughter fading when the door closed.

"Fuck." I let out a heavy sigh, pushing a hand through my hair.

"Asher Donovan," Meeka snapped, "tell me what the hell is going on. *Now*."

CHAPTER FOUR

Meeka

BESIDES THE FACT THAT Charles Brian scared the ever-living shit out of me, the new feelings tore through me over my best friend as well. Life was playing a trick on me because I knew there was no way Asher would just go ahead and give me to Charles. Who the hell does that?

I stood there with my hands on my hips, staring up at the eyes I had looked into since I was a child. Since we were in kindergarten together and all the way through high school. Asher didn't respond to my question. Why would he? There was only a monster who wanted to claim me as his own if Asher didn't train me accordingly. I felt like I had been sucked into a life that wasn't mine. My parents would lose their shit if they knew what I did to bring down those bastards. "Asher."

He moved to the couch, sitting down, and dropped his head in his hands. "Shit is getting out of hand," he mumbled.

"If you need my help, you need to give me more information." I sat beside him, touching his arm gently. "I need to know."

"I need to work out."

"No, tell me first. Something, at least," I insisted, sitting forward.

"What do you want me to say, Meeka?" His gaze hardened. "That I forced you into this shithole of a mess? That I have no idea what I'm fucking doing? That this isn't even my fucking job but Angel insists on me helping? That we're all so fucking desperate to bring down these bastards that we would do anything, no matter the cost?"

"Tell him you quit," I suggested, my heart thumping hard against my ribs. There had to be a reason why Angel would get Asher to go undercover. Something wasn't being said, but I wasn't sure how much information Asher could give out.

"It's not that easy. Angel is my brother. Whatever he needs, I am there."

"But you make it sound like you have no choice. Angel wouldn't do that to you." I didn't know Angel well, but I knew he cared about his brothers and would lay his life on the line to make sure they were protected and safe.

"I need to work out." He rose to his feet. "Are you coming?"

"I still don't know what's going on." I followed behind him as he led us to the gym at the back of his house. "How do you expect me to play along if I don't have any details?"

"You've done it before, Meeka. Look at what we both did with Violet." Rolling his shoulders, he hopped from foot to foot. Violet was Jay's twin and someone I wasn't allowed to see for fear it would be a trigger for her. Because of that, I would never forgive myself for using her the way we did. We brought down one of the corrupt men in the organization but losing a friend wasn't worth it.

"Yeah, and look what that almost cost us," I mumbled, holding the large punching bag in front of me.

"Everything worked out." Asher landed his fist against the bag, the sound reverberating through the room.

He made it sound so easy. Do something. Apologize. Move on. He wasn't stupid enough to believe life was like that, but there was no arguing with him when it came to Vice-One.

"Why are you undercover when SEALs deal with terrorists?"

Asher paused, his gaze sliding to mine. "We came across a bunker filled with females of all ages." His eyes flashed, falling back into his memory. "The smell ... So much death. It was putrid. It was something I never expected. None of us did. We had come across death before but," his face paled. "This was different. It made us keep going."

"And now?"

"I thought I would never smell it again." He cleared his throat. "Being undercover has nothing to do with me being a SEAL."

"You're right, because like you said, it's not your job. So why the hell is Angel making you do this? The FBI should be all over it. They have people for this type of job."

"Meeka, damn it," he snapped, punching the bag hard enough to push me back. "I don't want to talk about it."

"Well, I am *so* sorry," I rolled my eyes. "If you want my help, you will tell me. We can keep doing this song and dance shit but we both know that I'm going to win. Like I always do."

Our gazes locked, something switching between us. His chest heaved, his back stiffening. All I could think about was running my fingers over his smooth skin, feeling his muscles tighten and twitch beneath them.

I shook my head, ridding myself of that thought. *It is not the time, Meeka. Not the time at all to be thinking about your best friend and how good he would look writhing beneath you. Shit.*

"You need to get those thoughts out of your head, Meeka," Asher said roughly.

My cheeks burned. "I'm not thinking anything."

He grunted, hitting the bag once again. "I know when a woman is thinking dirty thoughts. Her eyes dilate. Her lips part. That dryness in your mouth? It's because you turned yourself on. As hot as the couple kisses we shared were, we have a job to do."

"You're so fucking sure of yourself, aren't you?" I bristled, scowling at the man who invaded my mind.

"I have every right to be sure of myself, Meeka. I know what your mouth tastes like." He shrugged. "Just wait until I taste your body."

Exasperated, I huffed. "Tell me what I have to do." I waved a hand in front of me. "What does Charles want?"

"He wants you perfect because I refuse to use one of his girls."

"Use one of his girls? For what?"

"You do know what he's involved in, right? What the operation is about?" Asher grabbed hold of the punching bag, staring at me intently.

"Human trafficking," I answered, my voice small.

He scoffed. "Trafficking women for sex, Meeka. They get kidnapped, drugged, and trained. They are then sold to anyone who is willing to spend the money so the females can live out their days serving their Master. Or until their Master gets bored and tosses them aside like shit."

"I …" I swallowed hard. "Oh, God."

"These men are so fucking vile God has given up on them." Asher paced back and forth in front of me, pushing his hand through his hair every so often.

"What am I supposed to do?" I shouldn't have asked the question. I didn't want to know the answer but I needed to find out. What my role was in the situation, how I could help my best friend bring down the bastards who had disrupted our small town. I needed to help Asher in any way I could, because as much as he had been trying to hide it, I could see something wasn't right with him after he came back from his last mission.

"Submit."

I nodded, lowering myself to the floor. Letting my head drop in my hands, I took deep cleansing breaths. Submit. *Ha. To whom?*

"Meeka," Asher said gently.

"Who am I submitting to?"

Thick fingers wrapped around my wrist, pulling my hands free from my face.

I glanced up, staring into Asher's eyes.

"Me."

A flush of heat washed over my body at the gruffness of that one word. Under normal circumstances, I probably would have laughed and teased him about it. I knew about kink. I'd read stories. Seen movies. But I didn't know the details. I wasn't naïve, but I also wasn't overly sexually experienced. It had been awhile. "How?"

His jaw ticked. "That's what we need to discuss."

"Tell me."

"Meeka." Asher rubbed his thumb over my pulse point in soothing circles.

"Please. I need to know. I want to help you, but I need you to be honest with me."

"Charles wants me to break you. That's what they do. They're drugged so they won't scream and fight back. Once the drugs wear off, pain is used to force them into submission. This lifestyle is sick and twisted, Meeka. They make BDSM sound like it's evil when it's really not. Bondage and submission can be a beautiful thing if it's consensual between all parties. But the organization is making up their own rules."

"People pay for this?" My heart raced, my palms becoming sweaty.

"Yes, Hummingbird. It's why we need to bring down these bastards. But until we can find out who and where the main hub is, there's shit we can do."

"And that's what you're doing?" I asked, even though I already knew the answer.

"Yeah. I'm so sorry for bringing you into it, but I don't trust anyone else." He glanced down at his hand in my lap.

"I know." I took a deep breath. "I'm pissed that you didn't come to me sooner. If you would have told me in the first place, it would have been less of a blow when you gave me that letter from Angel."

"How did you know it was from him?"

"I'm not stupid." I brushed my thumb over the tiny scars on his knuckles. "You also trained me, remember? I know you had no choice. Maybe I should be more upset, but we both know I can't stay mad at you."

A small smile tugged at his lips. "Probably doesn't help we both know each other so well, either."

I shrugged. Best friends turned lovers. It had happened, but could it happen to us? I wasn't sure, but if the kisses we shared were any indication, I was up for it.

"Let's continue working out before I lose my damn mind," Asher grumbled, rising to his full height. He went back to the punching bag. It was how he was wired. Whenever frustration settled in, he worked out. It had been like that for years.

I headed over to the treadmill. Running was my thing. No matter what happened in life, I always felt better after building up a good sweat. If that sweat could be from other things, it would be even more satisfying.

STAIN

While Asher lifted some weights, I pounded my feet into the mat of the treadmill. I couldn't help but wonder if he felt the same about those kisses. Did he kiss me because it was the only thing he could think of? Did he have the same reaction as me? God, I had never worried about that before. Even with the couple of guys I had been with, I didn't overly care if they were attracted to me. I could never understand why, but I just wasn't that into them. Maybe I was saving myself for that one, that special person who complemented me.

Suddenly, I felt a warm body behind me. A large hand reached in front of me, turning off the treadmill. I came to a stop, my heart racing hard against my ribs. My blood pounded, deafening me.

I didn't know what Asher's intentions were. But when his finger brushed down the side of my neck, a purr escaped my mouth. My body betrayed me. It was a small touch but it had been more than I had in months.

"You interrupted my run," I told Asher, gripping the sides of the machine.

"I did." The deep rumble of his voice washed over me, caressing my skin and squeezing my soul.

"Why?"

Asher spun me in his arms, curling his fist in my hair. "Because of this."

Before I could protest, his mouth came down on mine. I breathed him in, leaning into his touch. He tasted of mint, smelled of spice, and was hard as a rock. My senses became overloaded, and I couldn't help but kiss him back.

Asher curled his fist in my hair, pulling my head back to give him better access to my mouth. His tongue circled against mine. His free hand roamed down the side of my body before gripping my ass. He groaned, the sound rumbling from his broad chest.

The kiss deepened. Caging me in with his thick arms, Asher ground his pelvis into mine.

I gasped.

Lifting me in his arms, Asher wrapped my legs around his waist and pushed his hips into mine.

All I could do was hold onto him while he took control of my mouth and body. An ache formed between my legs, getting stronger as the kiss went on. He swallowed my sounds of pleasure, massaging his hands into the flesh of my body. Being held by him felt natural. Real. Needed. I couldn't help but give in.

Asher broke the kiss, his mouth trailing down the length of my jaw. A peck here. A nip there. With each touch, my heart jumped. Each breath, each moan, I opened myself to him.

"You are so fucking beautiful, Hummingbird," he purred against my skin.

"Asher," I moaned.

Shit. A moment of clarity struck me. "*No.*" I pushed him back, shoving out of his grip, and jumped off the treadmill. With a shaky hand, I brushed it through my hair, trying everything to compose myself. "We can't." As much as I wanted to continue—God did I ever want to continue—I couldn't. *We* couldn't. It wasn't right. We were best friends. It was a heat of the moment situation. He only kissed me to prove a point to Charles.

Hello, Meeka. He kissed you again, didn't he?

I shook myself. "I can't."

"And why not?" he asked, casually leaning against the treadmill with his arms crossed.

"We're best friends. It's not right."

"You say that, but yet you keep kissing me back."

He stood a foot away from me, but I could still feel him. His hard waist grounding into mine. His length pulsing against my inner thigh. Asher knew I had felt him. Growing. Heating with a fire that could no doubt make me burn with desire. But for him? Those feelings and thoughts were new and overwhelming, hitting me all at once. He must have been battling the same conflict by the look of sheer hunger in his bright-blue eyes. No one had ever looked at me that way. No one had ever kissed me like that. Asher knew I wasn't overly experienced after many drunken nights of me complaining about the lack of men lining up at my doorstep.

"Why do you keep doing that?" I asked, needing to break the unnerving silence between us.

"Doing what?"

"Kissing me."

"Are you complaining, Hummingbird?" He grinned, his gaze twinkling.

"I want to know what's going on." I took a step back until I hit the wall. With nowhere to run, I lifted my chin and stood my ground.

"I'll tell you when you answer my question, Meeka." He closed the distance between us, placing both hands on either side of my head. He caged me in, his big body towering over my tiny frame but I didn't feel small. No. With Asher, I felt like a woman who had been opened up to new possibilities. New control. He made me feel powerful even before we ever shared that first kiss.

"Meeka." He licked his lips.

My chest heaved, my nipples hardening at the husky use of my name. "Asher."

He leaned down, his mouth brushing over mine. It was so soft, a spark cracked. "I'm going to kiss you again. And you're not going to complain, are you?"

I shook my head so slowly I wasn't sure if it had moved or not.

"Words," he demanded, his voice rough. "I need your words."

Knowing what we were doing was new for both of us, I appreciated his holding back. But I found that I wanted to venture on that new journey with him. Even if it was just a kiss. I wanted my mouth to be owned by his lips. I wanted him to show me, teach me what it was like to truly be kissed by the person you trusted most in the world. My breath caught.

Fuck it. "Kiss me."

"Fucking a." His mouth crushed mine, moving fluidly and slow. Oh, so achingly slow.

I itched to touch him, but my hands stayed at my side.

Like I had hoped, he controlled me with just a kiss.

His tongue slid between my lips, dancing a path of pure lust and passion with mine.

The kiss was nothing like the previous ones. It was desperate. It hinted with a greater pleasure neither of us had ever experienced. It promised ecstasy.

I moaned, silently begging for more.

Asher repeated his movements every so often, causing more sounds of pleasure to leave my mouth.

I realized he did it when he wanted my moans. My purrs. The desire he built in me to grace his ears. They all belonged to him.

All too soon, he broke the kiss.

Our chests rose and fell with ragged breath.

His eyes glowed, searing into my heart. "Is that the kiss you were hoping for?" His voice came out gravelly. "Because, baby, I'd be happy to do it again."

I stepped underneath his arm, walking away from his passionate stare. I needed … I wasn't even sure, but those kisses … God, could he ever kiss. They were so damn good, they messed with my head.

"We … That …" I stuttered, brushing a shaky hand down my face. "We can't do that again." I kept repeating that statement but even I started not to believe it.

"And why not? Those moans leaving your mouth were not because you didn't like it, Meeka."

"We're best friends." I turned to him. "Our heads are not in the right place."

"Oh, I can tell you that my head is in the perfect place. But I do know of an even better spot." His eyes roamed down the length of my body. "You can deny it all you want, but I know you enjoyed that kiss and I also know, you want more."

"Asher." My cheeks burned.

"What, Meeka? Did you not like my tongue fucking your mouth? Because I am up for a do over."

"I …"

"Tell me, Hummingbird." He closed the distance between us and cupped my chin. "Are you up for a do over?"

"Yes," I responded without even hesitating.

He smirked. "Good." He kissed me hard on the mouth. "Because I am going to have the greatest enjoyment pleasing my body with yours."

CHAPTER FIVE

Asher

MOANS. PURRS. LITTLE WHIMPERS that were all meant for me. When my tongue slid into Meeka's mouth, it teased and caressed. It showed her who was in control. I demanded her pleasure when I deemed it necessary. I took her desire by the reins and gave her a hint of what I was capable of. But I knew it wouldn't last long. She may have pleaded for me to kiss her back, but she was stuck on the fact that we were best friends. Either way, I would fuck her. Eventually. I understood her hesitation but after the unexpected first kiss we shared, all bets were off. I wanted her. I had wanted her for years, but she didn't know that. I was too much of a fucking pussy to tell her. Every time I saw her with another guy, I would head to the gym. She was the main reason I had worked out so hard. Among other things.

Fisting her thick hair in my hand, I pulled her head back. It gave me better access to her mouth and while I swallowed her moans, I grazed my free hand down her side. Her sexy as sin curves made me harder. My cock threatened to explode in my pants if I didn't get inside her soon.

"Please," she muttered against my mouth.

I broke the kiss, mentally counting to ten before I spoke again. The woman was going to be the death of my dick. "Do you have any idea what you do to me?"

Meeka inhaled a sharp breath, her rosy cheeks reddening even more.

Someone was being shy. Well, she wouldn't be once I got through with her.

"No answer?" I grabbed her hand. "Fine, I'll show you." And placed it on the erection I sported in my pants.

Her eyes widened, her mouth forming an O.

That got her attention. "Do you feel—"

I was never expecting her hand to grip, to squeeze until a shiver shot straight up my back.

"*Fuck*," I groaned, leaning my forehead against hers.

"Do I feel how hard you are?" she whispered, rubbing me over my pants. "Yes, I do. I can feel you growing under my touch."

My breath came out in short gasps. I always found hand jobs boring, but with Meeka … Fuck me, she could rub one out anytime and I would beg at her feet like a fucking dog.

"Asher," she breathed, reaching into my pants with her other hand.

When her fingers came into contact with my dick, I jumped, letting out a hiss.

Whatever took over Meeka's actions, I wasn't sure. "Meeka, what … I thought … *Fuck.*"

"I wanted to touch you." She chewed her bottom lip, and it was the sexiest thing I had ever seen. The innocence, the timid shy girl staring up at me, begged for me to take over. To bring her to that precipice of pleasure she knew I could give her. But right then, I just wanted her to pull the desire from me. No fucking. No kissing. Just her hands.

"You feel … Your hands …" I stammered. I actually fucking stammered. This woman did that to me. She made me feel like a fucking virgin all over again who had no idea what the hell he was doing. My balls tightened. Her hands sped up. I was going to blow, and I didn't care that it had only been a couple of minutes. I knew without a doubt that it would be the best orgasm I ever had, and for that, I would never be ashamed to come so fast.

Not realizing I had closed my eyes, my gaze zeroed in on the face that was tugging the ecstasy straight from my body.

A moment of hesitation fluttered in the depths of her stare. She kept working my cock but something switched.

I grabbed her hands, pulling them free from my pants.

"What are you doing?" Meeka reached for my waist, but I stopped her.

"No." I would regret it. "I'm not having you give me a hand job because you feel like you have to."

"I don't …" She sighed.

"As much as I know I would enjoy it, I would rather have blue balls then make you feel fucking uncomfortable." I pinched her chin, forcing her to look up at me. "Why did you touch me when you have only pushed me away this whole time?"

"I thought …" Her shoulders slumped. "I'm not used to this."

"What?"

"This thing between us. Even with the other guys I've been with, this—" she waved a hand in front of her "—never happened."

My chest tightened. Ignoring the flutter of jealousy, I took a breath. "What do you mean?"

"I've always thought you were hot." Meeka blushed. "But I never allowed myself be attracted to you because I knew we were friends. But when you kissed me, everything seemed to shift."

I knew exactly how she felt but whatever was changing was still new. Settling down went against everything I believed in. I didn't deserve to be happy.

"I just don't want whatever happens to ruin our friendship," she continued, grazing her fingers down my stomach. "I know how you are."

What could I say? I had a history. A reputation of sorts. Was I proud of it? No. But having a shitty start to my life, I relied on the only thing that made me feel good. Sex. And lots of it.

"I don't need my lifestyle brought up," I said, a little more harshly then I had intended. Although I lived the life, I didn't want to be reminded of it daily. I was an asshole, and I treated the women I had been with like shit but they never said no. They begged for it.

Consent was key in everything I did and with everyone I had been with.

Meeka's back stiffened.

Way to ruin the mood, Asher. I was such a fuckwit.

"Tell me what's going on," she demanded.

And we're back to that again. I sighed. "You already know what's going on."

"Not completely."

"After we found Violet, even though Angel was pissed, he wanted me to continue looking. To do that, I had to get inside Charles Brian's home." If it was even his home. Who the hell knew anymore? All I knew was that there was a main hub we had to get into. If we could get there, we would find the ring leader, the Master, the darkness that started the whole operation. But no matter what we did, Vice-One could not find out any information about this person. From what we knew, the local police service and the FBI had a difficult time as well. But we all knew the Feds would keep their shit to themselves.

"So you got in and now he wants to meet with us both," Meeka stated.

It wasn't a question but I nodded anyway. My stomach twisted over the fact I had forced it on her.

"Fine." She pushed away from the wall, forcing me to take a step back. "Train me."

"We have less than two days," I told her.

"So? Train me as much as you can. After we meet with him, you can train me some more." Her mouth set in a firm line, her hands on her hips, and she was ready for business.

But I wasn't. I didn't want to train her. Not for Charles. Not for anyone else. For me? Fucking right I did. And I would. But I would have to get my cock out of the game and think clearly. Our lives and the lives of these girls depended on it.

Taking a breath, I crossed my arms under my chest and pulled the Dominant side from deep within. "Charles will want to make sure you can submit. You don't speak. You don't move. You don't do anything unless otherwise directed. You don't even ask why. And if it's something you don't like or want to do, you do it anyway."

I paused, expecting Meeka to argue. Instead, her gaze locked with mine. That was when she meant business. She had been undercover before when the FBI recruited her because of her size. She was small, tiny in comparison to the average woman. But her size meant nothing when it came to her strength.

She lifted an eyebrow, waiting.

Clearing my throat, I continued, "Forget everything you've learned while being undercover before. These men are nothing like what you've seen. They treat women, little girls, like the piece of shit on the bottom of their shoe. They have no problems hitting, cutting, slicing your mere soul into tiny pieces." I didn't want to scare her, but she needed to know exactly who we were dealing with. On the other hand, even I wasn't sure how far they would go to get what they wanted. "They will expect you to do as I say."

"What if I don't? What happens if I don't follow the rules?"

"Do you want to make this any more difficult than it has to be, Meeka?" She opened her mouth to speak but I only continued on my tirade. I could feel the anger bubbling up from my stomach, threatening to explode out of every single pore. "Do not underestimate these men. They have no fucking problems removing you from the situation if they don't like what they're getting out of you. I'm only one person. I can't take all of them on. I can't protect you against a dozen men." It could have been more but I only counted twelve on the way into Charles' place. If they were anything like my brother, Coby, the others would have been hiding.

"Are you trying to scare me?" Meeka's voice wavered. "Please tell me that."

"I wish I could." I stood a foot away from her, careful to keep my distance for fear of losing every inkling of control I had left. "I wish I could say that the females taken are treated well. Yes, they were clean when I saw them, but that was only after they broke."

"What happened *before* they broke?"

"You … uh …"

"Just tell me. You know I've seen shit. I need to know."

"I walked through a room filled with death before getting to the holding area. The ones who behaved would have to see the brutal horror every time they were taken from their cages. It reminded them to do as they were told." Memories of that room resurfaced, poking at my brain until it was all I could see.

"Oh, God." Meeka shook her head. "I can't."

That snapped me out of my nightmare. "Yes, you can. You have to."

"Why?"

"Because Charles saw you. We've been over it. If you don't come with me, he'll have his men hunt you down. You won't have to worry about impressing your sisters because they would never see you again."

The color drained from Meeka's face, her breath coming out in short gasps of air.

Moving quick, I helped her to a sitting position before she passed out and hurt herself.

I never meant to scare her. I didn't want to put that fear into her. But I needed to remind her what those men could do if she didn't do as I said. She needed to know. She needed to understand that it wasn't a game. It wouldn't be like the other undercover jobs she had been on. No. It would be worse. These bastards treated women as the lesser sex. They had no value in life. They were born to please a man and that was it. It was vile and corrupt, disgusting and cruel. I was guilty of using women in the past, but I would never take from a woman what she didn't offer.

"Asher," Meeka's shaky voice pulled me from my thoughts.

"Shh." I rubbed her back. "Breathe, Hummingbird."

"How am I going to succeed? What if I screw up?" She glanced up at me, her eyes rimming over with tears. "I'm not strong enough."

"Fuck that," I snapped. "You *are* strong."

She rolled her eyes.

My back stiffened, a hot tingle piercing my chest. Pinching her chin, I forced her to look at me. "Do not roll your eyes at me." I didn't want to be mean but I needed to show her that without her, I wouldn't be where I was today. I wouldn't be…free. "You need to understand something. You are strong. You helped me at the hardest time of my life. I would go to war and back if I didn't have to relive my fucking nightmare every damn night. You saved me from my step-father." I didn't want to drudge up the past because I knew it would ruin me later but Meeka needed to hear these words. I also needed to thank her but I couldn't form the proper sentence so instead, I sat there like a dumbass. I had never been good with words, and the silence that wore on proved how much I hated talking.

"I didn't do anything." She sniffed. "I'm not that strong."

I wasn't going to argue because at that moment, I had no idea what else to say.

"But I will do this for you. For those who couldn't. For Jay and her sister." Something flashed behind her eyes.

Jay had been taken months before by Eric Vega, our fucking boss. The bastard didn't own up to his mistakes and blew his head off instead. Because of that, Vice-One had never been the same. Jay became a recluse and moved in with Angel while Violet stayed at her old apartment. I could go on and on but this shit needed to get fixed. I had a feeling that it would take some time for all of it to get resolved.

"We will do this together," I said. "Side by side."

"What if something happens? What if—"

I shut her up with a kiss. I needed to think fast before she lost it and had a full-on panic attack. The touch was gentle. Although I liked it rough, I had to show Meeka that there were many different sides to me. Why I felt that way, I couldn't quite figure out. Instead, I allowed my lips to graze hers in a plea of acceptance.

When Meeka sighed into my mouth, all bets were off. Her hands wrapped around my neck, pulling me closer. The kiss deepened. Sounds stirred. My cock hardened. God, she was delicious, and it took everything in me not to throw her back onto the mat and taste the rest of her body.

***

STAIN

(Meeka)

The kiss was sweet, but it wasn't what I wanted. At first, I embraced it, kissing Asher back gently. But I needed more. With my arms around his thick neck, I moved myself into his lap. The hard length in his pants pushed against my inner thigh, giving me the courage to take control. To show him what I craved and needed.

Asher groaned, his hands slipping to my rear. His fingers massaged and kneaded, digging into my flesh. When our hips came into contact, I gasped.

"Fuck, Meeka," he said roughly.

"I-I want …" I didn't even know what I wanted but I knew I needed something more. Something more than just a kiss. A touch here. A touch there. I wanted to feel his passionate wrath. If he fucked like he kissed, I wanted to experience all of it. Every side of him. Every inch. Every hard muscle as he took me to new heights of pleasure and ecstasy.

"What do you want, baby?" He cupped my nape, pulling my head back.

"I …" I licked my lips, taking deep breaths. "I want you."

"Fucking a." His mouth crashed to mine. Lifting me in his strong arms, he carried me to the living room and placed me on the couch.

Wrapping my legs around his waist, I lifted my hips. Hinting, showing, letting him know that I needed him in ways I knew only he could provide. Never in my life had I experienced that kind of wanting need for another human being. I wasn't even sure it existed until then. But with Asher's big body between my legs, his demanding mouth on mine, I couldn't do anything but give in.

My hands trailed down his back, fisting his shirt, and I lifted it over his head.

Asher broke the kiss, throwing the offensive fabric on the floor. His eyes were dark. Hungry. They burned into my skin, making my body ache even more.

With trembling fingers, I unzipped my hoodie, revealing a white lace bra.

His tongue peeked out, licking over his bottom lip. He watched me undress for him, giving me the control for just a moment.

I shimmied out of the hoodie and threw it behind me.

Our gazes locked. Our breathing became ragged. Our friendship would finally take a different path. Already I had touched him. His length. How hard he could become for me. It was a brave moment. When he accused me of giving him a hand job because I felt I had to, I realized he had been right. I thought it would make sense. But now, I was doing it because I wanted to.

Asher grazed the back of his knuckles down the center of my chest before unclasping my bra with a flick of his wrist.

My nipples hardened in the cool air, sharpening to peaks.

He pushed the straps off my shoulders, letting his fingers brush over my pale skin.

Watching him look at me was fascinating. He stared with those bright blue eyes of his, burning a hole straight to the center of my being.

I wanted the next couple of moments to be fast and hard but I couldn't get over how his eyes followed the movements of his hands. His fingers trailed down my sides, forcing my skin to erupt in tiny bumps.

Arching beneath him, I felt the need to show him that I was into it just as much as he was. "Kiss me," I panted.

A small smirk spread on his face. Lowering his head, his mouth closed around a budding nipple. The growl that left his chest rumbled through my body.

I moaned, curling my fingers in his hair.

"So fucking sweet," he mumbled against my skin.

"Please," I begged. I actually begged. It wasn't something I did. Not that I had much experience with guys making me wanton with need. Never in my life would I imagine lying there with him. Oh, God. My stomach tightened.

"Hey, Hummingbird," Asher brushed a finger down the length of my jaw. "We can stop."

"No." I grabbed his face and kissed him. Hard. Screw slow. I wanted him now. I wanted him fast. I needed him … rough.

Asher growled. He actually growled. I didn't even know men could do that in real life.

"Get out of your head, Meeka," he demanded, pushing his hips into mine. "If you want me, prove it."

Holy balls on a cracker. What was I getting myself into?

CHAPTER SIX

Meeka

HE GROANED. HIS BODY was hard. He kissed me like I was the only thing he needed. I made him feel good. Me. Meeka Cline. A small town girl with big dreams. When he told me to prove how much I wanted him, I pushed him back and quickly took off my pants. As I was rising back up, he took hold of me backing us up until we hit the couch. I straddled him, gasping at the feel of his length rubbing at my core.

"Fuck, baby." His hand gripped my ass, moving me in a back and forth motion over his clothed erection.

I whimpered, a spark of desire exploding through me.

"Show me what you want."

Sliding my body up and down his pelvis, his cock brushed over my clit at the perfect spot. "Oh." I shivered, my hips circling against him.

"That's it," he coaxed, helping me ride out the waves of pleasure.

I jumped when his arm reached around my body and his fingers came into contact with my soaked panties.

"Soaked for me, Hummingbird?" Sliding a finger beneath the fabric, his knuckle brushed over my pussy.

"Please," I breathed, needing him to take it further.

He grinned. With his free hand, he cupped my nape and deepened the kiss. At the same time, his finger thrust into my body.

I moaned, shaking against him, and moved my hips in tune with his fingers.

He swallowed my cries, pumping hard and fast.

"Oh. Oh. God." I shook, not expecting to feel so good from just his finger.

He broke the kiss, staring intently into my eyes. "I want your orgasm. You're going to give it to me, aren't you?"

I swallowed hard. "Y-yes. Oh, please yes."

"Good girl."

The feel of him inside me only heightened the fact that I wanted to experience all of him. Every inch. Every muscle. Every movement down to his soul. I rotated my hips against his, rubbing myself up and down the length of his cock. He was still wearing his sweatpants, but the roughness from the fabric sparked a tingle throughout my body.

I broke, coming apart in his arms. He held me while I exploded with pleasure. My body tingled. Every nerve ending came alive with ecstasy. I felt him everywhere. All over me. Inside of me. Deep down into my soul. So much pleasure came from the mere touch of his hands. The moment we went further, I would surely combust.

In a quick move, Asher had me beneath him, his fingers still inside my body.

I groaned, arching under him. I hinted. Begged. I didn't care that we were best friends. I needed him in ways I never needed someone before. I needed him to show me how it felt to truly be alive. To feel every inch of my skin being touched.

"Tell me." Asher kissed up the side of my neck, circling his hips into mine.

"More. Please more."

Releasing me, he reached into his pocket and pulled out a condom.

My heart raced. With some maneuvering, I lowered my panties and kicked them off with my foot.

"Beautiful. Absolutely. Fucking. Beautiful." Asher pulled himself free of his pants, wrapping his hand around his thick length.

My breath caught in my throat. He was huge. The biggest I had ever seen. My mouth watered at the mere sight of him.

Sliding the condom down his hard cock, his gaze met mine. He paused, waiting.

That was my last chance. There was no going back, and I didn't want to.

At that moment, the phone rang.

"Fuck me," Asher snarled. Reaching for his phone, he checked the display and threw it back on the table.

"Don't you need to get that?" I asked, squirming under him.

"Nope." His mouth crashed to mine, ignoring the incessant ringing.

"It could be important," I said between kisses.

"Fuck them." Asher pressed the tip of his length against my opening just as a voice rang out around the room.

"Asher, answer your damn phone, fucker," Angel's deep voice boomed from the answering machine.

"*Shit.*"

I shivered. "It's fine." I pushed Asher back, pulling a blanket off the back of the couch to cover myself. "Answer the phone."

Asher grumbled, removing the condom, and righted his pants. "It better be important," he said, calling Angel back.

We both knew it was. Angel wasn't the type of man to just call out of nowhere.

"Hey, man," Asher greeted. "I was," he glanced at me. "Occupied."

My cheeks burned, the corners of my lips tugging into a tiny smile.

Pulling me to his side, Asher slid his arm around my shoulders. Things weren't weird. They were like they always had been. So we almost had sex. No big deal. Right? But I couldn't get the image of his naked body out of my mind. His cock thick with veins. Long and hard with pleasure. Because of me. But I also couldn't get the nagging feeling out of my head that I was just another notch on his bedpost. I knew I shouldn't think that way. I was different. I even knew that. He knew things about me others didn't. And the same went for him.

"We're meeting Charles the day after tomorrow if everything goes according to plan."

The mention of that bastard's name interrupted my thoughts.

"Yeah, the fucker likes to change things up." Asher held me closer. "Meeka is in." He explained to Angel that he didn't really give me a choice. But I knew if it came down to it and I did say no, Asher would have to deal.

"Nah, brother. I'm good."

"Ask him about the meeting," I said. "They should come here."

"Yes, she's beside me. You'll come here? Shouldn't you ask Jay first?" Asher scoffed. "Yeah, okay. She has you by the balls, man." He laughed.

My heart fluttered. The deep husky sound rumbled from his chest. It wasn't something he did often.

Asher said goodbye a moment later, letting out a deep sigh.

Sliding my fingers between his, I held his hand in my lap. "Maybe this wasn't meant to be," I said, breaking the silence.

"Everyone will be here by five." Asher rose from the couch, his back stiff and headed up the stairs. He paused, turning back to me. "Don't think this interruption is stopping me from getting inside your beautiful body. I made you come once. I will do it again. It's only a matter of when."

***

(Asher)

I almost fucked my best friend. It was bound to happen. I knew it, but I wasn't sure if she did. Platonic relationships didn't happen often. I was surprised at myself that I lasted this long. Meeka was beautiful. Thick hair that I would give my left nut to wrap my hands in and pull. Her full pouty lips. Her pale unmarked skin. My hands tingled with the need to leave marks on her body. I couldn't help but crave the feel of her skin warming beneath my touch. A spank here. A smack there. Her ass would be mine in no time.

My dick was still hard, but with having Vice-One and King's Harlots over in less than an hour, there was nothing I could do about it. Meeka needed to be savored. She had been with men but not me. The inner Alpha inside of me roared, springing to life at the mere thought of getting inside her delicious body. I could still smell her sweetness on my fingers. I could taste her tongue on my lips. Fuck, she was gorgeous, and she didn't even know it.

All of these feelings rushed together at once, leaving me breathless and out of control. The possessive need to throw her down and take that control back was overwhelming. Never in my life had I wanted to mark my territory like I did her. Was it normal? Did other men feel this way? I was acting like a caveman. The next thing I knew, I'd be pounding on my chest and grunting. I might as well have demanded that she cook me food and bring me beer.

After I got off the phone with Angel, something had switched between Meeka and me. Yes, she wanted me, but I also didn't want to make things weird. But the erection I was sporting didn't give two flying fucks about feelings and shit.

I spent the next hour taking several cold showers and focusing on Charles. But I was distracted. All of my thoughts traveled back to a tiny hot as hell woman that I suddenly could not get enough of.

Voices sounded from downstairs causing a tremor of frustration to travel through me. I loved my brothers. I loved my job. I respected Meeka's sisters but for whatever reason, I wanted to steal Meeka and disappear. Even just to talk. To spend time shooting the shit like we did as kids.

"He's upstairs," I heard Meeka say.

"I'm here," I grumbled, joining everyone in the living room.

"Well, don't you look fucking chipper." Dale clapped a hand on my back. "I feel …" He scratched his chin. "It's been way too long."

Vincent Stone laughed. The guy came on later in the game but fit in like he had been with us for years. Going by Stone, he had dealt with highly classified tasks before becoming a SEAL.

"I'm getting antsy," was all Coby said. The guy lived for the excitement even though you would never know by the emotionless numbing expression on his face.

"I need to work out," Brogan mumbled, dropping onto the couch beside Meeka. She linked their arms, leaning her head against Meeka's shoulder.

Angel and Jay were chatting quietly in the corner. Every so often, Angel would kiss her forehead. Jay's shoulders would slump, like she had taken on the weight of the world. I wanted to ask how her sister was, but I knew that was a touchy subject.

Meeka excused herself from the couch, slowly making her way to Jay. "Sorry to interrupt. Can I talk to you for a second, Jay?"

Jay frowned. "No." And turned back to Angel.

STAIN

Bitch. My back stiffened as I watched the hope drain from Meeka's face.

"What the hell was that?" Angel demanded, his brows narrowing.

"I'm not ready to talk to her," Jay cried.

"Meeka," I said, leaning against the wall.

Her gaze snapped to mine, her eyes rimming over.

"Come here, Hummingbird." I reached a hand out to her.

She walked into my outstretched arms, curling against me.

"She'll come around," I whispered, kissing the top of her head.

Meeka nodded.

I didn't like that she was hurting. She had tried so hard to impress Jay, and unfortunately, after a couple of wrong choices, it blew up in her face. She brought Violet home but possibly lost a friend. Their friendship had been rocky before. Now it was barely existent.

I could feel the eyes from our friends burning into me. What was I doing? Were Meeka and I a couple? Blah. Blah. Blah. Meeka and I were close but we had never let our friendship come to light until a couple months ago. No one had seen us together since we saved Jay's twin and revealed that we had been undercover. It was a shit move and we should have told our bosses but we didn't want to jeopardize anyone's lives.

Throats cleared and conversations continued.
That's what I thought.

I wasn't explaining what was going on between Meeka and me. My brothers would ask, it was a given, but I wouldn't tell them. Not until we were good and ready.

Angel whistled, silencing the room. "I know we haven't met up in a while. We're going to change that." He looked down at Jay. "Right?"

She rolled her eyes but nodded.

He whispered something in her ear, causing a flush of pink to caress her chinks.

"If you rolled your eyes at me, Meeka—" I kissed her cheek "—I'd spank your ass, not caring in the least if anyone saw."

"Somehow that doesn't surprise me," she muttered, leaning into my side.

"You know me well."

"I do." She smiled.

Even her smiles made my heart flutter. I was a man—our hearts didn't fucking flutter.

"Why are you looking at me like that?" she asked, frowning.

"Because you are driving me crazy." The fact alone that we almost had sex was enough to force me to drink. But her innocence sent blood shooting straight to the tip of my dick.

"Good. It's about time you had some feels."

"Feels? I always have fucking feels."

She laughed, elbowing me in the ribs. "Nope. It's because of me that you have them now."

"Are you teasing me, woman?" I feigned shock, gripping my chest.

"Maybe." She winked.

I opened my mouth to reply when a large form came into my view. Or several of them, actually. My brothers stood around me, but Angel was the first to speak.

"Meeka, will you excuse us please?" he asked, keeping his gaze locked with mine.

"Of course." She gave my hand a squeeze and headed to her sisters.

"What's up?" I crossed my arms under my chest.

"We leave in a week," Angel mumbled.

"How long?" It was the same conversation every single time, and it was one that I would have for the rest of my career. I wasn't ungrateful but sometimes I needed a rest.

"A month at least. Charles is making waves. You go in and do what you do best," Angel ordered.

"Wait …" I shook my head. "I'm not going with you?"

"No, and before you give me shit, you know why." Angel continued on but I didn't hear him.

This would be the first mission that I wouldn't be involved in. I never thought being undercover trying to bring Charles down would take me away from them.

"But we're brothers. How can you not expect me to go?" I met everyone's gaze before looking back at Angel.

"You know why you can't go," he said slowly, his tone firm.

Fucking guy. "And everyone else?"

"No one else knows except for us, and it needs to stay that way," Angel reminded me.

"I'm still trying to convince this fucker to tell us what is happening," Dale said, rolling his eyes.

"That won't happen because you can't keep your mouth shut." Stone punched him in the shoulder.

"We'll tell you," Angel interrupted their banter. "Just not right now."

"Then why the hell are we here?" Dale looked over his shoulder, his brows narrowing.

Max had been quiet the whole time, not making a peep since she stepped foot into my house.

"Patience, brother." I clapped a hand on his shoulder. "Patience."

Dale nodded, not responding. He was the fun and outgoing one, always joking and shooting the shit but his situation with Max had torn him apart. I could only guess the questions that traveled through his mind. But I was sure in time, everything would work out. It had to. For all of us.

CHAPTER SEVEN

Meeka

"OKAY, GIRL, SPILL." BROGAN had nattered on in my ear about how I never told her that there was something going on between Asher and me. But was there even something going on? Did I want there to be? Yes, I did. What we almost did an hour before was proof enough that we were attracted to each other. And the orgasm he gave me … An ache formed between my legs, making me squirm.

My neck burned. I looked up, catching Asher glancing my way.

His eyes darkened, a small smirk forming on his handsome face.

Would he always know when he turned me on? Was that normal? Maybe we were so in tune with each other that we could sense these things.

"Nothing is going on." My cheeks heated but I quickly continued before Brogan made a scene, embarrassing me further. "But you would be the first to know if there was."

"Then why is he being all sweet to you and kissing you on the head? And now he's looking at you like he wants to devour your soul. Did something happen? Something did. Didn't it?"

There was no point denying it. "Maybe."

"That's why he's being nice," she said a little too loudly.

"Seriously, bro?"

She laughed when everyone looked our way.

"But that's not the reason he's being nice." But it was nice getting the unexpected attention from him even though we weren't alone. It let me realize that he didn't care who saw. Whatever reason he had for the way he was acting, it made my heart sore and my body heat up. He had always been sweet to me over the years. I was the only one who knew the real Asher Donovan and the only one who could handle his temper. Now that he was older, he had a better control of his feelings but I knew a slow storm was brewing before he would explode again. It was only a matter of time.

"Well, either way, you two look cute together." Brogan smiled, crossing her legs.

I opened my mouth to respond when Jay came into view. My heart jumped when she sat beside me.

"I'm still pissed at you. I probably will be for a while. But I have a boyfriend who loves me and wants me happy and not having my sisters at my back makes me very upset." Jay raised her hand, stopping me from interrupting her. "I love you. I love all of you. You're my life and now Angel is a part of it as well. You have told me over and over why you did what you did but I still don't forgive you. You used me. Even though you brought my sister home to me, you fucking used me as bait."

My throat burned, and all I could do was nod. She was right. She was always right, and there was nothing I could do to deny it. I wanted to make it better. I needed to but all I could do was give her my best and hope she would eventually let me back in.

"Have we ever been close, Meeka?" she asked me, staring straight ahead.

"No," I replied, automatically. "Why am I in the King's Harlots?"

"Because you're best friends with Brogan."

I bit back a scoff, knowing it would just make things worse. "That shouldn't matter. That shouldn't …"

"What?" Jay turned to me. "What do you want me to say? That we can be all fine and dandy, go shopping and do each other's hair after you used me?"

"Jay, I never meant for it to go down that way," I pleaded with her, begging for her to understand. "Please believe me."

She shook her head, rising from the couch, and headed over to Angel.

My shoulders drooped, my chest tightening.

"She'll come around, Meeka," Max squeezed my shoulder before sitting beside Brogan. "Just give her time."

Time. I didn't have time. In less than two days, I was going to be facing an evil. The evil that threatened to destroy our small town. My heart raced. My palms became sweaty. A cold shiver of fear rippled down my back. Charles Brian would eat me alive.

"Meeka." Asher came into view, cupping my cheeks.

"I … don't leave me," I pleaded. If nothing else, he had to stay with me when we visited Charles. He needed to stay by my side for fear that they would take me away. I hadn't seen the girls. I didn't know what had happened to them while they were taken but I saw the pictures. The after effects. The moment after the life leaves them. They were better off. To remember the brutal way they were treated—it would destroy their mind.

"I'm not leaving you, Hummingbird. We're in this together. I promise you that." Wrapping me in a hug, he held me tight.

"Someone needs to tell us what the fuck is going on," Jay demanded.

Although we had our issues, I appreciated her boldness.

"Asher and Meeka have some business with Charles Brian," Angel explained. "I will explain when I can."

"You better explain now. I'm not dealing with this secret shit again," Jay told him.

"Woman, you better remember where we are." Angel stared at Jay, his thick arms crossed under his chest.

Jay's cheeks reddened and she was the one to look away first.

Never in my time knowing her would I have imagined her backing down. But Angel was her equal. I could see it. We could all see it. I wanted that. I craved it.

"You good?" Asher muttered, pushing a strand of hair behind my ear.

The back of my neck burned at the onslaught of stares being passed our way. "Yeah." I pushed out of his hold, needing to keep the distance before we stirred up any more questions. But it was too late for that, wasn't it?

Asher didn't respond, but his penetrating gaze burned a hole in the side of my head.

"I was going to have a club meeting, but Angel insisted on meeting here instead. Apparently, we're all now in the know of each other's business." Jay sighed. "Anyway, some shit is going down. Charles, the fucker that he is, is making it difficult for our suppliers to bring in their stock."

My head snapped up.

"I thought we were out of that," Brogan exclaimed. "We were supposed to be done with the illegal shit."

"There is a reason for it." Angel stood by Jay's side.

"But we will find out when the time comes," Brogan mocked. "Fucking ridiculous."

"Brogan." Coby's voice rang out around the small room. His eyes held her stare, his back straight. The dark, brooding man never backed down from my feisty best friend.

"Fine." Brogan grabbed her keys, rising from the couch. "I'll call you later. Be safe." She gave my hand a squeeze and left the house.

I gaped at the quiet man standing across the room. One use of Brogan's name and she complied. Since when?

Coby glanced my way, his lips tightening into a thin line. He didn't say anything. Just gave me a nod and met up with the rest of Vice-One. I had no idea what was going on there but something was off. It wasn't right.

"We're doing this so it makes it look like nothing has changed," Jay explained. "I don't want anyone thinking that we're letting our guards down. Creena is now a prospect and has been working at my shop for the past couple of weeks. I trust her but I need us all to feel her out."

"You know I'm in." Max linked her arm with Jay's. "Can we go now? I have a nail appointment."

"Of course you do." Jay rolled her eyes before they landed back on me. "I'm not a cold heartless bitch. I have my reasons for how I feel, and in time they will all be laid out. Looks like we all have to wait for something, don't we?"

Staring down at my lap, I let out a sigh. "I'll be in touch."

"Good luck. You're going to need it," Jay said dryly.

The guys continued talking while the rest of my sisters left the house. Jay's words hurt. The lack of emotion shown behind them bothered me even though I knew they were true.

Asher sat beside me once everyone left. "Listen, we—"

"I don't want to talk about what happened earlier." I couldn't deal with the thoughts and feelings racing through me on how much I wanted him. "I'm going to bed." I jogged up the stairs before he could argue and ran into the spare room I was staying in.

Slamming the door closed, I slid to the floor. What was I getting myself into? It had been the same question I asked myself over and over in the last day. Asher was a drug. One little taste and I wanted more.

CHAPTER EIGHT

Asher

THERE WAS NO FUCKING way I wanted to pressure Meeka but my lips still tingled from the way she had kissed me. I could feel her warmth wrap around me. Her coming apart in my arms. Damn that woman and what she did to me. It was too soon. Who knew what else would happen and we had the meeting with Charles to worry about. Fuck my life.

It had been hours since Meeka went to bed. I tried to do the same, but all I could do was stare up at the ceiling. Every time night came, I fell back into the nightmares that were my childhood. The constant screams pierced my ears. The sickening sounds of bones crunching, skin slapping against skin, the cries of anguish. I had tried so hard through the years. Counseling. Medication. None of it worked. Unless I spent the night with Meeka, I would never fall asleep.

Rising from my bed, I trudged down the hall to the spare room. Soft sounds of snoring crept through the closed door. Not wanting to wake her, I opened the door gently and padded into the room.

Meeka was curled onto her side, facing away from me. Her small frame was lit by the moonlight peering in through the window.

My fingers itched, tingling with the need to hold her. To wrap myself around her and tell her it would be all right when really, she was the one who always told me that.

Sliding onto the covers, I let out a heavy sigh. A moment of peace washed over me, just like it did as a child.

"Nightmare?"

I turned at the sound of the small voice. "Yeah."

"Tell me about it." She faced me, reaching out for my hand.

"I was ten, hiding in my closet." I closed my fingers around hers. Closing my eyes, I let the nightmare resurface. As much as I didn't like talking about them, it was needed. Meeka had pulled them out of me at a young age, forcing me to divulge the information I never wanted to tell anyone. "I was holding my teddy bear. Bobby. His name was Bobby. I was a silly kid trying to be a man." Ice cold fear gripped my spine. "There is a loud knock on the door. It's him."

"Asher."

My eyes snapped open, landing on Meeka's shadowed face. "Same dream."

"I know." She turned onto her stomach. "How do you feel?"

"I feel ..." The fear that had burned into my body years before, dissipated slowly. "Better."

"Do you remember the first time my father caught you in my bedroom?"

I chuckled, thankful for the distraction. "Yeah. I thought he was going to kill me."

"He would have if I wouldn't have stopped him." Meeka giggled, inching closer to me.

"If you come any closer, I'm not going to be held liable for what I do to you."

Her breath caught. "I just want to touch you. It makes you feel better, but it makes me feel better too."

"It does?" I brushed a finger down the side of her cheek before pinching her chin.

"Of course. You never asked anything of me. Never expected anything in return after all of those nights I helped you through your nightmares."

"I'm just lucky your parents were compassionate," I mumbled.

"You slept on the floor, and I didn't give them a choice."

"Why?" I had never asked before but I found the need to know. "Why did you help me? Did you feel sorry for me?" Pity was not something I was accustomed to.

"I helped you because I figured if I could do it for one person, at least I saved them. I may be small and I was even smaller then, but together, we stopped your step-father. That doesn't happen often."

Bile rose to my throat at the mere mention of him. The man who destroyed everything. Who took everything from me after my mother had given him so much. A new life. A job. A family. He took advantage of it when she was dying and destroyed my childhood.

"Asher." Meeka's soothing voice calmed my nerves.

She had no idea how much she saved me. From hurting myself. From hurting him. Even though I had wanted to. I wanted to end the evil that threatened to destroy my future. That was why I needed to help in any way I could. Jay wanted to help them because of her sister. I, on the other hand, knew what they were going through. I knew how it felt to be held captive, taken away from the innocence as a child.

"I remember thinking as a child that I would never make it to this age. I never imagined I would become a Navy SEAL." I also never pictured almost fucking my best friend. But I was too tired to think about that conversation that we needed to have.

"But you did make it. Look at you now. You're one of the strongest people I know."

Her words, although they meant well, I didn't believe them. How could I? I was broken as a child, forced to do things that would make the devil himself cringe. But I had no choice. I never had a choice. It was either that or be killed. I often wondered if the latter would have been better.

"I'm serious. You are strong."

"Go to sleep, Meeka. We have a long day ahead of us." I turned away from her, curling into myself like that of a newborn baby. My chest constricted, my throat burning with the lack of air. I couldn't breathe, but I wouldn't let her know that. I didn't let anyone know.

Meeka didn't press. Instead, she wrapped her arms around my waist, holding me against her. It was funny because I was much bigger than her but with her holding me, I felt small. Weak. Broken. Always so damn broken.

"You're powerful. You're strong. You inspire me to be a better person. I just wish you could see that about yourself." Meeka kissed the back of my head before the sounds of her breathing evened out.

Was she right? Could I ever see that about myself? I wasn't sure.

My eyes grew heavy. Thankful for the calm that Meeka bestowed on me by just her touch, I linked our fingers, finally falling into a blissful sleep.

***

(Meeka)

"Charles will want you to do everything I tell you. You have to kneel at my feet until otherwise directed. Keep your head down and your hands on your thighs at all times. Do not look at anyone unless spoken to."

Asher directed. I followed. The instructions he had been giving me all morning wore on my nerves but I had to listen in order for the operation to be a success. As soon as Violet was brought to safety, I quit, living on the income I made from working at a small bakery in town instead. I couldn't deal with secrets anymore. Even though I was pulled into the situation without me knowing, it would be the last one. But as always, something told me that it wouldn't end until the bastards were caught.

"Get out of your head, Meeka." Asher cupped my jaw. "I don't want you daydreaming and miss any instructions. It's your life we're talking about."

"It's not just mine," I reminded him.

"We're doing this for the women who have gone missing. I don't think you quite understand just what we're dealing with here."

"Of course I understand."

"Do you? Must I remind you what kind of men they are? Do you want me to go into detail about the smell, the sight, that fucking room that evil wouldn't even step in?" Asher released me, pacing back and forth. "I don't want to scare you, but if that's the only way you'll comply, I will."

"No, please continue the training," I looked down at my hands folded in my lap. "I'm sorry."

"Fine. When we walk into the house tomorrow, if directed, you'll be expected to follow like a dog. On your knees with a leash around your neck."

His words sounded around the room, but I could no longer focus on them. I would be treated like an animal. No, they probably got treated better. I would be garbage. Used for one thing and one thing only. How anyone could get off on this, I would never understand. Control and power, it was all they craved. They tortured females because it got them off. Because they could. Even the strong willed would eventually break. They always did.

"I will be there by your side at all times but just in case, you need to follow the demands of anyone who asks them of you," Asher continued.

"What if I don't?" I asked, my voice small.

"They'll hurt you. I can only protect you so much, Hummingbird. I will make it be known that if they touch you in any way, I will end them." Asher brushed his fingers down my cheek.

I tilted my head.

He placed a soft kiss on my mouth, his lips igniting a burning need. "Be strong. For me."

"Please don't leave me tomorrow. Whatever happens. I can only survive if you are there with me. We're in this together," I repeated the words I had told him years ago. When we approached his step-father. When we finally went to the police after much convincing on my part. His step-father broke, telling them he needed help, and that messed with Asher's head more than the abuse. It confused him, and he had never been the same since.

"I would never leave you. They'll have to pry my cold broken body away before I'll leave you alone with those fuckers." He leaned his forehead against mine, his breathing shallow.

"This brings back memories," I whispered. "Doesn't it?"

"I'm trying not to let it but yes."

"I wish we didn't have to go to Charles' place. I wish … I wish we were in a different life. Born in a different time."

"You're the only family I have," Asher whispered. It had been so quiet I almost didn't hear him. Clearing his throat, he rose to his feet. The solemn mood changed. He went from scared to dominating in a matter of seconds, and it threw me off. Ever since he was a child, he had been known to switch off his moods, his emotions. After what he experienced, I couldn't blame him. It used to bother me at first, but then, I got it.

"What time do we head out tomorrow?" I asked, knowing the conversation was over. It was time to get back into training. All of my years of experience couldn't prepare me for this. No matter how hard I tried, I wasn't ready.

"A car picks us up at—" A phone rang, interrupting the impending conversation. "Shit." Asher put the cell to his ear. "Yeah." His gaze met mine, his brows furrowing. "Fine. We also need to talk about some matters that can't wait. Your men, tell them to stop following me and sitting outside of my house. That's exactly what I said. You think I don't know? You clearly have no idea who you are dealing with, Charles. I have a lot of money riding on this. I already put half down, you want the rest? Get your men off my tail." Asher hung up the phone, closed his eyes, and waited. The phone rang again. "Deal?" He smirked. "Good. Now about tomorrow." He paced back and forth. "She will not be touched. If anyone, including you, lay a finger on her, I will break every bone, forcing you immobile. The only thing you will be able to do is stare at me while I peel every inch of skin off your broken body."

I shivered at his dark words.

"You think I'm kidding?" Asher chuckled. "Try me. I don't care who you are. I will find another way into the house. I don't need you or those bastards. Good. I'm glad we understand each other."

I left the room quietly, leaving him alone to talk to that man. He was a person I wanted nothing to do with, but unfortunately, life had a funny way of bringing people together. Asher and I had become closer because of the situation we were thrown in but would we remain the same once everything was done and taken care of. I didn't know. I couldn't know. And I refused to worry about it.

"Meeka?"

"I'm tired." My body hurt, my muscles straining over my bones.

"Sit." He led me to the couch, sitting us both down. "I could continue telling you all of the rules and what you should do and shouldn't do. What they will expect. What Charles will do if you don't listen. But, honestly, that shit doesn't matter. I need you to trust *me*."

"Of course I trust you." But my heart raced at his words.

"We are going in as one, and we are coming out as one. Whatever you see, whatever you hear, I need you to know that I will erase all of it. I will take it from your mind."

"You're scaring me," I said, my voice shaking. His pleading with me, his eyes darting back and forth, his hands gripping my arms. He was scared.

"Baby, I am only as strong as the woman beside me. You are beside me. Not in front. Not behind. *Beside*. We are equal."

"I don't know what you're talking about." I shook my head. "It doesn't make sense."

He grabbed my hands, rubbing his thumbs back and forth over my knuckles. "I'm not good with words."

"You're doing fine," I encouraged him to continue because I had no idea what was going on at the moment.

"I want more." He cupped my cheek, leaning his forehead against mine.

"What are you telling me?"

"Nothing," he shook his head, releasing me. "Forget it."

"Tell me."

He rose to his feet, brushing a hand through his hair. "I can't."

I gaped, watching him head up the stairs. *What the hell just happened?*

CHAPTER NINE

Asher

WHAT WAS THAT? GOD, I was such a moron. My words fumbled when I became nervous. I wanted to tell Meeka that I wanted more out of whatever we had. When everything was all said and done. When everyone was safe. I knew I shouldn't worry about it. It wasn't the right time, but me being the dumbass that I was, almost let the words slip out of my mouth.

"Asher?"

A light knock sounded on my bedroom door. Ignoring it, I crawled into bed. The cool satin sheets slid over my skin.

STAIN

Another knock. The knob jiggled, but I had locked it.

Eventually, Meeka went across the hall, shutting the door behind her, and left me in the loud silence of my mind.

What the hell was wrong with me? Was I that desperate that I almost screwed things up with my best friend? I didn't even know what I wanted. I wasn't sure what I was about to tell her. The kisses we had shared and the almost fucking part messed with my head. The nightmares were coming on strong, and Meeka was the only person who could calm me. She kept me sane. Made it so I didn't want to hurt myself or worse. I smiled to myself, remembering the first night I had broken into her bedroom.

"Asher, what are you doing?" Meeka's wide-eyed stare glared at me. "My dad will kill you."

"I couldn't sleep, Hummingbird," I explained, because that would make everything better.

"So you decided to break into my bedroom?" she cried, taking a step back.

"I'm not breaking in."

"What do you call it then? Why didn't you call me? I could have let you in the front door." Meeka placed her hands on her hips, jutting out her chin.

"Because it's after midnight, and your dad would have killed me," I stated, crawling through the window.

"What's wrong? Did something happen?" She chewed her bottom lip, closing the window behind me.

"Yeah." Something always happened when my step-father was involved. No one knew what I had been dealing with for the past several years. It felt like a lifetime ago since the first night he touched me. I wasn't stupid. I needed to tell someone. I knew that. But adults didn't understand. They always asked what you

did to make the other person upset. Implying it was your fault and looking at you with pity. I didn't want fucking pity. I wanted someone to listen as I told my story.

"What's going on?" Meeka asked, her question interrupting my thoughts.

I didn't want to tell her, but she was the only person I could trust. Becoming best friends fast, she knew things about me no one else did.

"Talk to me." She sat on the bed, patting the spot beside her.

"I don't need to give your dad more reasons to kill me," I said, sitting on the floor instead.

"Fine." She sat across from me, crossing her legs beneath her and waited.

"I …" I took a deep breath. There was no point in delaying the inevitable any longer. I had to tell Meeka. It was the only way I could move on. It was the only way I could deal with the bastard. "I don't know how to tell you." I picked at a loose string on my sweatpants. "I don't want you to judge me." I was surprised at the words leaving my lips. I wasn't one to talk. Never had been. But talking to Meeka felt normal. We had known each other since Kindergarten. She was the only person who didn't deal with my shit.

"Take your time, Asher." She smiled softly. "I'm not going anywhere." She stifled a yawn, wrapping her arms around herself.

I took that as my cue. "My step-father hits me."

The look of shock on her face was soon replaced with her telling me she wasn't overly surprised. She had said that I had a temper and my step-father was creepy. I made a joke that he didn't like girls so she had nothing to worry about. That didn't go over well when she had burst into tears. I never wanted her to cry. I didn't need her tears. I just wanted someone to talk to that wouldn't judge me. She never did. But she did become protective. As I was with her. Men were dicks. I knew because I was the same way. Except to her. Never to my Hummingbird.

My body was twitchy, my mind playing over and over again what would happen when we went to see Charles. I prayed he didn't touch Meeka, because I didn't know what I would do if he did. I had no self-control when it came to her.

"I want more." I had said those words, but I had no fucking idea what they meant. Falling in and out of sleep for the next couple of hours, I tossed and turned.

A light knock sounded on the door, jarring me from my confusing thoughts.

Meeka peeked her head into the room. "Are you awake?"

I only stared at her when I remembered that I had unlocked the door after waking up at some point during the night to take a piss. "I am." I sat up, pulling the blanket higher around my waist. I didn't need to make things more awkward between us if she knew I was naked. "What's wrong?"

. She chewed her bottom lip, ringing her hands together in front of her. "I couldn't sleep. Can I join you?"

My dick jumped at that, but being the gentleman that I was, I would have to learn to keep my hands to myself. She had a big enough day ahead of her. She didn't need me making it worse. "Of course."

Meeka breathed a sigh of relief and slid onto the bed beside me.

"I'll sleep on top of the covers like I used to." I wasn't sure why I felt the need to tell her that, but I needed her to know that I wasn't pressuring her into doing anything she didn't want to do. Yes, I wanted to devour her endlessly but that would have to wait. Holding her and letting her know that I was there and I wasn't leaving would have to be enough.

"We almost had sex, Asher. I think we've moved past sleeping on top of the covers." She patted the spot beside her.

"Are you sure?"

She nodded.

Rising from the bed, I pulled on sweat pants but not before I gave her a full view of my backside. My cock twitched at the small gasp that left her. I would be lying if I said I wasn't proud of the reaction my body caused.

Crawling under the covers beside her, I didn't give Meeka a chance to hesitate and pulled her against me.

"What are you doing?" Her hand slapped against my bare chest, not pushing but not letting me in, either.

"Shhh … I just want to hold you," I said into the crook of her neck.

"Why?" Her body relaxed, curling onto her side against me.

"You ease my nightmares, Hummingbird." I wrapped my arm around her waist, pulling the covers up and over us. "Just like you used to."

"You never held me before," she whispered.

"That's because I had to deal with your father but now, I don't." I kissed her cheek, letting my lips linger. I craved the day I could make her smell like me. To have the heady scent of sex as the pleasure seeped from her pores.

"I'm scared," she admitted, stifling a yawn.

"Me too, baby, me too." I didn't know what would happen the next. Or the day after that. Or even the day after that. Charles Brian didn't scare me but what he could do to Meeka did. I didn't have complete control, and that pissed me off.

"No. I'm really scared. Not just for tomorrow but for right now. This—" she rolled over onto her back "—whatever *this* is."

I didn't want to talk about it. Did I know what was going on? No. I had no fucking idea. But being with Meeka made me feel like I mattered. That after all the shit I went through as a kid, I had a purpose in life.

"No matter what happens tomorrow, know that I am here. Charles won't touch you. There's too much money riding on the line for him to take that chance."

"How can you be sure?" Meeka's hand grazed down my chest, her fingers brushing over my abs.

My cock twitched, begging for her touch. "I …" I couldn't focus on anything but her hand. It kept moving lower and lower until it reached the waistband of my pants. At times I thought she was innocent, but at this point, I knew she was distracting herself. "You need to stop doing that."

"Doing what?" She chewed her bottom lip.

In a quick move, I grabbed her hand and pulled her under me. Spreading her legs roughly, I knelt between her knees and ground my hips into hers.

Her back arched, a small gasp leaving her mouth.

"Your innocence makes me want to fucking rip you open," I snarled, pulling her arms above her head. "The way you look at me. The way you say my name. Fuck, Meeka." Grazing my teeth down the side of her neck, I nipped and sucked. This woman was driving me fucking wild. And I didn't know what would happen if I couldn't control my feelings. I didn't want to hurt her but the passion ensnaring around us shot straight to my dick.

"I'm not … I'm not experienced like you. Doesn't mean I'm innocent," she panted, wrapping her legs around my hips.

"Trust me, baby." I cupped her jaw. "Compared to me, you're innocent as fuck."

"Just—"

"Quiet," I snapped. "The only sounds I want leaving your mouth are cries of pleasure or my fucking name. You got me?"

She nodded quickly.

"Good girl." Lowering my mouth to hers, I sucked her bottom lip between my teeth, giving it a gentle nip. "By the way, I'm not fucking you tonight."

***

(Meeka)

To hear those words, I never actually thought I'd be disappointed. Asher was teasing me. He was showing me what he was capable of just by speaking. But I still had to ask. "Why not?"

"As much as I want to—" Asher sat back on his haunches, rubbing his hands down my legs "—I need some control because as soon as I get inside you, all bets are fucking off."

"I don't know what that means."

"Oh, Hummingbird." He smirked. "You really have no idea what you're in for."

"If you're trying to make me nervous, it's not working." I struggled beneath him, attempting to move out from under him. If he wanted to be a dick, by all means but I wasn't going to be a part of it. I pushed him one last time when I was flipped over onto my stomach.

"Where do you think you're going?" he asked, his voice rough. He pinned me beneath him, grinding his pelvis into my ass.

I moaned, holding onto his arm wrapped around my shoulders. "Asher."

"Fuck, I can't. God, Meeka, you're going to destroy me." His hips moved, his erection pressing into the flesh of my rear.

My lower body matched his movements. We were fully clothed but the scolding heat spread over us. "I want you," I whispered.

"I … Shit." His hot breath scorched my ear. "I don't want to hurt you."

"You won't." Spreading my legs wide, I hinted. I didn't care how; all I knew was that I needed him. I needed him to show me what it was truly like to be fucked. I didn't want slow. I wanted to forget. Everything. "Please," I cried out, shaking beneath him. "Fuck me."

Releasing me, Asher reached into his bedside table and pulled out a condom. "I'm not going to last long," he panted, tugging down my shorts.

"I don't care." I arched my hips, ready, sore, wet for the man hovering over me.

The phone rang. And rang. And rang.

"You have *got* to be fucking kidding me."

"Don't stop. Please." The phone could wait.

"I—"

It rang again. And again.

"Fuck my life," Asher growled and reached for the phone. "This had better be a fucking emergen—Coby, shit. Sorry, brother. What's wrong?"

My heart jumped. I stretched out my arms beneath the pillow.

"Thanks, my man." Asher tossed his phone onto the end table

I frowned. "What did he want?"

Asher laid down beside me, righting his pants. "He told me to have fun tonight because tomorrow is going to fucking suck and who knows how we'll be when it's done."

"Really? He said that?" I asked, raising an eyebrow.

"Pretty much."

The silence wore on. The passion still wrapped around us. The mood was done but definitely not forgotten.

"Maybe this isn't meant to be," I stated, breaking the silence.

"Oh, it's meant to be, Hummingbird." He kissed me hard on the mouth. "We just haven't found the perfect moment."

"This doesn't make things awkward?"

"Does it make it awkward for you?" He searched my face, his thumb brushing over my bottom lip.

"Not at all." But his words still struck a chord with me. He didn't want to hurt me. I didn't want him to hurt me, either, but something told me that he meant more by that then he led on. Did he mean emotionally or physically? Was he into something that I had no idea of? Not that I would know anyway. *Meeka, tangent.* God, the guy made me nervous. Well, that was new.

"Good." He pulled my shorts back up to my waist. "Because I will get inside you."

"We keep getting interrupted." I curled onto my side, allowing my eyes to flutter closed.

"It'll happen, baby." He wrapped himself around me, holding me close.

STAIN

A part of me went along with the charade because we kept getting interrupted. But what happened when we finally were able to have sex? Would it change things? My dark and dirty secrets would be laid out for him to see. It was almost worse than being naked.

"Sleep, Hummingbird." He brushed his nose into the crook of my neck, inhaling deep. "I'll leave you alone. For now."

CHAPTER TEN

Meeka

WE HAD BEEN SILENT since we woke up only a couple hours before. Going about our morning routine like nothing was about to happen; instead, we would be meeting up with Charles Brian. The epitome of evil who I wanted nothing to do with. Because finding the girls meant everything to me, I complied. Which I had been doing a lot of lately.

Asher suggested I wear something light and feminine. I would have preferred to wear a hazmat suit but understood what he was saying. So I threw on a floor-length, thin, maxi dress. It was black, slimming, and covered everything it needed to.

STAIN

As I was pulling my thick hair up into a messy bun, I slipped on my flip flops. The back of my neck burned, and I knew Asher was standing in the doorway watching me. "I didn't know what to wear."

"You look beautiful," he ground out. Something flashed behind his eyes.

"What's wrong?" I asked, smoothing my hands down the front of my dress.

Asher closed the distance between us and pulled me against him. Capturing my mouth in a hard bruising kiss, he wrapped his arms around me.

The kiss spoke so many words that neither of us could say.

His tongue slid between my lips, caressing, needing. The longer we kissed, the more desperate it became. It was rough, like he was taking ownership of his property. But I wasn't his, and I wasn't property. I wasn't an item to be tossed around and sold. These bastards took what they wanted and broke their toys until they were molded into what they wanted.

"Get out of your head, baby," Asher muttered against my mouth, pushing me back until I hit the edge of the bed. "Please, for me."

"I can't. I can't do this." But I couldn't stop kissing him. He felt so good. It felt natural. Real. Normal. It was everything I wanted it to be. Everything I needed in a man. Asher made me feel *alive*.

"I need you to know that you're safe. You're mine, Hummingbird." His mouth trailed down the length of my jaw, his hands cupping my rear.

I moaned, sliding my hands around his neck and waited. For him to take control. For him to shred my soul and piece it back together. I craved his touch and I knew it was only the beginning.

"You're mine," he repeated, laying me back onto the bed.

My heart stuttered. I broke the kiss, staring up at him. "Am I only yours right now?" I didn't want to ruin the moment but I knew how he was. How he had treated women in the past. He was bored. And I couldn't help but wonder if he would become bored with me.

"Please don't ruin this." He went to kiss me again but I pushed against his chest.

"Tell me. I need to know what is going on in your head." I lifted my chin, waiting.

"I want to fuck you. That's it. Right now, I'm stressed beyond belief, and I want to use your body to make me feel better. Is that what you wanted to hear? You want to hear how much your tight body can make me feel fucking normal?"

"Asher."

"Forget it." He shoved off of me and sat on the edge of the bed, dropping his head in his hands. "I've never had any problems fucking a woman before, but you, you mess with my head. I can't think straight. The only thing I worry about is getting inside of you."

I sat beside him, curling my hands around his arm. My heart raced, the back of my neck burning at his words. "I ..."

"You don't know what to say." He sighed. "Of course. The time I actually speak and have no problems saying anything, you can't say a fucking thing."

"What do you want from me? This whole thing between us is confusing and it couldn't happen at a worse time."

"Why the hell would you say that? It's happening at a time where we need each other. It's not like we're strangers, Meeka. I have known you forever and I knew you at a time where I needed you most."

"I didn't do anything," I mumbled.

"God, you have no idea, do you?" He turned to me, pinching my chin. "You helped me when I had no one else." He shook his head.

"I want you to fuck me." When the words left my mouth, I regretted them instantly. The look of shock on Asher's face made me second guess my thoughts. I had never—

A hot mouth crashed to mine. A hard body forced me back onto the bed. All feelings disappeared as we focused on the here and now.

Asher shoved my dress to my hips and ripped open the fly of his jeans. Rough hands bruised my skin, leaving marks on my body where I knew I would see them for days after. I didn't care. He could cover me in his touch, and I would forever be grateful.

"I'm going to destroy you."

"Yes," I begged against his mouth. "Do it."

He growled, spreading my legs. Breaking the kiss, he pulled the top of my dress down, exposing my breasts. Latching onto my nipple, he sucked and pulled until I was writhing beneath him.

I moaned, digging my fingers into his hair. My skin burned. My body hot and on fire.

With rough and needy hands, he pulled my arms above my head, holding me in place. His eyes roamed down the length of my body, his desire for me searing my skin. Without saying a word, he pushed between my legs, spreading them as wide as possible.

My chest heaved with ragged breath. The need to have inside of me, consumed my every waking thought.

My nerve endings tingled with desire for the man hovering me. "Please," I panted.

A wicked smirk spread on his lips. "I'm going to fuck you so good, Hummingbird."

His words turned me on. His body made me melt. His voice made me lose control.

Pulling a condom from his pocket, he sheathed himself and lined up his hard cock to the entrance of my body. Beating the heavy flesh against my mound, he pushed between my folds.

I moaned, writhing and tilting my hips. His cock moved over my swollen clit, an explosion of desire spreading through my body.

In a quick move, he thrust into my body, not giving me a chance to get used to his size.

I cried out, pain and pleasure mixing as one as his hips thrust hard and deep. "Oh, God."

"That's right, baby. Feel my cock inside your tight heat." Holding my arms above my head, his mouth moved over my collar bone. His teeth grazed my skin, nipping and biting a path in their wake. "You're so fucking hot."

No words left my mouth. I couldn't form a coherent sentence for fear it would come out a jumbled mess. Digging my heels into his rear, I pushed him into me as far as my body would allow.

"Fuck, Meeka. Can you feel how deep I am?"

"Yes," I whimpered. "Harder."

Letting go of my arms, he pushed my knees to my chest and pounded into me with a fervor I never knew existed. "Take me."

"God, yes!" I cupped his ass, rolling my hips upward, and met him thrust for thrust. "Harder. Please."

"Shit." He pushed into me. Hard. Fast. Rough. It bordered on violent. It consumed my thoughts. All I could feel was the man making me feel good.

"Asher," I cried out, a tingle spreading from my toes to my head. "Oh, yes."

"That's it, Meeka. Scream my name. Make me come so fucking hard."

"I'm …" I shook, my body vibrating.

Pulling me into his arms, he sat back on his haunches. "Ride me. Take what you need from my body, baby. Make yourself feel good."

Wrapping my arms around his neck, I slammed my hips against his. Riding him with everything in me, I kissed him slow but rough.

He groaned, digging his fingers into the flesh of my rear. "That's it."

An unexpected explosion set off inside me. His name left my lips on a scream, my voice cracking.

"Harder, Meeka. Fuck my dick. Hard," he shouted, slamming into me with so much force, I broke.

Our cries of pleasure mixed as one until we were spent and exhausted. We fell back on the bed, our bodies connected, our hearts racing together.

"Fuck me, Hummingbird. That …" He trembled, kissing me softly on the mouth. "You just ruined me."

I smiled, cupping his cheek. "Thank you." I no longer cared. About anything. Not what would happen when we saw Charles. Not what would happen the next day or the day after that. I didn't care. At all. Asher and I continued lying as one, and that was all I was concerned about. He felt good inside of me. It felt normal. Like we had been doing it for years. It was natural, and I found myself wanting to experience it over and over again.

"You don't need to thank me." He released me, disposed of the condom and righted his pants. He helped me fix my dress. "From now on, you are not to wear any panties."

I raised an eyebrow. "Why not?"

His eyes darkened. "Because they get in the way."

I stood from the bed and reached under my dress, pulling the panties down my legs, and tossed them to the side.

Asher watched my movements, his jaw clenching. "You like that."

"Like what?" I breathed.

"When I tell you what to do. Your eyes dilate. You love it when I boss you around."

A shiver raced up my spine. "Yes." There was no point denying it. He knew me well.

"Good." He stood, pulling me against him. "I love being in control. You will learn that more now." He kissed me hard on the mouth, cupping my ass. "I will make it so one demand from me and your body melts. Your pussy will be wet with just my words. You will be ready and waiting for me every time I desire it. I will fuck you whenever I need it and return the pleasure in ways you never knew existed."

I never imagined that Asher would be like that. *Was he like this with every woman? Was it just me? Did I give him what he wanted? What he craved?*

"I will help you get out of your head. If you trust me, I will unleash every dark and dirty desire inside of that beautiful brain of yours."

"Of course I trust you." But I wasn't sure just what kind of fantasies he had. "What do you want from me?"

"I want you to please me whenever I need it."

"What else?"

STAIN

He winked. "Oh, Meeka. There is nothing to worry over. I will return the pleasure more then you could ever know." His mouth moved down to my ear. "I know there's a dirty girl inside of you. I will have you begging me to take over your body completely. Every single inch."

***

(Asher)

Spending the last hour inside of Meeka was not something I was accustomed to. Meeka was perfect and she fit even better wrapped around my cock. Call me an asshole but her tight little pussy would make a fucking priest give up his celibacy.

I enjoyed watching the blush that had spread up her neck, reddening her cheeks into a rosy hue. She would glance my way every so often, and when I caught her looking, she would quickly go back to doing what she was doing. Her hands would flutter nervously as they smoothed down her dress. She squirmed, her body shivering slightly as a cool draft no doubt brushed beneath the fabric. The fact alone that she wasn't wearing any panties had me almost coming undone. And now that I'd had her? I wasn't letting her go. I wasn't one to fall easily, but with Meeka, I craved her gentle touch. Her dark eyes begging me to do all of the nasty things I had planned for her. She was the innocence I had been craving my whole life. She was pure where I was sin. I used women for my pleasure. I wasn't proud of it, but everything in me said that Meeka would turn me into a better person. She would make me want to be a better man. Could I be that man for her? Ever since our first kiss, I had asked myself that question over and over again.

A horn honked outside the house, interrupting the questions banging around in my head. Peeking out the window, I saw a black town car and knew instantly by the churning in my gut that it was either Charles or one of his bastards.

"We have to go," I told Meeka, reaching out for her hand.

She nodded, sliding her fingers in mine. She looked up at me through dark lashes, her teeth chewing her bottom lip.

I kissed her mouth, letting my lips linger. "Whatever you do, do not let go of my hand."

She nodded again, squeezing my fingers for added effect.

I didn't want to scare her but I knew how these men worked. They preyed on the weak and would do everything they could to get her alone. But I wouldn't allow it. It would be over my cold dead body before they harmed her.

"Let's get this shit over with." So I could spend the rest of the night showing her I wasn't an asshole. Not to her, at least. I felt like I was having a never-ending conversation with myself of should I or shouldn't I. She made me weak in the knees and my dick hard as a rock. Even before we kissed the first time. I always thought she was beautiful, but that kiss sealed the deal. She had to be mine, and I would do everything I could to make her see it.

"Don't leave my side," Meeka pleaded. "Whatever you do."

"I promise." We left the house, greeted by a large man in a black suit.

He didn't look our way but opened the door to the back of the car.

Holding Meeka's hand, I guided her into the vehicle, watching her face go from solemn to worried.

"Don't look so excited to see me, dear girl."

Charles. Shit. I was naïve to hope that he wouldn't be there and would be waiting back at the house. And as soon as I sat in the car, I realized that the windows were tinted past the point of seeing so I wouldn't be able to trace the way to his place. Fucking great.

"We're surprised you came to pick us up," I told him, holding Meeka against me. My nose burned, tingling with the scent of sex. She smelled like me. Under normal circumstances I would be proud of that fact, but knowing Charles could probably smell it as well, my inner Alpha beat on its chest with a possessive roar.

"I had nothing better to do." Charles smirked. "It smells like …" He lifted his nose in the air. "You two finally fucked."

Meeka bristled beside me.

"I have no idea what you're talking about," I bit out through clenched teeth. There was no way that I wanted to talk about sex with him. Especially not when it came to Meeka and me.

"I don't like a liar," he said, his voice dripping with venom. "But you're lucky I like you. Now, tell me, how is the training going?"

"It's not like you've given us enough time, but—" I cupped Meeka's jaw "—she's doing well."

"She," he repeated. "You're a better man than I because my toys are not referred to as human. They're toys. Playthings. And they are not female or male."

"That's where you and I are different. I don't play with toys, and I sure as hell don't fuck them."

Charles chuckled. "Touché." Pouring a drink from a bottle in a bucket of ice, he handed me the tumbler. "Cheers. To friends and playthings." Repeating his movements, he poured liquid from another flask for himself.

God, I hated the fucker. I didn't say anything and held the glass up to my lips, waiting for him to take the first sip.

He took his drink, his throat bobbing as he swallowed. "Give her the drink," he demanded.

"No." There was no point in asking why.

"Do it or I will force her to take a drink while my men hold you down."

Shit.

Meeka's eyes widened, looking up at me. Her gaze begged, pleaded with me not to let her take a sip. Who knew what was put in the amber liquid.

"What's in the drink?" Knowing there was probably nothing in it but I couldn't trust that. How would I know? The drink smelled like liquor. That was it. And if something else was put in it, there would be no way I could decipher the difference between the two.

"The fact alone that you think I put something in it hurts me." Charles grabbed his chest, his mouth curling into a wicked smirk. "Give her the drink. I'm not asking again."

"No," Meeka whispered, her eyes wide. "Please."

"Drink it," I told her, my voice firm. I held the tumbler to her mouth, cupping her jaw. God, please forgive me. My blood pounded in my ears, an icy cold shiver racing down my spine.

Something flashed behind her eyes. She took the glass from my hand, glaring my way before chugging the drink back.

She swallowed hard and coughed, shoving the glass back in my hand. So many words went unsaid. She was mad at me. She hated me. She never wanted to speak to me again. I could have handled it but her silence was worse. It drove me fucking insane not to hear what she had to say. I was the type of person who didn't speak. Meeka had done enough for the both of us over the years. I came to expect it and now, she was pissed. But alive.

I cupped her jaw, forcing her to look at me. Searching her face, I let out a deep sigh when nothing changed.

"I told you there was nothing in the drink."

CHAPTER ELEVEN

Meeka

THE LIQUID BURNED MY throat but heated my skin. My head became light and fuzzy but I was grateful. Yes, I was pissed beyond measures that I had to drink it but there was no point in arguing. Charles scared me. He looked at me like he could see inside of my soul. He was the monster that creeped in the dark shadows of my room and he had no problems showing it.

"Now that we got that out of the way, how is the training going? Anything I should help with?" Charles glanced my way, his face impassive. Crossing his leg over the opposite knee, he scratched the dark scruff on his strong jaw. "I'm experienced, Meeka. I know everything there is to know about training a woman into a toy for her Master. I'd be happy to go over some things with you."

"Like fuck," Asher snapped.

"Ah, there you are. I almost thought you had no emotion. You could have proved me wrong but your actions speak louder than your words." Charles shrugged. "You just ruined it for her."

"What are you talking about? I've done everything you have asked. If you want your money, you won't lay a hand on her."

"Oh, yes. Money. I almost forgot about that." Charles kept his gaze locked with mine. "How does it feel knowing you're worth a million?"

I gasped, clapping a hand over my mouth.

"Don't listen to him, Hummingbird. He's trying to get under your skin," Asher muttered in my ear. "And you're fucking worth more than a million dollars."

I bit back a smile, trying everything in me to play along with the twisted charade. I wasn't sure what was going on. Not being told much, I had to go with what was given to me.

"How much has Ash here told you?"

When I didn't say anything right away, I earned a hard look from Charles. "He-he's told me enough," I answered, my voice cracking.

"How much is enough? And don't you answer for her," he snapped at Asher. "I'm talking to your pet. If you want to keep her, you will shut your fucking mouth."

My stomach twisted, churning with disgust for the man sitting across from me. How could anyone just throw away another human being?

"Answer me, Meeka. What do you know?" Charles undid the buttons of his suit jacket, revealing the butt of a gun.

My eyes burned, but I refused to cry for him. He probably bathed in the tears of children. "I know you train girls. You break them, molding them into what you want, and then you sell them to prospective buyers." I didn't know how much of that was true, but I knew I had to say something. "I also know that I am supposed to do as I'm told."

"And do you?"

I swallowed hard, thoughts of only a couple hours before reigning my mind. "Yes." My cheeks heated. It was like I had given him every detail about the delicious experience Asher and I shared. It was disconcerting, knowing in his lifestyle that your sex life was not private. At all.

"Good girl." He sat back, taking a sip of his drink.

"Why do you care?" Asher asked, frowning. "She's supposed to be trained to be a toy. That's what you told me. Why are you showing interest?"

"So many questions." Charles winked. "You will soon find out." His gaze slid back to mine. "We all will."

Something had changed since the first time I saw him. Even though it was only a couple of days before, Charles looked at me like he wanted to eat me alive. Like he wanted to rip off my skin and cover himself in it. God, I watched too many movies. But by the sheer look of dark hunger in his gaze, I knew something had switched. I just prayed that whatever it was, I wouldn't be alone when I found out.

"Now, Ash. It seems to me like you're new to this industry. Let me tell you a little about how it works."

Charles pulled a manila envelope from his inside pocket. "These are contracts. For both of you. Every single item, you have to do at least once and mark it off. If you don't, trust me, we will find out."

"You have got to be fucking kidding me," Asher took the envelope and opened it. "Why do we need contracts? You already know I'm on the same page."

"What I know is that you're a quiet fucker." Charles pointed at me. "Bring her around and you open."

Asher shifted beside me, flipping through the pages of the contract. "You know you can't pull this on me if you want your money. You also know that I have connections. I can bring you more business. Meeka is the toy that keeps me satisfied." He smirked. "Trust me. You don't want to deal with me when I'm not happy."

I knew he had to be dramatic to get his point across, but I also knew that Asher meant every word. He had a temper problem. The school counselor had tried so hard to throw him into anger management but he only got into fights. He wasn't the type to talk about his feelings. Except to me. I could get Asher to open up and spill everything, but now that we had sex, I wasn't so sure.

"That may be true but it's worth a shot." Charles gulped back the rest of his drink before placing it in the cup holder. Giving me a dark stare, he nodded once. "Kneel. On the floor."

My jaw clenched, my hands curling into fists.

"Do it, Meeka," Asher said, giving my hand a light squeeze.

Complying, I lowered to the floor, kneeling at Asher's feet.

He kept his fingers locked in mine, careful not to let me go.

"I think we need to up the lesson. Come here," Charles demanded, his dark gaze piercing into mine.

"Not going to happen," Asher told him. "She only listens to me and no one else."

My heart raced on permanent overdrive. My skin prickled with tiny bumps of fear. It was only the beginning and already I was ready to give up. Charles scared me. No one should be held against their will to do things that would even make the Devil himself cringe. In my job, I had seen monsters, but never like him. All of the emotions Charles was displaying never reached his eyes. He was the epitome of a sociopath. No emotion. No heartbreak. It almost made me wonder what had happened in his childhood to cause him to be this way. Was he like Asher? Did he have a horrible start to life and just couldn't deal? With Asher, it helped him become stronger.

"Does she now? What if I separated you two?" Charles words dripped with venom and power. He was a Dominant man in the way he took control of the room with just a dark stare. The air was thick with superiority, the battle of Alpha male flying through the car. Asher didn't back down like Charles had hoped he would. When he looked away first, I mentally fist pumped the air.

"I think we need to make something clear." Asher cupped my jaw, leaning down to my ear. "Trust me."

I nodded slightly, giving him the reassurance that no matter what he said, I trusted him completely.

"Meeka is my toy. My pet. She does and says what I tell her to. She's already broken to appease me and no other man will change that." Asher's words were cold and uncaring. They sent a flutter of anxiety racing through me even though I knew he had more respect for me then he was letting on.

It's all an act, Meeka. Trust him.

I had to repeat the words over and over in my head. Asher was good at his job. He should have been an actor because I almost believed the words he was saying.

"Is that so?" Charles asked, raising an eyebrow.

"You're better off not second guessing me right now. If you want your money, you will understand the fact that Meeka is mine and mine alone. If anyone touches her and that includes you, I will rip off your head and piss down your fucking throat. What you do to those girls? It will be nothing compared to what I do to you. How do you feel about being skewered on a stick? No? Not your thing?" Asher feigned a yawn. "Didn't think so. Maybe you'll think twice next time before you threaten me and my toy. She's bought and paid for. I don't want to have to go through the act of training another one. I'm too old for that shit."

"And that's why you have us," Charles reminded him.

"Nah. Not my thing. I don't share, and I definitely don't play well with others. She was used once before me."

"Who trained her?"

"That's none of your damn business." Asher wrapped his hand around the base of my neck, rubbing his thumb up and down. That small touch was soothing, and it calmed my racing nerves. I knew Asher could take Charles but who knew how many more men he had under his beck and call.

"You're a difficult one to crack, my dear Ash." Charles pressed a button, speaking into the intercom. "Take us around the back. I have to remind our dear friends how we play."

"She already knows what happens if she doesn't listen, but if you feel the need to be extra dramatic, then by all means." Asher waved a hand in front of him. "You do realize, though, that if she misbehaves, what you show her will be nothing compared to what I do to her when I get her home."

"Oh, do tell," Charles clapped his hands together. "I love a little story of what happens to the toy that has been bad."

Asher laughed, cold and maniacal. "If only she bruised easily."

"Fuck, I love some pale skin that turns purple fast." Charles groaned. "Speaking of which, I need to show you a new device we got."

"And what kind of device is that?"

"Oh, you will see." Charles tapped the back of the window shielding the front seat from the back. It rolled down a couple inches, revealing two large men. "Well?"

"We're here," the one stated, his voice deep and rough.

I had no idea where we were going. I didn't know what would become of our situation. Asher being with me kept some of the fear at bay but his acting messed with my head. He would never speak to me that way under normal circumstances. Although he was demanding, something told me that I hadn't experienced all of that yet. His dark and dangerous desires could no doubt bring me to my knees. His dirty words melted me into a puddle of heated bliss. Once. Once was all it took for me to be begging at his feet, pleading that he do everything he wanted to me as long as he promised me the greatest pleasure in return.

My skin tingled, my nipples puckering at the memories of his mouth on me. It had been fast. It was nowhere near enough. An ache spread between my thighs, my body needing him back inside of me.

When we came to a stop outside of a large building, although the windows were tinted, I could see that the mansion was old. Weathered paint, vines growing up the sides of the house. It was a house taken out of a horror movie. It was eerily perfect for the solemn mood that had taken over the vehicle.

The car drove around the building, heading to the back of the house. A cloud had taken over, putting a permanent darkness above the rafters of the roof. If only the walls could talk.

"I shouldn't be so excited, but I am," Charles exclaimed. "I love it when a fresh pair of eyes sees what's in store for them if things go wrong."

"Nothing will go wrong," I blurted, snapping my mouth shut as soon as the words left my mouth.

Asher stiffened beside me.

"Ah, little thing has a voice. It's about time you spoke." Charles grinned. "Get out of the car."

Knowing I would probably hear of it later from Asher, I excited the vehicle. A part of me didn't care what happened, but then I had to keep reminding myself of the girls who had gone missing. The new victims. The old. Jay's sister. Jay herself. She had been taken and screwed up, having to take some time off for herself and Angel. God, I couldn't even imagine, and there I was being selfish. If Vega had been any indication of how evil these men were, Charles was the Master of it all.

Standing on shaky legs, I wrapped my arms around myself. Knowing I wasn't supposed to show any emotion, I held back a gasp at the sheer idea of what happened behind these walls.

A warm hard body stepped up behind me, fingers wrapping around my arm.

I inhaled. The scent of spicy cologne filled my nostrils mixing with the hint of sex. I knew it was Asher just by the firm but gentle hold he had on me. He was letting me know that I didn't need to worry. I was his. For how long, I wasn't sure. I couldn't think about that right at the moment. Although, it was a badgering question that wouldn't leave me alone.

"I need you to be strong. Not for me. But for you." He kissed the top of my head. "Let's get this shit over with before I kill him."

I nodded, letting out a heavy sigh. Maybe he didn't care about my outburst.

"And, Meeka? If you blurt out something again, I will bend you over my knee."

I swallowed hard.

Allowing Asher to lead me up the steps, I followed beside him. Not wanting to take any more chances, I kept at his side, careful not to make eye contact with Charles.

"Are you sure you don't want to leave her alone with me?" Charles asked, opening the front door. "I could take her off your hands while you make yourself at home."

"We're here for business. Not for your training techniques." Asher tightened his hold on me. "If I have to remind you again on who she belongs to, I will make it so you have to eat through a tube for the rest of your fucking life."

"So damn touchy." Charles chuckled. "I don't want to step on anyone's toes, of course."

It would be easier if they got along, but how could anyone get along with a monster? We all had our own vices, our own dark and dirty secrets, but when children—young women—were involved, it took things to a whole other level.

"Are you ready to see the room, pet? Asher saw it. I don't think he was a fan but, of course, he didn't say." Charles pushed through another set of doors, his two large security caging us in.

Asher didn't show any emotion as we were blocked in the hall.

He kept me at his side but that only did so much as we were surrounded.

"Oh, this will be so much fun." Charles nodded once.

In a quick move, his two men grabbed onto Asher, ripping his hand from mine.

"What the fuck?" he snapped, struggling to break free.

A shiver of fear gripped my spine when I was suddenly pushed forward. Charles grabbed my arm, holding me steady.

"It wouldn't make sense for you to be with us, Ash. It has a bigger effect if your toy is by herself when she sees what could become of her if she doesn't listen." Charles raised his hand. "No point arguing. You may be big, but no matter your size, you can't fight against a gun." Not waiting for Asher to respond, Charles cupped my nape and pushed me in front of him. "After you, pet."

CHAPTER TWELVE

Meeka

I DIDN'T WANT TO leave Asher, but I knew I had no choice. I may have been naïve at times, thinking the good in everyone, but I wasn't stupid. Charles scared me more and more every time he opened his mouth. I had been through shit in other undercover missions, but this time, it was worse. I had no problems playing the strong female, but when it came to being submissive and complying to the waking demands of men, I had to fight the urge to run.

When Charles opened the door to a second room, I had no idea what I was in for. But the scent of death hit me in the chest, knocking the breath out of me. It was strong and acidic. Bleach and other chemicals mixed as one making my throat burn. Closing my eyes, I didn't want to see what laid before me. I didn't want to see the victims, the females lying about after God knew what was done to them.

Charles moved behind me and placed his hands on my shoulders. "Open your eyes."

Nothing could prepare me for what laid before me. Everything evil was created from. Although the scent of death warned me that what was in the room was beyond anything I had ever seen before, when I opened my eyes, all I could do was stare. The walls were lined with stains of red. Some so dark, they looked black. Small cages filled the room, each holding a body. Even though the cages weren't empty, the room was silent. It was beyond eerie how quiet everyone was.

"Do you see?" Charles muttered in my ear.

All I could do was nod. The image before me would forever be burned into my mind. My darkest nightmares would be filled with what I had just seen. I prayed they were alive, but I was sure they would be better off dead. How could anyone move on? They would forever be broken, addicted to whatever Charles had forced onto them.

"Isn't it beautiful?" he purred.

Bile rose to my throat at the husk in his voice.

He pulled me back against him, wrapping his arm around my waist.

"Tell me how Asher feels knowing his boss was one of the front runners of the organization."

I attempted to pry him off of me, but his hold only tightened.

"Tell me."

"He … he was upset. He still is." I didn't want to talk about Asher and his feelings with the man holding me. I didn't want to reveal anything to him. I could have called his bluff. Would he hurt me if I didn't talk? Would he hurt Asher? Or worse? Chains clinked together in the large room but I couldn't make out where the sound was coming from. Relief floated through me knowing at least one was alive. If only I could save her. If only I could save all of them.

"Eric Vega was nothing. He was a fucking pussy for shooting himself." Charles pushed me further into the room. "If it were me, I would have had Genevieve begging at my feet, pleading for mercy." He chuckled. "She's absolutely beautiful from what I hear. I wonder what Angel would do if she was taken again."

"How do you know their names?" I asked, shoving from his grip.

"I have my sources." He shrugged. "You shouldn't be surprised, Meeka. I know everything that goes on in that club house. But the only thing I don't know is how you are associated with them."

I kept my face impassive, not wanting to reveal that I was a member of King's Harlots. If he didn't know, that might work to my advantage. "Why are we here?"

"Because Asher wants to work with me. I can't deny him that. He clearly has some fucking screws loose if he fights for his country but in his free time, tosses girls around like yesterday's trash."

That made me wince. Even though I knew it wasn't true, Asher was a good actor. He almost had *me* convinced. "How do you know all of this?"

"I have to find out everything I can about the people I work with."

"Does he know this?" I knew he did. Angel had made sure to stay one step ahead of Charles.

"No, and we're going to keep it that way, aren't we?" Charles led me into the room until we were standing in the middle of the vast space. "At first, I didn't think Asher was who he said he was, but when I brought him in here and saw his expression, I knew."

I swallowed hard. "What did you know?"

"That he was fucking perfect for the job."

"And … and what job is that?" Even before the question left my mouth, I knew what kind of job Charles would have for him.

"Why to take the girls, of course."

No. It couldn't be. "He would never. I don't care what you say." All of it was a ruse. It had to be. Part of me wondered why Asher agreed to any of it. He said he had no choice but when I spent the morning with him, I felt a different side to him. Maybe it should have made me nervous. But yet, it excited me.

"Oh, little girl. You clearly know nothing about your Master."

My Master. My stomach clenched. I didn't like that term when Charles used it. To be someone's slave? I was all for kink but being a willing slave was not something I was into. Asher hadn't mentioned anything about being my Master.

"I know enough," I muttered, trying to avert my gaze from the unmoving bodies lying in the cages.

"Do you?" Charles walked around me, pacing back and forth from cage to cage. His fingers grazed the bars, his eyes taking on a faraway distance like he was remembering a past memory. What happened to him that he felt the need to take these girls? Was it the stereotypical occurrence where his childhood was full of torture and abuse?

I was supposed to remain quiet. Only talk when spoken to. Only move when allowed. But I couldn't resist the words that fell from my lips. "Why them? What did they do to deserve this?"

"They lived." Charles met my gaze. "That's what they did. Women are for pleasure, that's it. Didn't you know that? Why do you think your boyfriend has slept with so many females?"

He was bored. "He's not my boyfriend," I mumbled, looking down at my feet.

"Good, girl. Keep your eyes down. You don't deserve to look at me."

My chest panged. I wanted out. I needed to leave before I said something else that would get me into trouble. I couldn't comply, falling victim to the wrath of Charles Brian. If that was even his real name.

"But because I'm a nice guy, I'll answer your question in more detail. These girls were easy. They were taken from a time in their life when they had no one else. Research after research was done on them. They weren't chosen at random, Meeka. Make sure to tell whomever you speak to that little piece of information. And next time I see you, you better be more submissive. I don't want a fucking word to leave your mouth or I'll shut you up myself." He laughed. "I don't think Asher would like that too much. Mind you, it would probably please me more having him watch as I fuck your throat."

My heart raced, my hands twisting and turning in front of me.

"But I'll leave you alone—for now." He snapped his fingers. "Look at me."

My eyes reached his. I bit back a gasp at the look of sheer evil in his dark gaze.

"I want you to choose a girl."

I shook my head. "Excuse me?"

"That is the last time you speak to me without permission," he shouted, banging his fist against the cage beside him. "Choose a girl or I'll throw you in a cage and you'll never see your precious Asher again. Now!"

I jumped. How could he expect me to choose? "I …"

"I'll give you to the count of ten."

"I can't," I whimpered.

"One."

"What do you want from me? You have all these girls. Just choose one yourself." *Shut up, Meeka.*

"Two," he smirked.

Gripping my hair, I pulled and tugged, the strands coming loose in my fingers. There was no way I could choose a girl and just hand her over like that. He may have had access to all of them, but I didn't want any part of it.

"Three." He took a step forward, forcing me to back up.

"Please."

"Four. Come on, Meeka. Time is running out."

"No. I won't play into your games."

"Five. You can refuse all you want, but I know you don't want anything to happen to Asher. I can see it in your eyes, pet. You love him."

"He's like a brother to me."

"Come on, Meeka." Charles stopped a foot away from me. "Unless you're into incest, we both know that's not true."

Either way, no matter how I felt about Asher, it was none of Charles' damn business. I wouldn't admit my feelings to him when I hadn't even told Asher how I felt. "I'm not telling you shit."

"Six." Charles feigned a yawn. "I'm getting bored. Trust me, we don't want that to happen. I'll choose a girl myself and force you to kill her. How about we play that game instead?"

When he went to turn around, I stopped him. "No! Please. I'll choose a girl, but please don't make me hurt them."

"Oh, Meeka." He patted my hand. "No matter what happens, it will be because of you they get hurt or worse. Seven."

Tears burned my eyes, my throat closing. "I choose the girl on the left. Fourth cage from the front door."

"Good girl. See? That wasn't so hard, was it?" Charles opened the door, calling in Asher and his security.

Falling to my knees, I let out a soft cry. My fault. It was all my fault. The girl would be killed because of me. How could I give in? How could I let Charles control me like that?

"Meeka." Asher knelt in front of me, pulling my hands free from my face. "We need to go."

"Not yet you don't," Charles interjected. "I have to show you my toy, that yours chose for me." Tugging a small frail girl in front of him, she wavered on her feet. Dark bruises marred her pale naked skin, her hair matted to her head. Her pupils dilated, her eyes glassy with whatever drug had been injected into her body.

"You got fifty grand out of me before we've even set anything up. We are leaving," Asher told him, his voice firm. Rising to his feet, he pulled me upright.

"You have no way back." Charles crossed his arms under his chest, raising an eyebrow.

"I just gave you fifty thousand dollars without any hesitation. I think I can afford a fucking cab." Asher moved in front of me, shielding me from whatever was about to take place.

"You're lucky I like you." Charles snapped his fingers again. "Bring her to the showers and have her cleaned. I want her primed before I fuck her."

The girl didn't make a sound as she was guided out of the room. Before she disappeared through the open doors, she looked my way. Our gazes locked. No emotion passed over her face but her eyes glowed, shining with fear.

Because of me, she was being taken away. To be prepped. Primed. Ready for Charles to do whatever he pleased. She looked no more than twenty but still so young. She would have had her whole life ahead of her but I sent her to her death instead.

CHAPTER THIRTEEN

Asher

MEEKA DIDN'T TALK. AT all. Not when I called the cab. Not when we took it back to my place. Not even when I asked her what had happened. She didn't tell me what Charles had said to her. She didn't tell me anything.

Although I had given Charles fifty thousand fucking dollars, he still made it difficult to leave. I didn't expect any less from him. The guy was all about making some extra cash and he would go through any means to make sure his addiction was satisfied. I also knew that he was aware of my job. He didn't know I was undercover. He assumed I had a sick desire. Maybe I did. But not when it came to little girls. That crossed the line. Charles should be shot and fucking pissed on.

When we reached my place, I paid the cabbie. Meeka didn't move. My gut twisted. Fuck me, I owed her big time. And I had to make sure she didn't lose herself. She was strong. Probably the strongest person I knew. I would not let that bastard break her down.

"Meeka." I opened her door. "We're here."

She nodded, leaving the vehicle, and walked up the steps.

I followed behind her, unlocking the front door.

"I'm going to take a shower," she mumbled, wrapping her arms around herself.

"Okay." I watched her slowly make her way up the stairs. Something was off. God, was I so selfish in needing to get everything resolved that I didn't see past her strength? Fear hid behind her eyes, and because of me, she was taken to the epitome of hell.

A darkness had settled inside of my house, ruining any chance I had of mentally unwinding.

My feet moved of their own accord. I needed to make sure she was okay. When I reached the bathroom door, I heard whimpers and soft cries.

Fuck.

Instead of knocking, I allowed myself in. Meeka was sitting on the floor of the shower, her arms curled around her bent knees. Water streamed over her, cascading warmth throughout the room that she probably didn't feel at the moment.

Taking off my clothes, I stepped into the shower and wrapped my arms around her shaking body.

She cried harder, leaning into me.

I didn't say anything as she cried in my arms. What could I say? Would I be able to tell her that it would be okay? That everything would work out in the end? How could she believe me? She watched a girl being taken. She saw others in cages like animals. I was an asshole for forcing her into this mess but as much as she would be mad at me, I wouldn't change my choice. Meeka was everything that I was not. And I trusted her with my life. She was the strength I needed to get through the job. Even with the missions, I knew I would have to go back to her. It kept me going when so many times I wanted to give up.

"I chose her," Meeka sobbed, breaking the silence. "I forced her to her death. Oh, God, Asher, she looked at me. I could see the fear. It's all my fault."

"It is not your fault," I said the words, but even I knew she wouldn't believe them.

"It is," she cried harder, her shoulders shaking with bone-wracking sobs. "There's no way I can go back there."

I held her tight and pinched her chin, forcing her to look up at me. "Yes, you can. But not because *I* need you to. It's because *you* need to go back there. I know you, Meeka. You won't settle until you find out yourself if the girls are safe and those bastards get caught. It's how you're wired."

"I'm not strong enough. I thought I was, but I'm really not."

"Yes." I kissed her softly on the forehead. "You are. You may think you can't handle it, that you can't go back there, but you can. Yes, it sucks. It sucks more than anything and it's the hardest job we have both been on. But we're doing it together. You and I. As a team."

She sighed, her shoulders slumping. She wiped the tears from under her eyes even though she was wet from the spray of the shower. It was out of habit but I found myself smiling. She was fucking adorable and beautiful beyond words. Not like I ever had many words to begin with. But with Meeka, I wanted to talk. I wanted to say everything on my mind.

"We do make a great team," she stated, rubbing my arm that was around her waist. "Why did you give Charles fifty grand?"

My jaw clenched. "He was being a dick, and I needed to show him that I meant business."

"He knows you're a Navy SEAL."

"I know, but he doesn't know that Vice-One has been after him for years. He thinks he has power when really, we wanted him to know who we are."

"You enjoy playing games with him, don't you?" She shivered, curling against me.

"We all do." I rose to my feet and turned off the shower before reaching out for her hand.

When she only looked up at me, my heart panged. "We're going to have a bath so I can wash the filth off of you. So I can erase the past couple of hours and replace those memories with comfort. I'll at least try."

Meeka nodded, her eyes welling. She placed her hand in mine, letting me pull her to her feet. We exited the shower and moved around the bathroom in silence. I drew a hot bath and Meeka brushed her teeth. We were both naked but not ashamed in the least. It made me proud that she was comfortable enough with me that she didn't need to cover up. We both had scars, flaws, things we weren't happy with in our bodies but that made us fucking human. I worked out as much as I could and ate a burger when I wanted to.

Meeka, on the other hand, was perfect. To me. She was tiny but curvy. Strong enough she could knock me on my ass.

She caught my gaze in the mirror, her eyes twinkling.

I smiled, enjoying the view of her holding the toothbrush in her mouth. It was later in the evening even though it felt like we were only at Charles' place for minutes. But it just proved that time stood still in that hell.

Clearing my throat, I slid into the tub, waiting for her to join me.

She finished brushing her teeth, letting out a heavy sigh when she was done.

"Come here, Hummingbird," I said gently, holding my hand out for her.

When she stepped into the tub, her whole body shivered. Sitting between my legs, she leaned her head against my shoulder.

"Better?" I asked, taking a face cloth and dipping it into the water. Brushing it over her shoulders and down her arms, I kissed her cheek.

"I want to forget the last couple of hours," she muttered, holding my other arm around her middle. "I want to forget that we're dealing with a monster. I just want to spend time with you and never leave this moment."

My dick jumped, twitching against her lower back. But it wasn't about sex. As much as I craved her body, I needed… whatever it was that we were sharing right then. "I'm here, baby. Whatever you need, tell me, and I'll make it happen."

"Make me forget."

I cupped her jaw, tilting her head, and covered her mouth with mine. The kiss was slow but deep, and it definitely didn't last long enough. "I wish I could make you forget permanently, but all I can do is make you feel better and help you through this."

"What if I don't want help? What if I just want it to end? I go back to my life and you go back to yours."

"Is that what you want?"

"I … God, no." She huffed. "But I don't … I'm scared. That's the truth. I want whatever this is between us, to continue and—"

"And what, Hummingbird?" I asked, hoping she had the same thoughts I did.

"I want more. From you." Her cheeks reddened. "I want you."

"Fucking a." My mouth crashed to hers in a hard bruising kiss. It wasn't the right time. We shouldn't have sex. But my dick thought different. Fuck me, her mouth tasted good.

"Asher," she breathed against my lips.

"I know," I panted, leaning my forehead against hers. "Sorry."

"Don't be." She smiled. "I like that you can't control yourself around me."

"Do you find it funny?" I joked, tickling her gently in the ribs.

She giggled, wrapping her arms around my neck. "Thank you."

"You don't need to thank me," I reminded her. "How many times have you saved me from falling into myself, Meeka? It's the least I can do."

She chewed her bottom lip, curling against me. "I never did it for anything in return. I did it because I care and your step-father was a sick bastard."

Her words registered home. They hit me square in the chest, wrapped around my heart like a blanket, and hugged me in a tight embrace. I knew she never protected me to get something out of it. It wasn't how Meeka was wired. She thought about others first. Her sisters. Her family. *Me.* She may have been going through issues with Jay at that moment but Meeka would still do anything to make sure she was safe.

The attraction I had for Meeka grew with each touch, each caress. We only had sex once but it was like we had been together for years. Everything seem to have fallen in to place. She was the strength I needed when I was weak. The power when I was frail. I loved her like family, but that love had grown into something more. It had been blooming before I ever kissed her. Being a broken man, I never knew how to act upon any of the feelings I had for her.

"What are you thinking about?" She moved to the other end of the tub, stretching out her legs in front of her.

"How beautiful you are." I grabbed her foot, rubbing my fingers into the heel. "I'm thinking how you force me to my knees with just one look. The sounds of pleasure that leave your mouth are because of me and that turns me on."

Her lips parted, her cheeks flushing at my words. "What else?"

I smirked. Lifting her foot, I kissed her heel and gave it a gentle nip.

She jumped, pulling from my grip. A giggle escaped her, causing my blood to stir.

In all of the years I had known Meeka, I never understood why I was so comfortable around her. I was a difficult person to deal with at times. *I* even knew that. The random feelings of want and need maybe weren't so random after all. I couldn't be sure. But as we sat in silence, whatever was going on between us only grew.

No touch and I could still feel her hands on my skin, gripping me as I took the pleasure from her body.

No sound, and yet her voice grazed my ears like a beautiful melody.

She smiled at me and rose to her feet.

"Where are you going?"

Meeka only held out her hand.

Not even hesitating, I slipped my fingers between hers and stood from the tub.

Leading us out of the large basin, she headed back to the shower. A shadow fell over her face, her teeth grazing her bottom lip. "I need you right now."

Turning on the shower, I pulled her into my arms and stepped under the hot spray.

"Please."

My stomach twisted. Whatever was going through her mind was weighing on her. Was it Charles? Did the sick fuck touch her? She wouldn't tell me, at least, not yet. Probably for the better anyway. If anything happened to her, I would rip him limb from limb and dance in his entrails. What those bastards did to the minds of females were far worse than the torture they inflicted on their bodies.

But I made the promise that I would do everything in my power to keep her safe. Meeka was the piece of me that was stolen as a child. She was the warmth and goodness I craved. If she only knew how I felt. But I wasn't a good man. She deserved better. She didn't deserve a broken man. *Fuck.*

Grabbing a washcloth, I rubbed it down her arms.

She leaned against me, her eyes fluttering closed. "I want you so hard, it hurts," she whispered.

My dick twitched.

Meeka had always been a good girl, but get her comfortable enough and a little vixen reared its head. This morning would be nothing like what I would do to her if she let me. And she would because she craved it.

"Why do you want me?" I asked, my lips grazing the shell of her ear.

"Because—" her breath hitched "—you can give me what I want and need."

"How do you know that?" I didn't want to ask the question but the words left my lips before I could stop them.

"Because I trust you. I trust you with all of me." She turned in my arms, grazing her hands down my chest and looked up at me. "You wouldn't hurt me."

"You don't know that." It took everything in me not to run away. My chest constricted. I wanted to be everything she needed, but it wasn't possible. My step-father stole that from me.

"What's wrong?" she raised an eyebrow. "You fucked me this morning, and now you're having second thoughts?"

"It shouldn't have happened." Shit. Even I didn't believe those words leaving my mouth.

"It shouldn't?" Meeka laughed, stepping out of my embrace. "I was the one who didn't want to have sex because it would make things weird. But you kept kissing me. God …" She shook her head. "I've never been kissed like that."

"Again, that shouldn't have happened, either." What the hell was I talking about? I didn't believe anything I said, but I couldn't stop myself. I was turning into a fucking pussy, falling into myself and getting emotional and shit.

Meeka frowned. "What the hell is going on?"

I huffed, shoving a hand through my hair. "We're best friends."

"Yeah, I get that, but the friend card kind of went out the window when you had me coming apart in your arms earlier." She crossed her arms under her full chest, narrowing her eyes.

Water drops hit her pale skin, sliding down the curves of her tits. Her nipples peaked, begging for my mouth and teeth. What was I doing? Why was I denying myself this beautiful creature standing in front of me? I had her once. She wanted me again. My body definitely wanted hers. Several thoughts bounced around in my head, poking and nagging. My mind was loud. *Fuck.*

Meeka's mouth parted, her pink tongue licking over her bottom lip.

Since that morning, I couldn't get the image of her arching beneath me out of my head. Whether I wanted to admit it or not, she was always at the forefront of my mind. It had been that way for years.

Taking a step forward, she slid her hands down her stomach.

My cock jumped to attention. Fuck me, she was absolutely breathtaking. Her dark hair, wet and knotty, just begged to have my fist wrapped around it.

"Fuck our friendship," I growled and charged toward her.

CHAPTER FOURTEEN

Meeka

THE DARK LOOK OF lust in Asher's gaze almost had me coming apart right then and there. I wanted him. Every single thing about him. Even though I got him the once, it wasn't everything he could give me. It wasn't enough. He had held back. I knew that. He knew it. And this time would be real.

He told me he wasn't good enough for me. Well, I would make damn sure he knew he was. But it would be about sex. The passionate need to consume each other's souls.

He dominated, took control, and I gave in willingly.

STAIN

When his hands grabbed my hips and lifted me in his arms, a wicked smirk spread on his face.

My stomach somersaulted. I was in for it.

Instinctively, I wrapped my legs around his waist; inviting him in to the spot I needed him most. But he didn't need an invitation. He knew I belonged to him whether I wanted to admit it or not. I had been his for years. I went through men just for something to do, but they mostly just ended up as failed dates. I was inexperienced, and I wanted Asher to show me everything there was to know about pleasure. What he could do to me. What desires he had and the dark fantasies he craved.

Our chests heaved, our breathing mixing as one. The cool tile bit into my heated skin.

"Please," I begged, circling my hips against his hard cock.

He didn't move. He only held me tight in his hands, his fingers digging into the flesh of my rear.

I whimpered. I couldn't take it anymore. The ache between my legs grew, burning with the need for him to take me to new heights I never experienced. I just wanted a little more. Maybe if I moved forward, I could get him inside me. My body shook. My feelings disappeared as the only thing I was worried about at the time was getting fucked. Not making love. I needed him to destroy me. "Please." We didn't have a condom. Maybe that was the issue. I was clean. I knew he was. "I want to feel you."

His eyes darkened. In one powerful thrust, he filled me to the hilt.

I screamed, coming a part instantly in his arms. His name left my lips on a guttural cry, my head slamming against the shower wall.

Asher took that as his cue and drilled into me with so much strength, I was coming undone for the second time in a matter of minutes.

Lifting my knees to my chest, he thrust hard and deep. So deep, I could feel him fuck my soul.

I cried out, holding onto his thick arms and dug my nails into his tanned muscles. "Harder," I whispered, spots dancing in my vision.

He leaned down to my ear, his hot breath scorching my skin. "You like it when I fuck you rough, my dirty girl. You wanted to feel my cock ripping you open. No condom, baby." His tongue licked along my jaw line. "You want me to come inside you?"

My heart sped up at his words, a moan leaving my lips. "Yes."

His hips pushed forth, our bodies slapping together. "All you will feel is me. For-fucking-ever, Meeka. You are mine." Dropping me to my feet, he spun me in his arms and pushed me up against the wall.

Leaning against him, I rubbed my ass into the raging erection.

"Don't fucking move," he growled, bending me over.

My hands slapped against the tile. My heart pounded so hard in my ears, I was surprised he didn't hear it.

Asher groaned, brushing his fingers down the length of my back before landing a swat on the cheek of my ass.

I yelped but wiggled my hips.

"So fucking perfect. You're mine, aren't you, Hummingbird? You wiggle that ass, teasing me, but you want me to fuck it, don't you?"

My eyes widened. He wasn't suggesting … *No, there was no way.*

He chuckled. "Look at me."

I looked at him over my shoulder, my mouth watering at the sight before me.

His hand wrapped around his dick, the tip angry and red. "Do you trust me?"

"Y-yes." I swallowed hard, not taking my eyes away from his long fingers pleasing the part of himself that had been inside me only seconds before.

"Then trust me to give you everything you want. You aren't ready for me to take your ass now. But believe me, I'll be fucking your ass soon enough. You can look at me with those beautiful eyes, but don't push me, Meeka. Remember who is in control."

****

(Asher)

She was soft where I was hard.

Pure where I was tainted.

Gentle where I was rough.

Her moans pulled me home, sheltering me in a blanket of bliss. She comforted me. Gave me what I wanted, and it was my turn to give her what she craved. My little sexual submissive did anything to please me. Her Master. I knew her inside and out. But at that moment, it was more. She fucked my mind, and in return, I gave her the sweetest pleasure.

Her moans wrapped around me, mixing with my grunts. Our sounds, the undying want took over as I forced her body to explode and her mind to break. She was mine. I took every inch of her and owned her like a true Master would.

The tight heat pierced me straight in the gut until all I felt was her.

"A-Ash … Oh, God."

I pulled her into an upright position, holding her against me while I was still seated deep inside her body.

As much as I knew I should go slow, I didn't want to scare her, I couldn't. There was a driving force inside of me, an animalistic need to mark her, and it took over. My hips thrust. Hard and fast.

She whimpered, her breathing coming out in short gasps.

Her body squeezed me in a vice like grip, begging me to let her come. So I complied. This time. With one arm around her waist, holding her up, I used the hand of the other to give her what she so desperately wanted.

"Hold on, Hummingbird," I whispered, grazing the scruff of my cheek against hers.

Meeka let out a breath of relief.

She wouldn't be relieved that quick. I smiled to myself.

Reaching between her legs, I pushed a finger through the wet folds of her pussy.

She jumped, whimpering.

With my cock inside her tight pussy, I flicked her clit, rubbing it hard and fast. Matching the movements of my thrusts, I had her screaming my name in record time.

"Oh, God. *Fuck.*"

She screamed again, but I didn't let up. The Alpha inside of me wanted her walking around tomorrow, letting everyone know that she had been fucked good and hard the night before. I wanted Charles to know that she was, in fact, mine. The possessive need to mark every inch of her took over, and I powered into her with so much force, I almost lost my grip on her wet body. Fuck. I needed to gain control. Spots danced in my vision. A grey cloud shielded my thoughts. I was driven mad with the need to destroy her.

"Shit." I didn't know what was going on, but the powerful hold her passion had over my body took over.

"Come, baby," she pleaded, pushing her ass back against me.

I groaned, tearing into her. Never in my life had sex felt that way. Powerful yet delicious. Pure fucking perfection.

"Please," she panted, meeting me thrust for thrust. "I—" Her words died on a scream.

And that was when I broke, my dick swelled, pulsing into her with hot jets of cum. "*Fuuuuuuck,*" I roared, my balls tightening to the point of painful.

I couldn't take it. The release was so fucking powerful, my vision faded in and out.

We both fell to the floor of the shower, breathing heavy and still connected.

Once my heart finally calmed down, I released Meeka and turned her in my arms.

Her eyes drooped, a small smile spreading on her beautiful face. "That was ..."

"Fucking amazing," I answered for her and kissed her softly on the mouth.

"Mmhmm ..." Her eye lids fluttered closed.

Taking her in my arms, I rose to my full height, but not before I noticed the crimson trail dripping down her inner thighs.

Shit.

CHAPTER FIFTEEN

Meeka

IT HAD BEEN YEARS since I saw the bright look of fear behind Asher's beautiful eyes. He had learned to mask his emotions by putting up a hard wall around him. I was the only one to ever break through, but even I had difficulty doing so sometimes.

In the last couple of minutes, he had gone from possessive Alpha male to scared timid little boy. My stomach twisted, my heart racing at the thought of losing him to the darkness inside.

"What's wrong?"

He shook his head, mumbling something about *monster* and *clean*. I couldn't understand him but as I neared him, he jumped.

"No," he cried. "Clean. I … have … I have to clean you."

"What are you talking about?" I reached out for him, but he only spun around.

Grabbing a cloth, he shoved it under the water, and before I knew what was happening, he was on his knees in front of me. "Clean."

What the hell is going on?

"Evil. So stupid," he continued mumbling to himself, rubbing the cloth over my skin. "Clean."

"I'm clean. Don't worry. I am," I insisted, kneeling in front of him.

"No," he snapped, attempting to force his hand between my legs. "Blood. Not clean."

"What are you talking about?" I followed his gaze, my eyes widening at the streak of red leaving my body and flowing down the drain. Oh, God. That was why. *Shit.* "Asher, I'm fine," I insisted, grabbing his hand from between my legs.

"*No*," he shouted, wiping the cloth over my aching core. "I hurt you. I made you fucking bleed." Although his words held an edge, his touch was gentle. So gentle it brought tears to my eyes.

My throat burned. "I'm fine, baby. I am. I promise you."

"I hurt you." His eyes shone. "I'm sorry. I'm so fucking sorry."

I didn't care that I had bled; I was more worried about the man breaking and losing himself before me. Throwing my body into his arms, I reached behind him and turned off the water.

He kept mumbling about cleaning and hurting me all the while holding me tight against him.

Never in my life had I thought his control over me would become a trigger for his past. The blood set him off but I wasn't upset with him. It happened. Asher needed me, but I didn't know how to make him see that I was fine.

Lifting me in his arms, he grabbed a large towel from the linen closet.

"Put me down. I'm fine to walk by myself." Although I was sore, it was the best feeling I ever experienced.

"Not gonna happen," he bit out, wrapping the terry cloth around me and carrying me to his bed.

"Asher," I squirmed in his arms. "I'm fine. Put me down."

But he ignored me and sat me on the edge of his bed. Brushing the soft material over my skin, Asher's brow furrowed in the middle. His big body, still completely naked, held no hint of the intense delicious sex we just shared. His cock was flaccid. I was tempted to touch him to see how he would react. When he knelt in front of me, taking my foot in his hands, I just sat there. Watching. I was confused as to what was going on and why things suddenly changed but after dealing with him for years, I knew to be patient. But it was different.

"I never meant to hurt you," he finally confessed, breaking some of the tension that had built up inside of me.

"You didn't. Yes, it was intense because you're—"

"I'm what?"

"Huge." My cheeks burned.

A hint of lust flashed in his eyes. "I should have waited. I should—"

"No." I took his hands and slid from the bed, straddling his lap. "I told you to fuck me. I wanted everything you had to give me. Nothing more. Nothing less. I wanted *you*." I jabbed a finger into his chest. "You gave me you, Asher."

"But I made you bleed," he cried, slamming his fist against the ground.

"And no matter how many times we have sex, you could still make me bleed, Asher," I told him. "I'm not fragile. I may be small, but I won't break. You have to see that. I loved everything that we did. Everything we shared because I knew it was meant to be."

He sighed, leaning his forehead against mine.

"Why does it bother you so much?" There was an underlining reason as to why he freaked out.

"I don't want to talk about it anymore." He rose to his full height, pulling me up with him. "We have another long day tomorrow."

I shook my head, shocked that he could go from upset to withdrawn in a matter of seconds. "We need to talk about this."

"I said, I don't want to talk about it." He raised an eyebrow, daring me to argue with him. His words lacked any emotion, any hint of the pain I had seen in his eyes just minutes before.

In a huff, I walked around the side of the bed and threw back the covers. He did the same but kept his gaze on me the whole time.

"Get in the bed, Meeka," he demanded, waiting.

Crossing my arms under my chest, I braced myself. I enjoyed challenging him.

He raised an eyebrow. "Do I need to repeat myself?"

I swallowed hard at the underlining threat in his voice.

"I will tell you, if I repeat myself, my dear Hummingbird, I will spank that beautiful ass until you soak my hand with your delicious cum. And after that, I won't stop."

Oh, gosh. A shiver rippled over my body. "I just want to make sure that you're okay," I said, sliding under the covers.

He joined me, wrapping his arm around my waist. "I know I need to talk about it. I get that. But right now, I want to enjoy this. I'm tired, Meeka. Help me sleep."

"Okay." I reigned soft kisses on his face. "Just promise me that we'll talk."

"I promise, baby."

***

(Asher)

Never in my life had I experienced what I just went through. The sight of the red crimson blood set me off. It was a trigger that I never knew would happen. It upset me to the point I blacked out, mumbling words that weren't coherent.

Meeka's wide eyes stuck with me. It would be engrained in my skull for the rest of my days. I didn't want to worry her. It was something I had dealt with for years, pushing feelings to the side like they weren't important. Triggers? Please. I was Asher-fucking-Donovan. I didn't have triggers. The Navy psychiatrist tried diagnosing me with PTSD and a whole bunch of other shit. Apparently, I had abandonment issues and social anxiety. It wasn't true. I just hated people. My brothers and Meeka were the only ones who could get into my heart, but even I knew it had never been completely. Until her.

With Meeka's sleeping form lying beside me, she breathed slow and deep. Content sighs left her lips every so often. She pushed her bare ass into my semi-hard erection that wouldn't go down since the first kiss we shared.

I pulled her closer. I knew I should be sleeping. I knew I should give into the dark slumber of rest, but I much preferred to stare at the gorgeous woman beside me.

"Sleep, Asher," Meeka whispered, snuggling into my arms.

"I prefer to watch you." I kissed her forehead, inhaling the sweet scent of her skin.

"Okay." Her eyes fluttered closed.

I smiled, placing a soft peck on her mouth.

She told me I was good enough for her. Although the words had left her mouth, I didn't believe them. I couldn't get over the fact that I would ruin her. I would destroy her soul and make her constantly worry over me. I didn't want that. She deserved better. A good man. As much as it pained me to say, I would give up everything to see that she was happy. My chest constricted. Just the thought of her being with someone else made me want to fuck her into submission and prove that she was mine.

The possessive need to control her every move was new for me.

I pulled Meeka into my arms, brushing my hand up and down her back. After all of the shit with Charles was done, I would end things with her. She didn't want to be with a broken man. How could she? She didn't deserve to be with someone who was so damn needy. It wasn't fair to her.

My throat burned. Fuck me. The pain threatened to swallow me whole. It hurt worse than getting fucking shot. How could I make her see that she deserved better? A thought came to me. Shit. It would work. As much as it would kill me, I had to do it. For Meeka. My best friend. The woman I loved.

CHAPTER SIXTEEN

Meeka

I WOKE THE NEXT morning wondering if things would be weird between us. You would think if it was going to be awkward, it would have happened already.

Asher wasn't beside me, but I heard him moving around on the main level. What we shared the night before changed things between us. It opened up a new possibility. Would this end after the mission was over? I knew Asher cared for me in the way he touched me. The way he handled my body, forcing me to succumb to the greatest pleasure I had ever experienced. But his fear that he wasn't good enough for me threatened to take over and consume his feelings.

Running my hand over the empty spot beside me, all I could smell was him. His spicy cologne was intoxicating. Mixed with the heady perfume of sex, it was downright drugging.

As much as he didn't want to, we needed to talk. And I needed to know why he freaked out. Blood wasn't the only reason, and I had to find out more. It was the only way I would understand.

Rising from the bed, I pulled his shirt over my head. It reached my knees, but the soft cotton comforted me as if the owner were wrapped around me instead.

With a moment of trepidation settling deep in the pits of my stomach, I trudged down the stairs. Not sure what I would find, I was happy when I saw Asher sitting on the couch.

He had his cell to his ear, talking quietly to whoever was on the other line. His back stiffened, his eyes looking up to meet my gaze. They roamed down my body, heating with fire.

My throat went dry at the look of pure lust staring back at me.

He crooked a finger, indicating for me to go to him.

My feet moved although I had felt like I was stuck to the ground in a puddle of wanton need. God this man and what he did to me.

He smirked when I complied, grabbing the hem of my shirt. "You have nothing to worry about, my brother. Yes. I know." He lifted the fabric, his nostrils flaring when he noticed that I wasn't wearing anything underneath. "Listen, man, I have to go; I'm about to eat my breakfast."

STAIN

***

(Asher)

Screams filled my ears. They were so loud they pierced into my soul. And that made me even harder. My cock threatened to explode, but I couldn't let up on the treat riding my face. Sweet juices flowed past my lips, over my tongue, and down my throat. All I could smell was the heady scent, and fuck if it wasn't divine.

Meeka's cries of pleasure were music to my ears and no matter how much she begged, I wouldn't let up. I was a man of my word when I told Angel that I was about to eat my breakfast. His deep chuckle proved he knew what I was referring to. I didn't care. I was a man and I loved eating pussy.

As much as I knew we had to talk, seeing Meeka wearing my t-shirt threw me off. It had set my blood on fire.

Mine.

It was the only word I could think of when I threw her down on the couch, practically ripping the offensive material off of her. Control. It wasn't warranted where she was concerned. All thoughts left me and for the third time, I had her screaming out my name.

Releasing her with a wet smack, I kissed her inner thigh before sinking my teeth into the flesh.

She cried out, a surge of wetness coating my fingers.

Hmmm, my Hummingbird likes it dirty. In a quick move, I had her under me and her legs wrapped around my waist. Her eyelids fluttered closed, a soft sigh of bliss leaving her beautiful mouth. Which reminded me, I needed to fuck it and soon.

140

"No falling asleep, baby. I've only had my coffee. Now I need my fucking eggs and bacon." I kissed the side of her neck, rubbing the juices from her body over her soft skin.

Meeka laughed, wrapping her arms around my neck. Her burning gaze seared straight into my heart. Her mouth brushed along the shell of my ear, causing a shiver to race down my back.

"Then feast on me and take all the sustenance you need, baby."

And I did. Twice.

***

(Meeka)

He moved from side to side, hopping from one foot to the other. It was a dance but also a battle. It was man versus weight. His fists swung. His legs kicked. He grunted. He swore. And he was all mine. *For now, anyway.*

Asher moved with a fluid grace, working out the muscles in his hard body until he was covered in a sheen of sweat. I could watch him for hours. It had been that way for years. I loved watching him train.

We were leaving to see Charles in an hour and heading to the clubhouse after. For whatever reason, Asher was finally letting me out of his house. Not that I had put up much of a fight. Maybe I had wanted things to change between us from the very beginning.

Every so often, he would look my way, his face grim and determined. The only hint of emotion was the twinkle of mischief in his gaze. I knew that look. It was the one where he told me to get ready and run.

"Don't poke the bear, sweet girl. I bite."

And did he ever.

Bruises marked my inner thighs where he had devoured me until I begged him to stop, telling him I couldn't handle anymore. But I knew he only let me have a break because he wanted to think I had some sort of control. I didn't. And I was fine with that.

There was still the issue of him believing that he wasn't good enough for me but with Charles being in the way, we had to depend on each other first. Taking the stresses of our jobs out on each other seemed only fitting.

My phone buzzed, vibrating in my back pocket. My heart jumped when I saw Jay's name flash across the small screen. "Hello?"

"Hey," Jay greeted.

"Is something wrong?" I had no idea why she would be calling, especially me.

"No. I will be honest, though; Angel is the one who convinced me to call you." She cleared her throat. "I'm trying here, Meeka, but with you not around, it makes it hard."

"I know." I sighed. "We're stopping by tonight," I continued when she didn't say anything. "I miss you. All of you. This shit sucks."

She laughed. She actually *laughed*.

Relief flooded through my veins at the mere sound. I slid down the wall until I hit the floor, curling my knees against my chest. "I'm happy Angel convinced you to call me."

"Yeah, well, that man of mine is too fucking smart for his own good sometimes." She cleared her throat again. It was her signature move whenever she became nervous. "Max wanted to have a party tonight, but I told her to just have the guys and us there."

"I agree. I need to see my sisters."

"How are things there?"

I laughed. "I have a dark brooding man who won't leave me alone, and it's confusing as hell."

"Sounds like you got a problem," she teased.

"A delicious one," I whispered, leaning my head back against the wall.

"Listen, whatever you do, whatever is going on between the both of you, don't be stupid like I was and push him away."

"Why, Jay, are you giving me advice?" I teased back, the light-hearted humor a nice change for us.

"Yeah, I guess I am."

"Baby, who are you talking to?" came a deep voice in the background.

"Meeka," she replied.

"God, woman, it's about damn time," Angel grumbled.

My heart swelled that he had been rooting for me. Jay and I had a lot of shit to work through but the easy conversation set us on the right path to being friends again. "I'll let you go, Jay. Thank you again for calling me."

"See you tonight." And with that, she hung up.

"Who was that?" Asher asked, standing over me.

"Jay." I held my phone in my hand, staring at the screen. Did we really just have this conversation? Was it a dream? Was I so desperate for Jay's respect, that I imagined the whole thing?

"And?" Asher frowned.

"It was good. Angel convinced her to call me. It was nice. Really nice."

He pulled me to my feet, placing a chaste kiss on my lips. "Good. I'm glad."

I sighed, wrapping my arms around his hard waist. The scent of sweat and sex filled my nostrils, making my core clench.

"When do we leave?" I asked, clearing my throat and stepping out of his embrace.

"Half an hour, but first, I'm going to fuck my woman."

And he did. But the only thing I could focus on was the fact that he said I was *his*.

***

(Asher)

Everything in me said to tell Meeka that we needed to end things before we both fell deeper into this confusing-as-shit mess. But my body acted before my brain did. The soft curves of her body made every inch of me want to fall deep inside her and never leave. She was my comfort when my anxiety threatened to ruin me and bring me to my knees.

Charles had one of his men pick us up a half an hour after I made use of Meeka's body to please my own. God, I was such a dick. I was using her, but I couldn't stop myself. I tried, fuck me, I tried, but she kept me calm when I wanted to combust. It was about to happen. It would. Eventually. It was like an elastic band being pulled tight until it snapped. I just prayed Meeka wouldn't be on the receiving end.

"Are you okay?" Meeka's soft voice pulled me from my thoughts.

"It is what it is," I answered, kissing her forehead.

"You know the boss would shit if his whore spoke out of line." The driver frowned.

"She is not a whore, and I don't fucking care what your *boss* says or thinks," I threw back at him. "My pet is just that, *mine*. As long as she listens to me, I could give a fuck about anything else."

The driver chuckled. "I think that's the most words I've ever heard you say."

Shit. I was losing my ever-loving mind. I sure as fuck couldn't break role, especially where Meeka was concerned. It would be the end of everything if Charles or one of his men found out we were working undercover.

I harrumphed and pulled Meeka closer to my side.

"Thank you," she whispered, chewing her bottom lip.

My gut twisted, a sharp pain piercing me straight in the heart. What the hell had I brought her into? Was I that fucking selfish that I thought of only myself?

I was sick of this shit. I needed the mission to be done and over with for fear of blowing it for everyone. My feelings were never worn on my sleeve, but it wouldn't take a smart person to know that I felt something for the tiny thing sitting beside me.

The rest of the drive to Charles' place was quiet. It took everything in me not to tell Meeka how I felt. Even though I had convinced myself that I wasn't good enough for her, the constant war raging inside of me was enough to drive a sane person mad.

My cell vibrated, indicating an incoming text. It was about damn time.

Angel: U there?

Me: Yup

STAIN

I responded as soon as we pulled up to the big mansion that housed enough secrets to our operation that would no doubt end this organization.

Angel: Good. Get me everything u can.

Me: Like u expected any less from me.

I could almost hear his deep chuckle that would be followed by an "ass". My heart panged. I missed my brothers. I missed shooting the shit, working out at the gym, and just doing nothing. They hadn't left for the mission yet that I was no longer allowed to go on. If I had it my way, I would throw Charles in jail and do my job. That wasn't what I got paid for. We did an old boss a favor before he blew his head off in front of Jay. Angel lost his shit that his girlfriend was taken in the first place. He almost went all Liam Neeson on the fucker.

I realized then that we never mourned. Not together. We got pissed off, a new boss, and went about our daily lives like nothing happened. We never talked about it.

"Looks like the boss is antsy," the driver mumbled.
I followed his gaze.
Charles was on the phone, his eyes hard and cold.
Fucking great.
Opening the door, I stepped out of the vehicle.
Meeka followed suit, instantly grabbing hold of my hand when her feet touched the ground. With her eyes cast down, her fingers remained locked in mine. We had a quick training session before the car picked us up. Not like I had much time when all I could focus on was her heat wrapped around me.

"Why hello there," Charles smiled down at us from the top step, putting his cell in the inside pocket of his jacket. "You must be wondering why I had you dropped off at the front of the house instead of the back as per usual."

"It crossed my mind." Cupping the back of Meeka's neck, I guided her up the steps until we were standing face to face with Charles.

"I would usually have your toy in the holding room while you and I discussed business but—" he crossed his arms under his chest "—I have a feeling you would make that rather difficult."

"You are correct." I pulled Meeka closer to my side. "Where she goes, I go. Besides, when it comes to business, my toy, as you like to call her, needs to know where she stands."

"And why is that?" Charles moved to the double set of doors, leading into the large mansion.

"Because it's her life we're talking about." I shrugged, playing it cool like her life didn't matter when really, it mattered more to me than my own.

"She's a toy. Her life shouldn't matter. Bruce!" Charles called out, not waiting for my response. The fucker was smart because if I had it my way, he would be long dead in the ground before he took his next breath. Meeka was not a toy. None of the girls were but I had to act. And fucking act I did. God, I needed a vacation.

A large man, who I could only guess was Bruce, appeared in the hallway. "Sir."

"Bring me the papers. Our dear friend Ash here is a little impatient." Charles winked at me. "And make sure to bring me the collar as well. I don't want his toy getting out of hand."

STAIN

Meeka stiffened beside me.
Fucking fucker.

CHAPTER SEVENTEEN

Meeka

I WAS BRAVE. I was strong. I was a woman, and no one could mess with me. Standing beside Asher proved just how much of that was actually true. I bit back a scoff. I didn't believe the words chanting in my head, but I sure as hell tried to.

While he and Charles discussed business, I used it as a distraction to scope out my surroundings. Much to my dismay, the collar Charles had placed around my neck, thankfully giving Asher the chain, held my head in place. The contraption was stiff. The metal around my throat was thick, making it almost impossible to look around me without moving my whole body. But I couldn't do that for fear Charles would notice. I could only guess that Asher was checking out where we were. From what I saw, the mansion was old. The little research I had done was that the place had been in the family for centuries. Charles Brian was heir to a prestigious line of bastards, and if he didn't meet the requirements that had been set out for him, he wouldn't gain what he felt was rightfully his.

Charles may have not been the sole leader of the organized crime but he was as high up as we could get for the moment. Asher had been trying to get into the house for weeks. I wasn't sure which house it was or who exactly we were dealing with. If the main person was as terrifying as Charles, we were officially screwed.

When we had walked into a sitting area, Asher indicated for me to kneel at his feet while he sat comfortably on a couch. As much as I didn't want to submit when Charles was there, I knew I had to for Asher's safety. The bite of the cool marble flooring sent a shiver over my heated skin. Much like the metal wrapped around my throat, all I could do was sit and hope for the best that the meeting would be over soon.

I tried paying attention to the words flowing between Charles and Asher but my mind kept drifting to my past. A past that had always involved Asher. A past where he had spent as much time with me as possible so he didn't have to go home. I never knew what hid behind the walls of his house. I only knew that he came to me at night and slept on the floor of my bedroom and left before the sun rose in the morning. I never asked what his step-father did to him or made him do. But if the incident in the shower was any indication of the triggers his nightmares had conjured up, my best friend needed me in ways I never knew existed.

"Meeka," Asher barked out my name, pulling me from my thoughts.

"Looks like she is ignoring you." Charles laughed.

"Sorry." My cheeks burned. "What was the question?"

Asher leaned down to my ear, his hot breath scorching the side of my face. "As much as this is an act, I will punish you if you embarrass me again."

I swallowed hard, a flush of heat roaming over my skin. "I'm sorry."

"Now answer the question," he demanded, sitting back in the couch, and pet his hand over my head.

"How much do you think a life is worth?" Charles asked, finishing the sentence for him.

"It's priceless," I answered automatically, meeting Charles' gaze.

"And why is that?"

"Because no one should have a price on their head. No matter what. These girls are worth more than the money you spend on them. Their training, the people who want to buy them, and so on." I was rambling but I couldn't help it. I needed to let Charles know that although I was absolutely terrified of him, I wouldn't back down. For Jay, for her sister, for King's Harlots. For every fucking female in the damn country. I would fight Charles until every last one of them were saved.

"You think so? Do you think their life is worth more than yours? How about Asher's?" Charles raised an eyebrow, challenging me. "What if I said that these girls were thrown away like next week's trash? Addicts, whores, the lowest of the low when it comes to the human life."

"Clearly, they didn't have anyone to help them," I countered.

"And what would you do to help them, pet?" Charles asked, sitting back in the couch and crossed his ankle over the opposite knee.

"I would make sure they have a place to go." I shrugged. "Maybe they have no one."

"You, dear girl, are way too nice." Charles nodded once. "What have you been teaching her? To love others as you love yourself?" he scoffed. "Fucking please."

Asher shifted behind me, keeping his hand wrapped around my nape. "Unfortunately, she still has a mind of her own."

They both laughed.

As much as I knew Asher wasn't serious, the coldness in his chuckle sent a shiver racing down my spine. Never in my life had I heard such a dark evilness when it came to laughter. Between him and Charles, I wasn't sure who was worse. Every now and again, I had to remind myself that this wasn't Asher. This wasn't the man I had feelings for. Yes, I loved his Dominant side, but this took on a whole other level when it came to control.

"You need to get on that," Charles reminded him. Snapping his fingers, he smirked. "How about I show you what happens when a girl is finally broken?"

My heart picked up speed when the sound of a door opening from the other side of the room jarred through my thoughts. Chains rattled. Feet shuffled.

"Ah, yes, here she is." Charles rose to his full height, closing the distance between him and a frail girl. Her dark hair was pulled back into a messy bun, loose curls framing her pale face. Her bright-blue eyes twinkled. She swayed on her feet but she kept her gaze locked with Charles. A white, sheer night gown hugged her curves. A flutter of shock ran through me at how healthy she looked. Besides the drug-induced haze, she appeared normal.

"Our clients don't want to receive a broken and damaged package. Not physically, at least." Charles moved around the girl. "Eric Vega was a rookie."

Asher shifted slightly at the mere mention of his old boss's name.

"He didn't follow the rules. He assumed that he could do whatever the hell he wanted just because of who he was. But he made the wrong choice when he took the twins."

Jay and Violet. My throat went dry.

"You see, in this line of work, you can't take someone who will be missed. It doesn't work that way. Eric got a head of himself and wanted to showcase his power." Charles laughed. "Which clearly, it didn't work out for him."

The girl wavered on her feet.

Charles pulled the chain, forcing her to knees with a thump.

The sound vibrated through me. Although landing on the hard floor probably hurt like hell, no emotion showed on her face.

Charles sat forward, holding the end of the chain tight in his hand. "I have a feeling that in a couple more weeks, you'll be allowed into the main house."

"A couple more weeks?" Asher snapped.

"Watch the tone. You may be huge, but I'll still kill your ass if you continue to step out of line," Charles sneered. "And you wouldn't want that. Meeka would then be left in my possession. Oh, the things I could do to her."

I shivered at the venom dripping from his voice.

"How much?"

Charles grinned. "It's always money with you, isn't it?"

"That's because it's the only thing that makes you see reason. How much?" Asher repeated.

"I don't want any more money but my boss might." Charles looked down at the girl kneeling at his feet. Something passed behind his dark gaze. Regret? Sorrow? Pain? I wished that was what I had seen, but it wasn't. Whatever the emotion was, it sent bile burning up my throat.

"The mind is a fragile thing," Charles stated. "It's built up of tiny wires, and if one of them crosses, so much can happen. You can break it down, mold it, make the mind what you want it to be unless the victim is strong." His gaze met mine. "You're strong, aren't you? That's why Asher has a hard time training you, even though he won't admit it."

I shifted on my knees, not liking to talk about Asher when he was right behind me. He trained me like Charles had demanded, but there was only so much that can be done in a short amount of time. All of the other undercover operations I had been on required months of learning your role. It was next to impossible when I was thrown into the mix and demanded to submit to Asher because I was the only one he trusted.

"Tell me what I have to do to get into the house," he said, not bothering to comment on Charles' accusation.

"You'll see." Charles scratched his chin. "In time."

Asher rose to his feet, pulling me along with him. "Fine. We're done."

"You think you are, but you aren't." Charles snapped his fingers.

Two, large, beefy-looking men appeared almost out of nowhere. They grabbed hold of Asher, pulling him from my grip.

"What the fuck?" he snapped out.

"You see." Charles rose to his feet, petting his hand along the girl's head which was probably the only nice thing she would get from him. "I have to make you understand that you do not call the shots. If I want you in the house, you will get in the house. I may have a boss but I'm trusted with making decisions. And you don't scare me."

Charles took a step toward me, his saunter demeaning and controlled. "Keep your eyes on me. If you so much as even glance his way, I will hurt him. And I know you don't want that, now do you?"

"Please," I whispered.

"I'm sorry." He cupped his ear. "What was that?"

"Please don't hurt him," I said, louder.

"I won't as long as you listen to me." He wrapped his arm around my waist, pulling me flush against him. "Let's begin, shall we?"

CHAPTER EIGHTEEN

Asher

SEEING MY WOMAN IN another man's arms should have had me falling apart. It was what Charles wanted, but I refused to break. I wasn't one of his victims. I was a fucking Navy SEAL. I didn't crack under pressure. I was trained by the best.

Falling back into the training I had gone through years ago, I listened to the voices in my head and kept myself calm. Angel's demands were engrained in my skull, much like the rest of my brothers. It was normal for us to use our training in daily activities but it didn't happen often. Not until recently.

While the two fuckers held onto my arms, keeping me in place, I kept my gaze on Meeka. I willed her not to look my way. I could take a hit. But I didn't want her to see it. She was strong but she was going through enough shit without me adding to it.

Charles kept his hold on her, his hand moving ever-so-slowly down the length of her back before it cupped her ass.

As much as I tried to hold it in, a growl escaped my lips.

Mine.

"Ah, yes." Charles glanced my way. "There's the possessive male attribute. A growl. The only time our true animalistic nature comes out. Or so we think. You see if you embraced that side of you, you could have so much more. You act like you want it, but I don't see it in your eyes. Although—" Charles grinned, keeping his arm around Meeka "—I do see something there. Something darker that I might be able to use." He pinched Meeka's chin, forcing her to look up at him. "Do you see it? That darkness inside of him? I wonder what his story is. Do tell me. I sure love a good history. Was he abused? Did he get thrown into the system?" He glared my way. "Did your step-daddy give you a good beating? Were you not loved?" He paused. "Poor Asher was all alone until he met you. Isn't that right, Meeka?"

"You have no idea what you're talking about," she said, her voice becoming firm.

"No? Tell me then," he shoved her head forward, forcing her to look at me but much to his dismay, her eyes closed. "Smart girl." Charles chuckled. "You felt sorry for him, didn't you? That was the only reason you let him in."

"No." She shook her head. "That's not true."

Fuck this guy and all he was worth. "Let her go," I demanded, struggling against the bastards who held me.

"Oh, I will," Charles smirked. "But I want her to admit it."

"I have nothing to admit." Meeka pushed against him but his hold only tightened.

"Tell him." He pinched her chin, forcing her to look at me, and that time, she did. "Tell him you felt sorry for him. Admit it."

"Fine," she cried. "Yes, I felt sorry for him, but that—"

"You see, Asher." Charles grinned. "People only let you in because they feel sorry for you."

"No!" She shoved out of his grip. "That's not true."

My skin vibrated, my heart beating hard against my ribs. She felt sorry for me. Back then and probably even now. I was broken, and she wanted to fix me. It was the only reason we had become friends.

"That's not true," she repeated, shaking her head.

A growl escaped me, not realizing I had spoken out loud.

Fuck everyone.

***

(Meeka)

Pain etched in Asher's dark gaze. A shadow crossed over his face. His body was hard, ready to fight a battle. No, a war. He was bordering on the edge of sanity. I had seen that look in his eyes before. A time in school when the bullies were picking on me. Or when a guy wouldn't leave me alone and I wasn't strong enough to push him off. Asher had lost it then, and he was about to lose it now. Charles and his band of bastards didn't know what they were getting with him when they pushed him too far. They thought he played it cool, didn't care about anything or anyone but himself. I wasn't even sure if Vice-One knew Asher had a darker edge to him. One he didn't jump off often, but when he did, it was hard to bring him back and I had been the only one who could. I couldn't understand why. But right then, Asher was pissed. At me. Probably at the whole world. Whatever it was, I needed to get us out of there.

"Hmm, looks like he wasn't expecting that answer." Charles chuckled. "Let him go." He moved to the couch, pulling the girl into his lap, and snapped his fingers. "Leave. I'm bored."

The men let go of Asher, and before I could process what was happening, he grabbed my hand and tugged me out of there.

I ran alongside him, not looking back, but with his long strides, I couldn't keep up.

Asher noticed and scooped me into his arms, holding me against his chest.

The next thing I knew, we were in a cab. How we got there, I couldn't be sure. I didn't remember a single thing as he stared out the window and held my hand tight in his.

Everything was foggy. A haze had crushed me in a blinding hold. I wouldn't lose it. I refused. He was pissed but he would get over it. We were safe. *For now.*

Asher's mouth moved but he stared straight ahead. Was he talking to me? The driver? I couldn't hear him. A loud buzzing settled in my brain, my hands became sweaty. My heart raced. *Thump ... thump ... thum*p. It didn't let up the further we got from Charles' place.

The next thing I knew, I was sitting outside on the picnic bench in front of the clubhouse. How did we get there so fast? With shaky hands, I dropped my head and took deep cleansing breaths. I was losing it. I never lost it. I was always in control of my feelings. I was strong. Jay had taught us to be tough in this male-dominated world. We had nothing to prove, but unfortunately, others didn't see it that way.

Mumbled voices pulled me from my thoughts.

I looked up and saw my sisters standing around me. Jay spoke in a low voice to Asher, but I couldn't make out what was being said with his back to me.

Brogan sat beside me, wrapping her arm around my shoulders. "Bad day?"

"You could say that," I croaked out. Giving myself a shake, I rubbed a hand down my face, massaging some life back into myself. I wouldn't let Charles get his way over me. But I could still feel his hands on me. His dangerous gaze as it raked over my body. His rough fingers while they pinched my chin. My skin tingled with memories of the touch.

Asher turned to me, his dark eyes narrowing. "You good?"

The question was meant to be caring but it hinted at a coldness that took my breath. I felt sorry for him. God, how could I have been so stupid to admit that?

I didn't respond and slid off the table before heading into the club. I didn't check to see if he followed because I knew he would. Although he was pissed at me, he wouldn't want me to be alone. And knowing him, he would stake his possessive claim over me since another man touched me. My body tingled in all the right places, a flush of heat warming my skin. Asher was difficult but he was mine. He knew it. I knew it.

I went to the bar and grabbed a bottle of water.

"Do you still feel sorry for me?"

I jumped, spinning on my heel at the deep voice coming from behind me.

Asher loomed over the counter before sitting on the barstool, his intense scrutiny piercing into me.

"No," I mumbled, handing him the bottle.

He chugged back the rest of the cool liquid and threw it in the recycling bin. "Come here."

That same tingle shot straight to my core and I found my body listening to his command before my brain caught up. I rounded the corner and stepped between his legs before planting my butt on the stool beside him. "I didn't become friends with you because I felt sorry for you. We were kids."

"We drifted apart at one point, and then you started talking to me again. Did you feel sorry for me then? I was the loner. The bad boy all the girls wanted to date but were too scared to ask. You had the balls to talk to me. Why, Meeka? What was so special about me?"

I swallowed hard at the badgering of questions he threw at me, but I wouldn't back down. "We were neighbors. I missed being your friend and hanging out. The guys left me alone when I was friends with you."

"So it was for selfish reasons."

"No! God." I shook my head. "Stop. Fine. Yes, I felt sorry for you. In the beginning. I saw a boy who looked sad every damn day and I found I wanted to make him happy. I was just a little girl so I had no idea how to make that happen. And then puberty hit and you started ignoring me. That's why we drifted apart."

He grunted, a small smirk tugging at his lips.

"What?"

"I had the biggest crush on you all through school. That's why we drifted apart. I couldn't handle seeing you in those tight little shorts or those jeans that hugged your ass perfectly."

"Are you—" I couldn't believe it. "Seriously?"

He chuckled, rubbing the back of his neck. "Yeah. That's why I became distant. Not for any other reason."

"I thought you hated me. I couldn't figure out what I had done." I was still blown away. *He had a crush on me?*

"God no." He grabbed my hand, kissing each of my fingers. "Every time I saw you, I wanted to bend you over and drive my body into yours. But you were under eighteen at the time and I had enough shit to deal with. I didn't need statutory rape added to that pile."

"Why did you wait so long?"

"Life happens, Hummingbird." He shrugged.

"And now? Do you still have a crush on me?"

His eyes twinkled. "The need to own you consumes my every waking breath. I can feel you before you walk into the room. My cock hardens at the mere sound of your voice. Does that answer your question?"

"Yes," I answered, breathless.

He grinned.

I opened my mouth to say something when a loud bass started booming through the speakers.

"I need a fucking drink," Jay rounded the corner and headed behind the bar. "Hey," she said to us, grabbing a bottle filled with dark amber liquid.

"Grab a bottle and bring it back to your room," Angel called out from the hallway.

"Not gonna happen, baby," she yelled back. "I'm getting drunk with my sisters tonight. You can join me if you wish."

He appeared from the hallway and heaved out a heavy sigh. "Fine. If I must."

She laughed. Standing on tiptoes, she gave him a soft kiss on the mouth. "Come." She grabbed his hand, leading him to one of the larger booths at the front of the room.

"I guess there's a party tonight?" Asher asked, nodding his head toward the door.

Cars started pulling up outside, followed by the deep rumble of bikes. "Max throws parties when everyone is stressed," I told him. "It's her way of cleansing the aura around here."

He grunted. "I'm not one to drink away my problems. I'd rather fuck them away." He met my gaze. "You game?"

My cheeks heated. "I haven't seen my sisters in a while," I laughed, rising from the stool and stepped between his legs. "But later—" I kissed his mouth "—you can fuck all your problems away with me."

He grinned, and I swore my heart melted.

****

(Asher)

An hour later, the party was in full swing. It reminded me of the days back in college. People showed up every hour on the hour filling the location to the brim. The club house overflowed with people. Bikers, women dressed in barely-there clothes, and us. Jay had tried to make the party just be Vice-One and King's Harlots, but after the word got out, everyone and their dog showed up.

Meeka stood off to the side, laughing every so often with Brogan. Although the music was loud and deafening, I could still hear her full-bodied chuckle. It could have just been my imagination, but I liked to think that whatever made her happy at that moment was because of me.

A part of me held a tiny bit of anger that she had felt sorry for me. My confession changed things. I had a crush on her. Who wouldn't? She was so damn shy and naïve that she never knew just how hot she truly was. I remembered in school the cat calls, the whistles, and even the evil sneers from the popular girls. But Meeka never noticed. Some called her a snob but I knew that she actually didn't hear them. She never knew they were referring to her.

Meeka met my gaze every so often, her eyes becoming glassier by the minute. She was on her fifth beer, and eventually, I would have to drag her off to bed before she passed out in the middle of the room.

I didn't know who anyone was besides my brothers and King's Harlots, but I noticed how the other men watched out for them. Jay had been headstrong in trying to make her club blend in with the other bikers, but it had been hard when they were women. Those men, though, looked at them with a sign of respect. And as much as it grated on my nerves that they knew another side to Meeka that I didn't, I had to appreciate the protection she had when I wasn't around.

Meeka's laugh interrupted my thoughts.

Every possessive bone in my body hardened when I saw a strong hand grip her shoulder. Some asshole had his hands on my girl.

She giggled, shaking her head. It was innocent enough on her end but the dark look of lust in his gaze sent me over the edge.

I rose from where I was perched when a heavy hand cupped my nape.

"Think about what you're going to do before you do it," Coby said, his voice flat and cold.

"He has his hands on her," I ground out, a grey cloud shielding my vision.

"He does but she only has eyes for you," he pointed out, giving my shoulder a light squeeze. "Remember, one word and he's gone." And with that, Coby walked away.

My heart jumped.

Coby meant what he said. He may have had the nickname Ghost for most of his career, but I knew that he was more like the executioner. He was also smaller than me but he sent my nerves on edge.

One word.

One command and the fucker who had his hands on my woman would disappear. As much as I was inclined to have Coby follow through with his promise, I wouldn't do that to Meeka. But I would fuck her until all she thought about was me. All she would *feel* was me and I wouldn't regret taking her from the party at all.

****

(Meeka)

Why was I so damn nice? I didn't know who the guy was that had spent the last hour talking to me. What

165

was he even saying to me? Oh, yeah, he was talking about the club. He kept saying over and over how impressed he was that women ran an MC when I knew he was just trying to get in my pants. Or panties, rather, when I wasn't wearing any pants. *Oh, God. Where are my pants? Oh, yeah.* I looked down, noticing the dress that hugged my curves. I needed to stop drinking. I chugged back the rest of the beer and grimaced at the disgusting taste. It was piss warm. How long had I been nursing it? *Gross.*

"So what do you say?" the guy asked me, raising an eyebrow. His finger traced down the length of my arm.

I followed the movement, wondering what Asher would do if he saw. "About what?"

"I don't suggest repeating your question," a deep voice boomed from a foot away.

I guess I would find out sooner rather than later.

"And you are?" The guy stiffened beside me, rising to his full height before he noticed who was talking to him. "Uh … I'm gonna go." He pushed off the wall, and before I could ask what the hell was going on, he was out of the club in a matter of seconds.

I laughed.

"What's so damn funny?" Asher bit out, crossing his arms under his broad chest.

"You scared him half to death." I laughed harder. Maybe it was the alcohol but it was damn funny.

"Woman, he had his hands on you," he growled, clenching his fists at his sides.

"Yeah, so? He wouldn't do anything because I wasn't going to let him."

"You are too damn nice." Asher pinched my chin, forcing me to look up at him, and leaned his arm against the wall above my head. "Do you know what it made me want to do when I saw him touching you?"

"No," I breathed out. "But I can imagine. You go all possessive." It was hot as hell. All laughter had died then as I stared into the dark heated eyes looking down at me.

"He was touching what belongs to me," Asher bit out through clenched teeth. "I don't share well with others."

"Who says I belong to you?" I threw back at him, the liquid courage giving me some back bone. I never had any problems telling him how I felt but when it came to our relationship, I was confused as hell.

"Don't test me, Meeka." Asher stepped in front me, brushing a hand down my side. A shiver traveled along with it, and as much as I hoped he didn't notice, he did. With a firm grip on my hip, he lifted me until I was straddling his knee. "I own you. Every time you scream my name, I own you. I own every single fucking inch of you. I make you come. I make you scream. And I make you beg for more."

"What … what if I don't want more?"

Asher's eyes darkened, challenging me. "You are very lucky that you're drunk right now."

"Or else what?" I asked, my chest rising and falling at being restrained by his hard body.

"I would bend you over my knees and spank your ass for denying what rightfully belongs to me." He lowered his head, his mouth brushing over the shell of my ear. "You gave me every inch of you. You begged *me*. Remember?"

I shivered, memories of where he had been clouding my vision. He was right. I had begged. God, had I ever begged. I couldn't get enough of him.

"Ah, yes. You do remember." Asher smirked, brushing his mouth along mine. "I also seem to recall that you demanded I fuck you harder." Something flashed behind his eyes, but it was gone before I could question it.

I knew what it was about, though; he was remembering when he freaked out. Some childhood nightmare had taken him back in time at the sight of the blood. He still hadn't told me what it was about.

"Don't," he demanded, digging his fingers into my hips. "Don't go back there."

"We need to talk about it," I insisted, cupping his thick arms.

"I can't."

I searched his face. Well, that just ruined my buzz.

"What was that?" he asked, frowning.

"Nothing." I patted his chest. "Put me down."

"I don't take kindly to demands, little girl."

And there it was. The Asher I had become accustomed to. The man who had invaded my space for the past week or maybe it was more. Less? I wasn't even sure anymore. Time seemed to stand still when it came to him. And I couldn't wait to get lost again. Lost. Yes. That was what I wanted from him.

"Hmm …" He smirked, lifting me until both of my legs were wrapped around his hips. He moved us to a dark corner away from the crowd with the heavy music still buzzing around us. "I can feel your heat, Meeka."

Oh, God. Tightening my hold around his waist, I hooked my fingers in his belt loops and pulled him closer. So close but not enough. Never enough.

A groan sounded from the back of his throat.

Pulling his head down to meet my mouth, I crashed my lips against his. Forcing my tongue between his lips, I had control. For a moment. And then he took over.

Asher gripped my hips, pushing between my legs until I felt every inch of him. He grew beneath my touch.

All thoughts disappeared as our mouths moved as one. Asher kissed me like he fucked me. Demanding. In control.

I breathed him in, lost in the desire he built in me.

"Get a room, you two." Dale chuckled, walking past us. "I don't think anyone here wants to see you two bumping uglies."

We broke apart, the sudden desire fading to a dull roar.

"Where's Max?" I asked him, raising an eyebrow.

He frowned, grumbling as he walked away. "Sass. So much fucking sass. Damn women and their sass."

Asher shook his head and placed a soft kiss on my nose. "You make me want to fuck you in public. I lose all control and I don't care who's around."

"I'm … sorry?"

He laughed, placing me on my feet. "Don't be. My inner caveman comes out when I'm with you. If it wasn't frowned upon, I would fuck you in the middle of the room so everyone knew who you belonged to."

Now *that* was an interesting image. "Baby, I'm all for public display of affection but that might be a little much."

He laughed harder, wrapping his arms around my waist, and pulled me back against his chest.

I smiled, pushing my ass into his pelvis.

"Fuck, woman, you're going to be the death of me."

And no matter what happened, no matter what life threw at us, I had a feeling our new road together was only just the beginning.

CHAPTER NINETEEN

Meeka

"SO ..."

I glanced up at Brogan. "So ... What?"

She sat on the stool beside me, leaning against the bar. "How are things with Asher?"

"Fine." My heart skipped a beat at the mere mention of his name. "Why?"

"Girl," she huffed. "Do I have to rip it out of you? What's going on with you two? I'm your best friend and you don't talk about him."

"He's my best friend, too, and I don't talk about you with him," I pointed out. After the most recent kiss, the drunken haze left my body like Asher sucked it out of me. A flush of heat traveled up the back of my neck remembering other parts of my body he had sucked.

"That's different. We're women. We're supposed to talk about the men we're sleeping with."

"Are we now?"

"God, Meeka, tell me," she cried.

I laughed. "What do you want to know?"

"The guy's huge. Is he ... you know ..." She waggled her eyebrows. "Well proportioned?"

Oh, God. "Um…"

"I think you should just leave her alone," Creena said from behind us.

"Why don't you go back to doing your job, prospect?" Brogan said, her eyes twinkling in the dim lighting of the room.

Creena laughed, shaking her head, and left her spot behind the bar. She continued serving drinks, getting help from frequent regulars every so often. Random women showed up with the other bikers, moving from man to man faster than they changed their panties. Some even propositioned us.

"Earth to Meeka." Brogan snapped her fingers in front of my face.

Raising an eyebrow, I slowly met her gaze. "I have no idea what's going on between us. But when I do, you'll be the first to know."

"Fine." She sighed dramatically, jumping off the stool. "Just know that I'm very jealous."

I laughed. "You don't need to be. You can get any man here."

"Yeah." She frowned, her gaze moving around the room.

"Are you looking for Coby?"

Her eyes snapped to mine, her cheeks reddening. "I have no idea what you're talking about."

"Yeah," I scoffed. "Okay."

"Coby wants nothing to do with me so I'll just live vicariously through you." Her mouth set in a firm line. "And I'll just wait for you to tell me what's going on between you two." She winked, blowing me a kiss, and headed to one of the tables. She walked by where Coby was sitting with Dale and Stone and gave him the finger. At first, I didn't think he noticed, but I then saw the small smile tug at his lips. Huh. Guess the guy wasn't so emotionless after all.

Brogan wanted the details on what was going on between Asher and me. Well, she was going to have to wait because I had no idea. If I said it out loud, a part of me feared it would be over. It would be too real. We were best friends having sex, but would we still be having sex if he never kissed me the first time?

"Stop thinking so much, Hummingbird." Asher's voice slid over me like melted chocolate.

My face heated, the desire for him tingling between my legs. I squirmed, squeezing my thighs together and hoped for the best that he didn't catch my reaction. But when I looked up at him, a slight smirk had appeared on his face.

"I'm always thinking," I mumbled, ignoring the scrutiny from the man who had invaded my thoughts.

He pulled my stool closer to him, leaning forward. He placed his hands on my thighs, moving them up to my hips ever-so-slowly. The path caused a burn—a painful ache that set my body on fire.

"Let me take you out of your head," his head moved down to my ear, his hot breath scorching the side of my face. "*Pet.*"

STAIN

(Asher)

Feeling Meeka tremble gave me the confidence I needed. The back of my neck burned from the eyes staring at us, but I didn't care. I didn't care about any of them. I only cared about the woman sitting in front of me. The woman who had invaded my bed the past couple of nights.

Meeka stared up at me with wide eyes, her full mouth parting slightly.

I gripped her hips. She shivered, giving me the reaction I craved. The power play between us sent blood rushing through my body. Something switched. In that moment, that time and place, it became more than just us fucking. I wanted to devour her. Own every inch of her skin. Feel her deep within my soul.

"Asher," she panted, placing her hands on my forearms. Her nails dug into my skin. We were hardly touching but I could feel her all over me.

I didn't say anything as I pinched her chin. Brushing a finger over her bottom lip, I smiled when she inhaled a sharp breath.

Oh, little girl. What I could do to you. What I want to do to you. Our time together has only just begun.

"Asher," a barked command came from behind me. As much as I didn't want to turn around and lose focus of the sight in front of me, that voice belonged to the one person I shouldn't mess with.

"What?" I reached for Meeka's hand, giving her the option of linking our fingers or not.

She smiled up at me, sliding her hand in mine.

"We have a problem," Coby stated. "Angel needs us."

"What's going on?" I asked just as Dale and Stone jumped up from a table and headed outside.

"Meeka—" his gaze slid between us "—you should come as well." And with that, Coby followed our brothers out of the club.

"He's intense," Meeka muttered.

I bit back a scoff. If she only knew.

Rising from the stool, I pulled Meeka with me and led us out of the club. The moment we stepped foot outside, my gaze zeroed in on the reason everyone had left the club.

"What the hell are you doing here?" Jay snapped, pushing back Tyler Bone. The fucker was her ex, and he didn't leave her alone. A couple weeks before, he had tried blaming Vice-One for the disappearance of her sister and for the others.

"I heard there was a party." Tyler's gaze moved around the crowd watching their little spat. "It seems like the party has come to us."

"What's going on?" I asked Angel, stepping up beside him.

"The bastard thinks he can show up whenever he wants. Causing problems for me and my woman." he grumbled, crossing his arms under his broad chest.

"Need us to take care of it?" I asked, watching Meeka walk up to Max and Brogan who were huddled by Jay.

"Not yet." He jerked his chin toward Jay. "Jay seems to be handling it."

***

(Meeka)

STAIN

My hands clenched into fists at my sides while the rest of me stood on guard. Waiting. I was ready to jump in at any moment if Jay asked me to. We may have had our problems, but she knew I was there for her no matter what. It was an unwritten code between all of us. If one goes down, the rest follow. We were a unit much like Vice-One. None of us were blood related but we were family.

I did a quick scan of my surroundings, making sure nothing or anyone was out of place. Asher stood by Angel, both of them watching Jay. Probably to see if she would need their help. I admired that in them. We had dealt with men trying to knock us down because we were women. There couldn't be a female MC. It wasn't normal. We weren't tough enough. Blah, blah, blah.

"Why didn't you invite me to the party, Jenny?" Tyler asked, using the name only he was allowed.

Please. The guy was a douche nozzle and controlling as shit.

"Did you have something to say?" He glared at me.

Asher took a step forward.

"Not yet." I moved in front of him, placing a hand on his chest. "Don't."

Tyler chuckled. "You men call yourselves Navy SEALs? I wouldn't want you protecting my country. You're worthless as shit and you let women tell you what to do."

"We don't let anyone tell us what to do, but we're also not stupid enough to go against them." Angel stepped up beside Jay, placing his hand at the small of her back.

She stood taller, jutting out her chin. "You're not welcome here, Tyler."

"You see, the funny thing is that I'm always welcome. You don't have a choice in the matter because your dad still owns this property." Tyler smirked. "I'm right, aren't I?"

What the hell?

"What's he talking about, Jay?" Max asked, placing her hands on her hips. The movement caused her tiny bump to become more pronounced. That was when I caught Dale's lingering stare on her lower belly. Those two had problems of epic proportions. I couldn't even begin to understand what was going on with them.

"He's not talking about anything," Jay bit out. "You're full of shit, Tyler. My dad has nothing to do with this place. I am the one who bought it. I am the one who pays to keep this fucking place maintained. You can tell my father *that*."

"Oh, he already knows," Tyler leaned forward, brushing a strand of hair behind her ear. "Do you think of me when he fucks you?"

A deep growl came from Angel. "You mother fucker." He charged for Tyler, pushing him back a foot. "I'll kill you."

"Try it, asshole." But Tyler only laughed. He actually laughed at Angel. Even I had to chuckle knowing it would be the end for him.

In a quick move, Asher had his arms around Angel's shoulders, pulling him back.

A flutter of disappointment traveled through me. Tyler deserved everything he got. He was a chauvinistic bastard who had his clutches in Jay for years.

"You need to leave," Jay said, her voice calm. "Right now. Before I tell Asher to let Angel go."

Tyler threw his head back and laughed. "God, you haven't changed. Always depending on others to fight your battles for you."

Seriously? "I've had enough," I interrupted. "You come in here, expecting a grand entrance, and when you don't get the reaction you want, you get pissy. Or maybe you did get the reaction you wanted. Were you trying to get a rise out of Jay? Does it turn you on knowing her boyfriend is ready to kick your ass? *I should just tell Asher to let him go.*"

"Who do you think you are, little girl?" Tyler snapped at me.

"She's my fucking sister so you leave her the hell alone." Jay got in his face. Even though he was a head taller than her, she didn't back down.

"Oh, yeah, Jenny." Tyler licked his lips. "I remember how our fights went. Maybe we should give your boyfriend a little show." Before any of us knew it, he kissed her.

Angel pulled them apart, his fist flying into Tyler's jaw. He pummeled him to the ground, hitting and beating Tyler like he was the punching bag in our gym.

If it were me, I would have screamed and attempted to pull Angel off of Tyler but Jay only stood there. A darkness passed behind her eyes, her jaw clenching. Other than that, there was no reaction as to what was taking place before her. Her and Tyler had a dangerous history. Rumors went around, but I didn't know what actually happened between them. All I knew was that it was toxic.

"Should we stop him?" Dale asked.

"Not yet." Coby looked between the duo on the ground and Jay.

Jay closed her eyes, took a deep breath, and nodded once.

"Now," Coby demanded, his voice gruff.

Asher and Stone pulled Angel off of Tyler.

Much to my surprise, he didn't fight them, but when he walked past Jay, she kept her gaze on Tyler.

Angel leaned down to her ear, saying something only she could hear. Her breath caught.

Dale and Stone picked Tyler up off the ground. He only smirked, rubbing his jaw. A dark bruise had already started to set in. Blood was dripping from his nose. He may have just been beat but by the grin on his face, you would think he won the lottery.

Jay didn't say anything as Dale and Stone pushed him forward.

"You need to leave," Dale barked. "*Now.*"

"What's going on with you two, Jay?" Max asked, grabbing her hand.

"He's an asshole," she mumbled.

"No, I mean with you and Angel."

"Yeah." Jay's eyes welled. "I know." And with that, she walked away.

"Um, is it just me, or was that really weird?" Brogan stepped up between us.

"It was weird," I agreed; something odd was going on. Jay and Angel were like the hierarchies of our two groups. When they were fighting, a shift in our universe was felt between all of us.

Nothing mattered anymore when we were all tense. It was so thick it could be cut with a knife. As clichéd as that sounded, it was the damn truth. Angel and Jay were having problems with Tyler. I didn't know how far that went but he had always been a man who didn't take no for an answer. As sick as it was, he loved her.

STAIN

We followed Jay into the clubhouse, and much to my dismay, she went up to Angel and pushed him. He only glared down at her, shrugging off his brothers who hadn't let him go.

"What the hell was that?" she demanded, pushing him again. "You can't do that, Angel. I don't need men after you because you're fucking jealous."

"I am not jealous." He frowned. "You are mine, and no man, I don't care who the fuck he is, gets to lay his mouth on you."

"That doesn't mean you should beat him within an inch of his life," she shouted, smacking him in the chest. "You have no idea who he is or what he's capable of."

"Please." Angel rolled his eyes. "He's still alive, isn't he? I've been to fucking war. You think I'm scared of some bastard who can't let my girlfriend go?"

"I don't care about that shit." She grabbed his shirt, pulling him close. "I care about you. That's it. It would kill me if something happened to you."

"Nothing will happen to me as long as he stays the hell away from you."

They stood there in silence, staring at each other.

My heart raced, not knowing what to expect next.

"What if he doesn't?" Jay asked, crossing her arms under chest. "I can't control what they do, and you can't jump him every time he comes by."

"Then he needs to stay away."

"He's the vice-president of my dad's club. That's not going to happen."

"Make it happen."

"Angel," she bit out. "You know I can't do that."

"Are you sure?" Angel raised an eyebrow. "Or is it because you don't want to?"

Jay's mouth opened and closed. "Are you seriously asking me this?"

"I am. Tell me, princess."

Jay moved past him. "I'm not talking about this with you in front of everyone. You have an issue with me, be a man and talk to me, but don't accuse me of shit."

"Fuck," Angel muttered, following Jay to her room at the back of the club.

"Shit." Dale whistled, rubbing a hand over his head. "That's some heavy shit right there."

Stone grunted. "And this is why I'm glad I don't have a crazy ex."

Coby pulled out his phone, sent a text, and put it away a moment later. "I'm taking a walk." And with that, he left.

"He does that a lot, doesn't he?" Brogan asked, staring after him.

"He does." Asher slid into the booth, meeting my gaze, and patted the empty spot beside him.

I sat down, a soft sigh leaving my mouth at the feel of his arm brushing against mine. It was safe. *Home.*

"He's trained to protect," he explained. "When I go into battle, knowing he's at my back is all the strength I need to fight."

"Truth," Dale agreed. "I remember one time where we didn't see him for three days but we knew he was around."

"How did you know?" Brogan asked, a keen interest for the man we hardly knew anything about shining in her gaze.

"The bastards kept dropping like flies." Dale chuckled. "It was the greatest thing. Those fucks had no idea what was coming to them. You should have seen their faces."

Asher shook his head. "Dale gets off on other people's misery."

"Maybe." Dale winked at me.

I had come to know that Dale hid behind his joking exterior. He and Max had their own problems when she told him she was falling in love with him and that she was having his baby. A double whammy at its finest. Unfortunately for Max, he didn't feel the same way and wanted nothing to do with the kid. That was the rumor, but I didn't believe it. He was a good guy. I couldn't imagine that he would just toss Max aside when she was having his kid. He was better than that. At least, I hoped he was.

The crowd that had filled the large room of the bar dissipated as time wore on. Angel and Jay had disappeared, hopefully calling it a truce or working out whatever was going on between them.

"Well—" Dale knuckle rapped the table "—I'm calling it a night." He slid out of the booth just as Max walked by. He paused, staring back at her.

"Whatever you are thinking, don't say it," she told him, her voice dripping with venom. "I don't want to hear it."

"I wasn't going to say shit," he bit out and turned back to us. "I'm definitely out." He made his way to the door, slamming it open before heading out into the night.

"Well, that was fun," I muttered.

"Training is going to fucking suck tomorrow with these shit heads not in the right frame of mind," Stone grumbled, rubbing a hand down his face.

"Asher."

I jumped at the deep voice coming from beside us, surprised to find Coby standing there.

"He does that." Asher laughed. "What's up?"

Coby handed him his cell.

Asher took it, his eyes moving over the screen. The smile left his face when he glanced up at Coby. "When?"

"Now."

"Shit."

CHAPTER TWENTY

Asher

"WHAT'S GOING ON?" MEEKA asked, looking between Coby and me.

"I'll tell you later," I told her, motioning for her to move so I could leave the booth.

"Why can't you tell me now?"

The thought of lying to her crossed my mind, but I knew it wouldn't work. She knew me better than I knew myself at times. Only she could set me straight and bring me to my knees without me knowing.

"It's work related." That was partly true. Sort of.

"Yeah," she scoffed, sliding out of the booth. "Okay." Crossing her arms under her chest, she frowned.

"I can't tell you now." I pinched her chin, forcing her to look at me. I didn't want to leave it like this between us. Our friends were already going through shit without our problems being added to the pile. "I will explain later." I kissed her fully on the mouth, not caring in the least who saw. She was my woman, and I was damned determined to make her and everyone else see it.

She sighed, kissing me back before she pushed out of my hold. Her cheeks were flushed, her eyes glassing over with lust. "Later."

I nodded. "Damn straight." Clearing my throat, I swallowed down the urge to bend her over the table and take what rightfully belonged to me.

Out of all the women I had been with, none of them had me going all possessive caveman. If Meeka didn't enjoy the fact that I physically needed her, I would have toned down the Domination raging inside of me. But when I realized she was sexually submissive, that Dominant part of myself took full control. It was something I had been searching out for years, and I finally met my match.

"Asher." Coby was at the door, waiting.

I followed him, not giving Meeka the chance to ask me anymore questions for fear that I would spill everything.

"You'll have to tell her eventually," Coby stated.

"I liked it better when you didn't talk at all and just disappeared into the night," I mumbled, following him.

"I only talk when I have something to say," he stopped, waiting for me to catch up and stared up at the dark sky. "And right now calls for me to talk."

"I don't tell you my shit, and you don't tell me yours," I reminded him. All of us were close, but we had spent so many days and weeks together, day in and day out, that we needed to keep some things to ourselves. Like Meeka and myself.

"I have nothing to tell." Coby continued walking.

"Why aren't we driving?" I asked, ignoring his statement. He had something to tell. A story of his own. But none of us knew what that story was. I only knew that my shitty childhood was perfect compared to his. "We would get there faster."

"We're walking," he said, his voice final.

I dropped the subject. We continued to walk in silence until we got a couple blocks away from the club. After Angel and Jay had a run-in with Tyler, a silent agreement passed between Coby and me. We had worked together for so long that no words needed to be said. When Tyler was forced to leave the grounds, I had already decided that I was going to confront him. I didn't care who he was or how tough he may be. He didn't scare me. I had come face to face with the Devil himself. Tyler was a fucking pussy compared to my step-father.

"The girls are going to be pissed and Angel is going to hand our asses to us for this." I shoved my hands in my pockets, the cool air whipping around me.

Coby smirked.

I shook my head. He lived for excitement. Silent in the night. You didn't see him coming until it was too late. As cliché as that sounded, it was the truth. He was the ghost in the night. The shadows in the corners of your bedroom. He was a good man, but cross him and he would put you out before you knew what was happening.

We hadn't discussed what we would say to Tyler but we would get a couple hits in before words left our mouths. My bones vibrated, my heart racing in anticipation of what was to come.

"One more block." Coby popped the collar on his black leather jacket, his stance becoming relaxed and calm. This was his time. Between the two of us, I was the talker, and that was saying something when the only person I tended to talk to was Meeka.

When we walked that last block, I was shaking with the need to hit something, and I couldn't wait for my target to stand in front of me.

"He's inside." Coby glanced at his phone, pressed a couple buttons, and put it back in his pocket before turning to me. "Ready?"

"Fucking a."

The building was booming with a loud heavy bass. The walls shook, vibrating from the sound of the music. As Coby and I casually walked into the clubhouse, no one approached us or said a word. It was almost too easy.

"Did you show up for the women or for me?"

That voice. Fuck me with a rusty chainsaw.

Coby caught my reaction and turned around slowly.

I followed his gaze, my eyes landing on Charles Brian. What the hell was he doing there?

Charles smirked. "Surprised to see me?"

Coby frowned, no doubt wondering how Charles knew me.

Shit. A part of me was thankful that I had left Meeka back at the King's Harlots clubhouse. Charles would have eaten that shit up otherwise.

"And who do we have here?" Charles asked Coby. "I have some toys that would be perfect for you."

Coby's jaw twitched. "Your *toys* as you say, couldn't handle my kink."

"Ah." Charles' eyes brightened. "Well—"

"We aren't here for you," I told Charles, my palms becoming twitchy. Just as I was about to question my brother over the odd statement, two large men came up behind him. *Well, this night just got a whole lot better.*

"Ah, so you're here for Tyler." Charles nodded. "Makes sense seeing as his ex is dating your brother."

"How the hell do you know that?" I demanded.

"Now, now, children, play nice." Tyler came up behind them, his eyes narrowing. "Follow me."

I opened my mouth to argue. My hands clenched into fists at my sides.

"Calm, my brother," Coby whispered in my ear, clapping a hand on my shoulder. "Remember the reason we are here."

I nodded once.

We followed Charles, Tyler, and the two large mother fuckers down a long narrow hallway. The bass from the speakers jarred my thoughts. Why were we there in the first place? Would it really help? Angel would be pissed. Blah, blah, *fucking* blah.

Every so often, Tyler looked back at us until we reached a double set of doors. He stood off to the side, waiting for whatever was behind door number one.

"After you," he sneered, crossing his thick arms under his chest.

Charles pushed through the doors, the music becoming louder as we stepped over the threshold.

I tried … I tried so fucking hard not to see. Without averting my eyes and making it obvious, I stared straight ahead. But out of the corner of my eye, I saw *them*. Girls. Boys. I would bet my life on it that they were all under the age of twenty.

If Coby was affected by the sight before us, he didn't say or do anything. No reaction crossed his face. He would have his own way of dealing with things when we left.

Everything in me said that Tyler had something to do with what had been going on over the past couple of months. I didn't know how. I didn't know why. I made a mental note to mention it to Angel. If he knew anything about Tyler being mixed in with this shit, he never said. Tyler was a dick but men like him still had a line they wouldn't cross.

"So you came because you wanted a piece of me." Tyler grazed his hand over the ankle of a young girl curled into a ball on a tiny stage. She whimpered, escaping him. He only chuckled.

Bile rose to my throat. We needed to get out of this room before one of us ended up dead. And it wouldn't be me or Coby.

"You caused problems at our party," I told him, my heart jumping when a door closed behind us.

"What the hell did you do at their party?" Charles demanded, leaning against a large oak desk in the far right corner of the room.

"I made an appearance." Tyler scratched his jaw. "Nothing special."

"That's not what it looked like to me." I glanced at Coby. "You?"

He shook his head. "Nope."

"What gives, T?" Charles pulled a file off the desk and threw it at Tyler. "I have enough shit falling into my lap. I don't need the problems with your ex-girlfriend added to the pile."

"I only talked to her." Tyler opened the file, a grin forming on his face. "Well, it looks like you have been busy," he told me.

"I have no idea what you're talking about." There was no way any of them would know about our undercover operation. Hell, even the Captain had no idea. Angel didn't do things by the book and even though it wasn't my job, he recruited me because he knew I could take care of it. But when my gaze landed on the photo staring back at me, my world crumbled around me. The black and white photo showed my bedroom, my bed, and two very naked bodies on it. My chest panged. Red seared across my vision. These fuckers had been watching us the whole time. Words formed on my tongue, but they wouldn't leave. I couldn't even begin to say what I wanted to. Meeka. She was all I cared about. She would be pissed and disgusted that this happened. That *I* let it happen.

"I wonder how your little girl would feel if we showed her this." Tyler pinched the edge of the picture, swinging it back and forth. Taunting me.

My back stiffened, rage bubbling from the deep pits of my gut.

"She won't find out, now will she?" Coby interrupted. "You want to know why? Because you are a pussy. It's why you showed up earlier when Angel wasn't alone. You knew that we would pull him off of you. Did you have your crew hiding? Were they waiting for you to make the call?" Coby took a step forward.

"You see, if it were me and *I* wanted to make an appearance to see my ex-girlfriend and scare her new boyfriend, no one would see me. I would show up during the night when everyone was asleep. Catch them off guard. Maybe show up in her room when the boyfriend went to take a piss, or better yet, when he went back to his place." Coby's voice dripped with venom.

Tyler stared at him, locked on the man looming over him. And *that* was the reaction Coby was going for.

Charles wouldn't stop him.

"I would scare her a little bit," Coby continued. "But I wouldn't hurt her. I'm not a sick fuck like you people are. I don't prey on women."

"They're the weaker sex," Tyler added.

Coby laughed, the deep maniacal sound turning into a growl. "The women I know would eat you for dinner."

And that was so fucking true. Meeka may be small but she was feisty as shit. She could definitely knock me on my ass.

"You are weak then," Tyler countered.

"We're weak. Hey, Asher," Coby said. "Did you hear that?"

"I sure did." I grinned. It was funny seeing that side of Coby. Anyone who didn't know him, would think this was him, but I knew it wasn't. He was acting. No one knew the real him. Even us, his squad and brothers—we only knew that he was quiet but lethal.

"All right, gentlemen." Charles picked up another file off his desk. "Do I have to show you more pictures? Or did you want to get right down to business?"

"How do I know that's even me? It could be doctored."

"Yeah, because other couples are going to end up naked in your bed." He rolled his eyes. "Come on now. You're smarter than that."

I couldn't bring Meeka back to my place. Not until this was over with and all the cameras were gone. The place would be swept for bugs, and after, I would sweep it again to be sure. But I would have to tell her. As much as I didn't want to, she deserved to know. The picture didn't show all of her, thank fuck for that, but it showed enough.

I was going to kill him.

As soon as Angel gave me the go ahead, Charles would be mine.

***

(Meeka)

An hour after Coby and Asher left, I sat at the bar while Creena cleaned up. Max and Brogan had ushered everyone out of the club so we could spend the rest of the night in peace and quiet. Angel and Jay never left her room. There were no sounds of yelling so I hoped for the best that they were talking through their problems. Or they could have been like Asher and me and just have sex instead.

"Hey, boss," Creena greeted, wiping up the counter.

I spun on my stool, finding Jay standing at the entrance to the hallway. Her shoulders drooped, dark bags circled under her eyes. She yawned, rolling her shoulders back and forth.

"What's going on?" she asked, her gaze moving around the now empty club. "Where is everyone?"

"Max kicked everyone out," Brogan jabbed, sliding onto the stool beside me.

"Good." Jay nodded once. "Where are the guys?"

"Stone left shortly after Dale did," I answered. "And both Coby and Asher went to take care of something."

Jay raised an eyebrow. "What?"

I shrugged. "I'm not sure."

Angel came up behind her, kissed her head, and whispered something in her ear.

She tilted her head, waiting.

He smiled, placing a soft peck on her mouth. "I love you, princess."

"I love you, my king," she muttered.

If I could gush without sounding like a dork ... *Oh, screw it.* "I think that's the most romantic thing I've ever heard."

Jay's cheeks reddened, her eyes twinkling as she watched Angel head out the front door.

"Everything okay?" Max grabbed two bottles of water, handing Jay one before taking a sip of her own.

Jay inhaled a sharp breath. "It will be."

CHAPTER TWENTY-ONE

Meeka

WE HAD EXPLAINED TO Jay that Coby and Asher had somewhere to be. They wouldn't tell us what or even who they were meeting.

When Angel left, Jay couldn't stop pacing back and forth in front of the bar.

"Something isn't right," she said. "I can feel it."

As soon as those words left her mouth, the door banged open. Asher and Coby both barged into the large room.

"Um … I think he needs something," Brogan muttered.

Waiting for her to make fun or joke about exactly what Asher needed, I swallowed hard when she didn't continue.

His gaze moved back and forth over the room before they landed on me. His fists clenched and unclenched at his sides. His nostrils flared. His mouth set in a grim line. But what caught my attention was the look of pure hard lust in his eyes.

A sheen of sweat coated his brow, his shirt wrinkly and unkempt. His gaze roamed down the length of my body, heating my skin on fire. I had heard about that. The power of erotic desire taking over so all thoughts fizzled out into nothing. That drive to ignore everything around you and just be. The tension cracked between us. I always imagined what it would be like to experience that loss of control. To be stressed to the point you just needed to fuck your way out of it until you felt better.

Rising from the stool, I waited. I wasn't sure what Asher's next move would be, but I would be ready.

Charging forward, he didn't give me any time to comprehend what was happening. He hooked an arm around my waist and threw me over his shoulder.

Gasps and muttered voices sounded from around us, but all I could focus on was the man needing something from me.

When we reached my room, he threw the door open.

"Asher." My voice trembled, but my body was on fire. I didn't always know what to expect with him. He was intense, rough around the edges but he always thought of me first. He pleased me in ways I only read about in my filthy romance books. He took pleasure to a whole new level.

He didn't say anything. He kicked the door closed and in two large steps, had me on the bed. Ripping open his jeans, he pulled me to the edge of the mattress.

I had no control. Over my body. Over Asher. Over the raging emotions coursing through me. It had nothing to do with how we felt about each other. It would be pure hard sex. He needed me. He brought me along for the ride, making sure to take what he wanted to make himself feel better.

Asher lifted my dress to my hips. "*Fuck,*" he snarled, his fingers cupping my bare ass. "You listened to me." Lowering to his knees, his mouth was on me before I could comment.

Arching beneath him, I gripped the blanket. Heat swam over me. Pleasure forced my brain numb.

Asher's tongue thrust inside me, sucking and licking until I was crying out his name. He didn't let up, giving me another shattering release before he flipped me onto my stomach.

Panting, my core was still tingling from the scruff of his jaw and the ecstasy he had built in me since the very beginning.

"I'm going to fuck you until you beg me to stop," his voice rumbled over me, vibrating through my bones.

A moan escaped me, my fingers digging into the blankets.

A belt buckle clanked. Heavy breathing filled my ears. The next thing I knew, Asher loomed over me and grabbed hold of my hands.

He grunted, slamming into me in one full thrust.

I cried out, spots dancing in my vision at the unexpected invasion.

He didn't let up. With each powerful thrust, my hips lifted off the bed. His body was hard, full, and throbbing for me.

He towered over me, pumping hard and deep.

I was trapped between him and the mattress, my feet dangling over the edge, but all I could feel was him. His power. His strength. His need for me. He forced the pleasure from my body, breathing it in and using it to make us both feel better.

Asher's mouth moved down the length of my neck, his hot breath scorching the side of my face. His low grunts rumbled deep, vibrating through his chest. "I need you," he groaned. "So fucking much I can feel it deep in my bones."

"You have me," I panted, arching beneath him.

"Break for me, Meeka. Fall apart, and let the pleasure consume you."

And I did.

****

(Asher)

I didn't want to hurt her but the urge to drive into her so fucking hard took over my mind, body, and soul. After we got back from seeing Tyler, I was on edge. Coby noticed and told me to get my girl. I had every intention of being honest with her and tell her how I felt. But when I laid eyes on her and she smiled at me, all bets were fucking off.

With her trembling and writhing beneath me, I would claim what was mine. The fact she listened to me and didn't wear panties almost made me come undone right then and there. Feasting on her body would never get old. Her sweet taste made my head swim. Her moaning my name while I lapped at her pussy like a starved man sent shivers racing to the tip of my cock. She deserved to be savoured. And I would do anything to show her that she belonged to me.

I would make her mine.

Forever.

CHAPTER TWENTY-TWO

Meeka

I WOKE A COUPLE of hours later to the mumbled sounds of Asher speaking. A light glowed from the phone in his hand. Sitting up, I moved behind him and placed my hand on his back.

His body relaxed. His gaze met mine, his eyes softening. "Listen, brother. I have to go. Yeah. She's awake. No. We'll be out in a bit."

"Who was that?" I asked when he hung up.

"Coby." Asher kissed my forehead, letting his lips linger. "Are you okay?"

I stifled a yawn, nodding. "Why wouldn't I be?"

"I was rough, Meeka."

"Yeah, but I wasn't complaining." I sat up, cupping his cheek. "We've had this discussion already. I like your roughness."

Placing his hand over mine, he leaned into my palm. "I couldn't control myself."

"After you came back with Coby, I knew something was wrong."

"We went to see Tyler."

"You did?"

"We went to stop him from causing anymore shit for Angel and Jay, but—"

"But what?"

"Charles was there."

My heart jumped in my chest at the mention of that man's name. "He-he was?"

"Tyler is working for him. He has to be. It's the only thing that explains why Charles was there in the first place."

"No!" I shook my head. "That can't be possible. He's a douche but there's no way."

"He's a sadistic fuck, Meeka." Asher rose from the bed, pacing back and forth. "I'll admit that we were shocked to see him but it all makes sense now."

"So what happened when you saw him?"

"It eventually ended up with my fist landing against Tyler's jaw." Asher smirked, rubbing the bruises on his knuckles.

"You have to tell Jay," I insisted. "Even though none of this makes sense, she needs to know what's going on."

"No. We can't. Not yet. I'm telling you because we're working together."

"Is that all we're doing?" I asked, taken aback at his words.

"What else would it be?" His eyes darkened, challenging me.

"Are you fucking kidding me right now?" I jumped from the bed, pulling on my dress. "I can't believe you."

"Hummingbird."

"No!" I spun on him. "You go on how you *need* me and I'm yours and all that shit but you act like this is going to end after the mission is over. Is that what you want? Are you only using me while we search out Charles and bring his operation down?"

"You know that's not true." Asher's jaw clenched, his chest rising with ragged breath.

"Then *tell me*," I shouted. "What the hell are we doing? I can live with the nightmares from your past. I can help you through that. But I refuse to be used just so you can get your dick wet. Is that all you think of me?"

"I'm not using you," he repeated slowly.

"Then what the hell are we doing? We keep going back and forth. Talk to me."

"You know I hate talking." He closed the distance between us, wrapping his arms around my shoulders. "But I want to try."

"Tell me why you're so scared of hurting me." I gripped his shirt, breathing in the scent that was all him. No cologne. No body wash. Just pure hard male.

"I can't control anything when I'm with you. Tonight scared me. All I could think about was getting inside your body whether you were prepared or not."

My heart jumped. "Well, with you, I'm always prepared."

"Fuck, that's not …" He moved us to the edge of the bed. He sat with me standing between his legs.

"That's not what I meant." Leaning his head against my chest, his hold around my waist tightened. "I needed to get inside you because I knew you would make me feel better. You keep me calm when that darkness wants to come out and destroy everything in its path."

"Does that darkness want to come out often?" I asked, brushing my fingers through the hair at his nape.

"Not until tonight. I'm stressed. I needed something to relieve it."

"What would you have done if I hadn't been here?" I knew he wouldn't have gone to another woman, but I needed to ask. I needed to hear him say it for fear that I was wrong.

"I would have found you or worked out until I passed out," he muttered, his voice muffled by my shirt.

A breath of relief left me, a twinge of guilt twisting in my stomach.

Asher lifted his head, glancing up at me through his thick lashes. "Did you think I would fuck someone else?"

"I'm not sure," I admitted, chewing my bottom lip.

"I guess I deserve that." He lifted me, placing me on his lap and kissed my forehead. "I don't want anyone else but you. But I will be honest and say that I don't know what I want out of this."

"Let's just take it a day at a time." I straddled his lap, curling my fingers around his neck. "But you need to talk to me. I need to know what's going on."

"I do talk." He glanced down at his hands in my lap.

"Not like before you don't." I braced myself. "Tell me why you freaked out in the shower."

"I hurt you." He went to move but I only held on.

"You did not hurt me." I cupped his jaw, forcing him to look at me. "You've been with enough women, Asher. You should know that bleeding can happen."

"That's not the same." He pushed me off of his lap. Reaching for his sweat pants, he pulled them on, his back ridged.

"What do you mean?" I didn't want to push but he hadn't talked about it. I also couldn't help him if I didn't know what the hell was going on.

"I … Fuck. I don't want to talk about it." He started pacing back and forth, brushing his hand through his hair. "With all of the shit going on, secrets between us is not going to make anything easier."

My heart picked up speed.

He took a deep breath. "I haven't told you everything about my step-father and what he did. I told you he abused me physically but there was more. So much more." A dark shadow passed over his face as his mind took him back to his childhood. "He used to hit me before my mom passed, but after, it became worse. He said he loved her and blamed the abuse on the fact he lost his wife, but I think it was more than that. I believe he was waiting for a time where he could inflict as much pain on me as he wanted. He fucked with my head. Made me feel things I shouldn't have. Made me see and do things no boy should experience."

"What kind of things?"

"He had a room in his basement." Asher's gaze took on a faraway look. "I wasn't allowed to go in it at first, but then after a while, I would get in trouble if I *didn't* go in it."

"What do you mean?" I asked, kneeling in front of him and grabbed hold of both his hands.

"I had to clean up the messes."

Oh, God. What kind of person would even think of bringing a child into the terrors of hell only to satisfy their own personal needs? It was all starting to make sense. "W-what kind of mess?"

"The mess after he finished with a woman." His breathing became shallow, coming out in short bursts of air.

"Asher," I whispered.

"I didn't know what happened to the women, but they never looked the same after he was done with them. He forced me to clean up. He drove my face into blood. All I could smell was the putrid scent of puke …" He was rambling, not making any sense as his chest began to rise and fall.

"Okay." I pushed to my feet, wrapping my arms around his shoulders and cradled his head against my chest. "That's enough." My throat burned, my eyes welled, but I refused to cry. I had to be strong. He was always there for me, and now I would be there for him. But if I ever came across that man, it would be the end of him. No matter what it took, I would destroy his step-father.

***

(Asher)

The moment he left me alone with them, I fell to my knees, praying to whoever would listen that I could leave this nightmare.

Mom, why did you leave me?

Why couldn't you have stayed to protect me from him?

I asked those same questions over and over again, but I never got a response.

I blamed her. It was all her fault. She should have known. I was her baby boy. Couldn't she see the marks on my tiny body? The handprints on my arms when I wore a t-shirt?

The teachers at school called her about it, but she denied everything. She was always in denial. She never even confronted my step-father.

I loved her but I needed her more. I needed her when he came into my room each night and beat me.

Mommy, why?

"Come back to me."

The sweet sound pulled me from my thoughts and brought me back to the present. A sheen of sweat coated my skin. It was a memory. A fucking nightmare but the putrid scent of death caressed my nose once again. Even though it had been years ago, it would always linger. It was a smell I would never get out of my head.

"I can't." My voice cracked. Was that me talking? "*Fuck.*"

"Asher." Meeka's brows narrowed, her hands gripping mine in a tight hold.

I tried. I tried so fucking hard to forget.

The pain. The anguish. The screams. But they were so damn loud. Cries of terror stabbed me in the chest with memories of women begging for their lives. They pleaded with me to help them but I was so young. I couldn't do anything. I was small, a fucking bean pole. What could I have done? It was my fault. All of my fucking fault. I should have done more. I should have called for help. I could have ran to the neighbors. But I didn't. I didn't do anything.

My eyes widened, my heart racing hard against my ribcage.

"Listen to their cries, boy." My step-father took a deep inhale. "It's music to my ears. Now clean up this mess." He

pushed me forward. "I want the room spotless. It makes the women nervous when they see the blood."

"No. I can't."

"Yes, you can, and you fucking will." He shoved me to my knees. "You're lucky I don't make you clean this shit up with a toothbrush. Now get to fucking work."

He left but he didn't take the woman with him. Her muffled cries pierced my ears, growing louder and louder until all I could hear were her screams.

Stop.

Stop screaming.

I couldn't take it anymore.

Holding my hands over my ears to muffle out the sound, I rocked back and forth. I prayed, pleading with her to stop.

Please. Stop.

****

(Meeka)

"Stop. Please stop."

Bile rose to my throat at the look of sheer terror written all over Asher's face. When he had fallen to his knees, the breath was knocked out of me. He told me it had been bad, but I never knew how much. The mental did more damage than the physical and with his job, it didn't help. He finally cracked under the pressure

He rocked back and forth, holding his hands over his ears. He kept muttering for something to stop, but I wasn't sure what he was talking about.

"Baby." I grabbed his hands from his ears and cupped his face, placing soft kisses on his mouth. "Please. Come back to me." I didn't know how to help him. I didn't know what he needed. He lost the battle to the demons that had threatened to destroy him for years. They won. His step-father won. He succeeded in ruining this man's life whether he knew it or not.

"Asher," I said, my voice shaking. "They're memories. They're not happening. Please, baby. Come back to me."

His arms suddenly wrapped around me, pulling me against his hard chest. His head pushed into the crook of my neck, his body trembling.

My heart picked up speed. Tears rolled down my cheeks. I couldn't stop them. I had no control over the emotions flooding through me.

I would give anything to take away his pain. To help him move past the nightmares that he relived over and over every time he closed his eyes. It was naïve of me to think that would ever happen. Even with years of therapy, an abuse victim was always just that—a victim. Maybe not to the abuser but to the nightmares they left behind, engrained in the person's mind.

"I'm here. I'm always here." I rubbed soothing circles on his back.

"I'm sorry." He held me tighter.

"You have nothing to be sorry about. You would do the same for me."

He sat back, leaning against the edge of the bed. "I would but—"

"What?"

"I would go out and find him and then I would kill him but not at first. I would make him suffer. I would rip off every body part that laid a hand on you."

"Um, okay, well, how about we just take our pain out on a punching bag instead?" I offered, attempting to lighten the mood.

His lips twitched but he looked far away.

STAIN

Asher brushed the back of his knuckles down my cheek. The touch was soft and gentle.

"I don't deserve you," he whispered. It was so quiet, I almost didn't hear him.

I opened my mouth to argue, but the words never came out. I just sat there, willing him to believe that he deserved all of the happiness in the world. He wasn't a monster. He wasn't his step-father. He was so much more. He was one of the best men I knew. And I would do everything in my power to make him see that.

CHAPTER TWENTY-THREE

Meeka

ASHER FINALLY FELL ASLEEP an hour later. His tanned back rose and fell with ragged breath, and I prayed he was having peaceful dreams.

Rising from the bed, I got dressed. Although we didn't have sex, he insisted on me being naked beside him. He had told me that touching me calmed him. I didn't quite understand what that meant, but I didn't argue. Giving him what he wanted, I wrapped myself around him until his breathing evened out.

When I was certain that he was asleep, I kissed his cheek and decided to talk to Coby and find out what the hell had happened. Asher had snapped. Although I didn't mind him taking it out on me, it still worried me.

He was losing himself, and I didn't know how to help him remain strong.

"Hey, girl." Brogan came up to me as I closed my bedroom door. "How's that man of yours?"

Under normal circumstances, she would have teased me about Asher throwing me over his shoulder. Her lack of jokes sent a flutter of unease twisting in my stomach. "Um, he's sleeping."

She nodded, frowning. "Everything okay?"

"It will be." It had to be. I knew by the questioning look on Brogan's face, that she wanted more answers, but I couldn't give them to her. I didn't even know what they were. Asher needed my help, and no matter what, I would do everything in my power to be strong for him.

"If you want to talk, I'm here." She patted my hand when her phone rang. Pulling it out of her back pocket, she slid it to her ear before locking eyes with mine. "Yeah. Okay, when? Now? Yup. She is. Okay." And with that, she hung up. "We have to go."

"Where?"

"The basement."

My heart jumped. To get to the basement, you had to go outside and to the back of the building. Jay had a high tech security system built in. The only time we ever went into the basement was for an interrogation. And even that didn't happen often. Something about us being women and all that shit.

I followed Brogan out the front door, my heart picking up speed by the second. We never went into the basement. That meant that Jay found something out.

When we left the club, the cool night air bit at my skin. The guys weren't around; Asher was still sleeping and who knew where Angel was.

"Meeka." Brogan snapped her fingers in front of my face.

"Sorry." I shook my head. "What?"

"I know you and Jay have had your problems but she needs you right now. We all do."

"Of course. Just tell me what to do."

"Creena's going to watch and make sure no one unexpected shows up. We have to keep this from Angel until after or else he's going to lose his shit."

"Does this have to do with Violet and what we did?" I asked, not sure if I wanted to know the answer. Luckily for us, everything turned out in the end and Jay wasn't hurt. She was the strongest woman I knew but Angel would definitely put an end to this.

Brogan knocked once on the metal door, smiling back at me. "It's time."

Taking a deep breath, I followed her into the dark hall that held stairs leading down into the basement. It was your typical run of the mill unfinished basement and creepy as hell. That was why Jay kept it the way it was instead of renovating it.

Creena came up the stairs, nodding once, and stood at the closed door. "Angel went home to feed Buck. Dale and Stone went to a local gym the Navy uses. Asher is …" She glanced at me.

"Sleeping," I answered.

She nodded. "And Coby is … around."

"That man is like a ghost," I muttered, taking a couple steps down the stairs.

"Isn't that his nickname?" Creena asked.

That caught Brogan's attention. "You think?"

"You should ask him," I said, gently elbowing her.

She scoffed. "Please."

STAIN

"Ladies," Jay barked from the bottom of the stairs. "Get down here. *Now*."

Brogan and I headed down the stairs. Once we walked into the large open space, I saw a chair in the middle of the room. A cold sweat raced down my back at seeing the man sitting on the metal chair. His hands were tied behind his back, and his ankles were tied to the front legs of the chair. Max stood off to the side, and Jay moved in front of him.

The question of what was going on tingled on my tongue, but the words wouldn't leave me. Jay was desperate. It had been hard for her to run a female MC but we all stuck together and made it work. We were a team like Vice-One. The thought of Asher slid into my mind. Every part of me ached for him.

A loud crack sounding through the air interrupted my dirty thoughts.

Jay leaned over the man, peering into his eyes. "Tell me what you know about the men who took my sister."

"I'm not telling you *shit*," he spat. "You think you're so fucking tough because you're the president of an MC. Little girl, you have no fucking idea who you're playing with."

"Tell me," Jay demanded. "Or, *little boy*, I will gut you like a fucking pig."

My mouth went dry. I had never seen Jay like that. She was always put together but … a darkness took over.

The man laughed. "I'm not scared of you, bitch. All of your little whores would make great toys."

"Shut up!" Jay shouted, landing her fist against the man's cheek.

He spat at her feet, laughing harder. "You do have a hell of a punch. I'll give you that. I know some men who would love to play with you. You would be a challenge for them. Is that what Eric Vega liked about you? You put up a fight? How did it feel being chained to his wall?"

"Tell me who took my sister," she said, her voice cracking.

"Your sister put up a fight too. You know what men would pay to have twins? I can guarantee you a million."

A couple shocked gasps sounded around the room.

"Who are you?" Jay asked. "Were you the one who blew a hole into our club? Tell me that. Tell me *something*."

The man sneered. "I'm just a man who makes it so my boss gets what he wants. And that hole? I have no idea what you're talking about."

"You're lying." Her fists clenched at her sides. "Tell me."

"I'm not telling you shit."

"Who took Violet?" Brogan demanded, coming up to Jay's side. That small movement sent Jay standing taller. She liked to think that she could do everything on her own, but she couldn't. It's why we all worked well together. We needed each other.

"What the fuck are you going to do? Smack me to death? Look at you. You're tiny as hell." The man threw his head back and laughed. "You're a fucking sprite."

In a quick move, Brogan cupped his jaw and dug her fingers into his cheeks.

He cried out.

She sneered. "I love it when a man is forced into submission." She licked her lips. "Now, you're going to tell us who took Violet Gold."

"Fuck you," he spat out.

Brogan's grin grew. Pulling out a switchblade from her back pocket, she flipped it open and waved it in front of his face. "You see, my sister here—" she pointed at Jay "—is nice, but I'm not." Suddenly, she dropped her hand, stabbing the knife into his thigh.

The guy screamed. "Fuck! You bitch."

"Hurts, don't it?" she twisted the knife. "Now, tell us what we want to know. Who took Violet, and who blew that big ass hole into our club?"

"Listen, whore. You can do what you want to me, but I won't say shit," he said through gritted teeth.

Brogan twisted the knife again, pushing it further into the muscle.

He screamed, shaking in the chair.

I winced, looking away when my gaze caught a shadow on the stairs.

Coby stared straight ahead, looking directly at Brogan. No emotion showed on his face, but I caught something in his dark eyes. The hint of pure unmistakeable lust peered from him. For Brogan?

Well, that was new. I knew she had a crush on him, but I never thought it would be reciprocated. Unsure how he got by Creena, I took a step back and stood beside him.

He nodded once, crossing his arms under his broad chest.

"You will say something because it's how men like you are," Brogan continued. "You're trying to show them that you'll do whatever it takes to get their approval but you will also do anything to get to the top.

If it means taking them out, you won't hesitate. Will you?" When he didn't say anything, Brogan went on. "That's what I thought." Pulling the knife from his thigh, Brogan wiped the blade on her pants and took a step back.

"My sister has a temper," Jay told him. "If you don't give us what we want, I'll let her kill you." She wouldn't, but it still made my heart skip a beat. None of us had ever killed anyone. Most MC's dealt with violence and corruption, but we tried to stay on the straight and narrow even though it was damn hard at times.

"I don't know anything," the guy finally said.

"Tell us who you deal with," Brogan tapped the knife against her hand.

"Doesn't matter if I tell you. You'll kill me either way."

"No, we won't." Jay crossed her arms under her chest. "I want you to take a message back to your boss. Let him know that no matter what, we will come after him."

The guy scoffed. "Please. You going to have your boyfriend do your dirty work?"

"No," a deep voice boomed from the stairway. "My girlfriend does her own shit."

All heads turned Angel's way. He stood on the stairs, staring down at Jay.

"Ah. It seems my boyfriend wanted to come and play," she said, her gaze locking with Angel's. Something flashed in them. Worry? Fear? I couldn't be sure. They had been going through some issues. The human trafficking shit was causing problems even for the strongest of couples.

"Oh, I want to play," Angel trudged down the stairs. "But my girlfriend apparently likes doing things by herself."

"Well, it looks like you two have some shit to deal with," the man said, struggling against his binds. "Why don't you let me go and I'll relay your message."

"Shut up," Angel demanded, walking up to Jay. Cupping her nape, he tilted her head back and smacked a hard kiss on her mouth. He muttered something in her ear. Her eyes widened, heating with desire for the man holding her.

Angel released her, walking by me. "Take care of her," he told me.

"I will." And I would. At times, Jay was like a bomb, and I was just waiting for her to go off. No matter what happened, we would be there to pick up the pieces.

When Angel headed up the stairs, he clapped Coby on the shoulder, whispering something to him. Coby nodded once, gave Brogan one last look, and followed Angel.

Once the door shut behind them, Jay shook herself and focused back on the man sitting in front of her.

"Are you going to kill me or let me go?" The man feigned a yawn. "I'm getting bored."

Jay shot her fist out, landing it against his jaw.

The sound reverberated through my body.

"Fuck. What the hell?"

"Tell me who you report to," she demanded, her voice calm and even.

"Ask your boyfriend," he nodded toward the stairway. "I'm sure he knows."

"Fine." She turned to Brogan. "He's all yours."

****

(Asher)

A sheen of sweat coated my skin, my clothes sticking to my aching body. My muscles jumped, protesting with each movement I attempted to make. Rolling over onto my back, I let out an agonizing breath. I tried to replay the last hour in my mind. I remembered charging for Meeka, throwing her over my shoulder, and taking my frustration out on her. Bits and pieces of our conversation after came to mind, but other than that, I was a fucking lost cause. It was like a movie had been playing and someone cut out a scene. The memories were dark, and I couldn't figure out what the fuck happened. All I knew was that I felt better. At ease.

I didn't black out often and my breakdowns were few and far between. But seeing Tyler, knowing we had to tell Jay her ex was in on this trafficking shit bothered me.

A sharp pain pierced between my eyes, reminding me that I didn't have the control I thought I had.

Leaving the bed, I headed to the bathroom to take a shower. To wash away the filth of the nightmare that had become my life.

Stepping under the hot spray, I quickly washed the sweat off of me. After drying myself off and getting dressed, I went in search of Meeka. I needed to apologize and try and explain what had happened. I needed *her*. My cock twitched. And my body did as well.

"Your girl is in the basement," Angel called from the gym doorway. "You should head down there before she's a witness to murder."

"Murder?" I frowned. "What the hell are you talking about?"

"Apparently, the Harlots found a guy who is a runner for the organization you and Meeka are working to bring down."

"We're not the only ones," I reminded him.

"Maybe not—" he crossed his arms under his chest, leaning against the wall "—but they'll see *you* first before they see us."

"Did the guy recognize Meeka at all?"

"It didn't look like it."

"Shit." *Why the hell wouldn't she have thought of that?*

"Because Jay asked her to do something, and Meeka will do anything to get back in her good books."

"True," I mumbled, not realizing I spoke out loud.

Angel pushed off the wall. "Remember who you're dealing with. Not just Meeka, but the club she belongs to as well. You hurt her, and those girls will attack as one."

"I don't plan on hurting her." My brows narrowed.

"Maybe not, but you also haven't told her how you feel or what's really going on."

"What the hell am I supposed to say? That my past is catching up with me and I don't know how to fucking handle it? Or that I love her but I'm terrified that after, it won't be the same?" Where those questions were coming from, I had no idea. I never spoke about my feelings. Not even to my brothers.

"I don't know what's going on with you or what your past consists of. I know you'll tell me when you are ready but you need to protect her. I was selfish when I asked you two to go undercover for me."

"You needed me," I reminded him.

Angel rubbed the back of his neck. "I know." He took a breath. "Listen, you are my brother. Not by blood but by breath alone. I love you, man. And I don't say it enough. You guys are my fucking life."

"What's going on?" I frowned. "Do you know something that I don't?"

He shook his head. "I wish I fucking knew something. Jay is losing her shit over not being able to get the information from her sister. Violet has turned into a fucking vault. She won't say shit."

"Did someone threaten her? Since we brought her home?" Meeka and I had brought her back to her sister. Even though we almost lost our friends over it, Violet was safe, and that was all we cared about.

"No, not that we know of." Angel came up to me, placing his hands on my shoulders and peered into my eyes. "If you want out, just say the word. We'll figure out some other way to bring these bastards down."

"I found out information," I blurted. I had wanted to tell Jay first, but maybe if Angel knew, he could help sweeten the blow.

"What sort of information?"

"Coby and I went to see Tyler."

"Fuck." Angel released me and started pacing back and forth in front of me.

"We wanted to let him know that he isn't welcome here."

"What did you find?" he asked, closing his eyes and pinched the bridge of his nose.

"Charles Brian was there."

"Shit."

Exactly.

CHAPTER TWENTY-FOUR

Meeka

I NEEDED SOMETHING TO occupy my thoughts. To distract me from the image that had been burned into my retinas. When Jay had told Brogan that the guy was all hers, Brogan did what she did best. She fought. She hit him over and over. I could still hear the sounds of bone crunching in my mind. We weren't your average MC but shit on our doorstep and we were sadistic just like the rest of them.

Brogan may have been the smallest, but she could pack a punch. I also knew that she wouldn't kill him, or anyone, for that matter, but I didn't like seeing that side of my best friend. It was the part of her she couldn't control. There was a darkness in her that she never let out until it was needed or too late.

"You came up here without them."

I jumped at the deep voice coming from a few feet away and found Coby staring back at me. "I … They're just doing an interrogation, so I wasn't needed."

Coby nodded once and picked up a cloth. He started wiping down the counter before sitting on the bar stool in front of me.

Clearing my throat, I handed him a beer and took one for myself.

He clinked the bottle against mine and took a swig, his eyes peering at me. "Ask me," he finally said, placing the bottle back on the counter top.

"What happened when you went to see Tyler?"

"Asher told you."

"Yes." It wasn't a question, but I felt the need to answer anyway. "But he didn't tell me what exactly happened."

"We saw Charles Brian, and Asher lost his shit."

"What did you do?"

"I stood back and watched."

"And you let him go at Tyler?" I demanded, my voice raising.

"Before you accuse me of shit, little girl, you need to get your facts straight." His voice came out even and in control. "I stood back until my brother indicated that he needed me. Asher knows what he is doing. Yes, he's had a shitty start to life, but with you, he's kept going."

"Wait." I shook my head. "You know?"

"I don't need to know anything."

"But—"

"I saw it in his eyes, and I've also seen how you two are together."

"You are a very confusing man," I blurted, my cheeks heating at my outburst.

"Maybe so, but I do pay attention. I'm trained to watch and listen." His eyes twinkled.

"Is that why you don't say much?" I asked. "Sorry, I'm being really nosy."

"I like you for him. I wish we would have met sooner, but Asher liked to keep that part of his life a secret."

"Yeah," I agreed. "He never told me much about you guys." Asher had always been a private person. Even when he used to sneak into my room at night. He would tell me that he needed some peace and quiet. I never argued or asked him what was going on. I didn't have to. I knew he had a shitty childhood. I met his step-father. One look at the man, and you could tell he didn't care about anyone but himself.

Coby rose from his spot at the bar and knuckle rapped the counter. "Have patience with him." He turned to leave. "Oh, and please tell your friend to stop trying."

"Brogan?" I frowned.

"Yes."

"Why?"

His back stiffened. "I'm not good enough for her." And with that, he walked away, heading out the front doors of the club.

My heart panged for him. Much like Asher had told me, Coby felt the same way. But knowing Brogan, she wouldn't give up. There was something about Coby that was good for her. He may have his secrets, but I knew she could help him see that he was good enough.

I sighed, going back to cleaning behind the bar. What was with these men who felt they weren't good enough?

Distracting myself, I bent over to put the empty beer bottles back in their box when a rough groan sounded from behind me.

Smiling, I rose to my full height slowly and turned around. "Something you like?" I asked Asher, making a point to let my eyes roam down the length of his body.

"Fuck, woman." He took a step toward me. "You keep looking at me like that, and I'll bend you over right here and fuck that sweet pussy of yours."

"Yeah, yeah. Promises, promises." I laughed, continuing to put the bottles away.

"Is that a challenge, Hummingbird?" he stepped up behind me. "Because I'm always up for the task."

"As much as I want to, I have to finish cleaning."

"It's almost three in the morning, Meeka."

"It's distracting." My shoulders dropped. Rubbing a hand down my face, I stifled a yawn. "I didn't want—"

"I know." He pinched my chin, tilting my head up to meet his mouth. "I get it. Jay is desperate and is willing to do whatever it takes to find the bastards who took her sister."

"I wish I could help." My heart jumped.

"You *are* helping. You were there with her."

"I don't like seeing that side of them."

"Is that why you left and decided to clean?" he asked, raising an eyebrow.

My jaw clenched. "It is. Brogan loses herself. She goes to a dark place, and then the violence takes over."

He nodded. "I know how that feels."

Running my hand down his chest, I leaned against him, breathing in the scent of *him*. Asher had always smelled good. Whether it be due to cologne, sweat or sex, I could devour him. A soft purr left my mouth, a shiver of desire enveloping me in a soft cocoon.

"Meeka," he said, his voice husky.

Clearing my throat, I leaned back, looking up at him. "Coby told me to tell Brogan to leave him alone."

"Really?" Asher cupped my nape, brushing his thumb up and down the side of my neck. "Why?"

"He's said the same thing you have." I swallowed hard. "He's not good enough for her."

Asher released me and took a step back, shoving his hands in the front pockets of his jeans.

"It's not true," I reminded him, knowing he was agreeing with Coby. "You know it isn't."

"Meeka."

"No," I huffed, placing my hands on my hips. "Damn you. You can't do this. Neither of you can."

"I'm not talking about Coby and Brogan," Asher grit out, his eyes darkening.

"Fine. You want to talk about us? Okay. We'll talk. I like you. You like me. We fuck. But I know you have feelings for me. Whether you care to admit it or not."

"Of course I fucking have feelings for you, Meeka. I wouldn't still be here if I didn't. I wouldn't be working with you and having you live at my house while we try and bring this organization down."

"Tell me you're good enough for me then. Tell me you want more when this is all over."

"Fuck, Hummingbird." He shook his head. "I can't. Not yet."

My eyes burned, a heavy lump forming in the back of my throat. Turning away, I picked up a cloth and started wiping the counter. I wanted more. I wanted him to admit he cared for me. I knew he did, but I needed to hear him say it.

Asher wrapped his arms around me, holding me against his hard chest. "I don't want to jinx it. You are the only woman I want. I've wanted you for years. You know that."

"But I want *more*."

"I know, baby." He squeezed me hard. "Of course I have feelings for you. I wish I could go into more detail, but I don't even know what these feelings mean."

"I don't want this to end." I leaned my head back against him, gripping his arms. "After all of this undercover shit, I want this to continue. I need *you*."

"And I need you," he muttered.

I turned in his arms and cupped his face. "You have me. Please know that."

"You will always deserve better."

A hot shiver shot up my spine. I wanted to yell and scream that he was wrong. He deserved all the good things in life.

"Please, don't—"

A loud bang sounded throughout the room, making us jump apart.

Brogan, Max and Jay came through the front door. Heavy bags appeared under their eyes. They looked exhausted and spent.

"I'm going to bed," Max mumbled, rubbing her tiny baby bump. "I can't handle this shit," she muttered to herself.

Jay didn't say anything and followed her down the hall.

"I'm going to go hit something." Brogan cracked her knuckles, stretching her arms over her head.

"Bro," I called out before she disappeared around the corner.

"Yeah?" She stopped suddenly.

"Um …" I remembered Coby's words. "I think you should stay away from … from Coby."

She raised an eyebrow. "Did he tell you to say that?"

"No." I ran my hand through my hair, pushing it back off of my face. "I just thought it would be best. You know, looking out for you and all."

She nodded once. "Thank you." She took a step forward. "Oh, and Meeka? You fucking suck at lying." Before I could respond, she headed down the hall.

I sighed, turning back around to face Asher. "Coby mentioned it to me. I was trying to be nice."

"Coby has some shit he's dealing with," Asher said gently. "He doesn't want to bring Brogan into his mess."

"I talked to him."

Asher leaned against the counter, crossing his arms under his chest. "And?"

"I asked him what happened when you went to see Tyler. I … I wanted to know what made you snap."

He looked away, the muscle in his jaw clenching. "We all have a darkness that we deal with. Whether it be pitch black or grey, whatever the fucking shade is, it's there. Nagging at us. Forcing us to do things we don't want to do. Sometimes we let it win. Sometimes we can control it. Sometimes we can't."

"What are you saying?"

"I'm saying that I need your help to control my darkness. I don't want this to end. But we need to bring Charles down before we decide to make our relationship official."

My heart skipped a beat. It was better than nothing. Although I wanted him to admit his true feelings for me, I wouldn't push. I wasn't even sure how I felt about him. I was attracted to him. I had feelings for him. Blah, blah, blah. It was a known fact that I couldn't resist him. No matter what he did, my never-ending desire for the man wouldn't go away.

"Meeka." He crooked a finger, indicating for me to come closer.

So I did.

***

(Asher)

She wanted me to admit how I felt about her. She begged for the words to leave my mouth. But I couldn't for fear that she wouldn't feel the same. It was unjustified of me because I knew that Meeka cared for me.

When she stood in front of me, looking up at me through those thick lashes of hers, my cock twitched. From that angle, I could see the smattering of freckles on her nose where the sun had kissed her skin.

She was absolutely beautiful. In every single way. Without even trying, she was so damn appealing. So why couldn't I tell her how I felt? Oh, yeah. Because I was a fucking pussy. I made up the excuse that we needed to get this shit with Charles behind us first but the truth was, I was scared. Meeka could break my heart harder than any woman before her. I never let them in. But her, she knew all of me. Every single inch, and I wouldn't know how to come out of it if she destroyed me.

She licked her lips, grazing a hand down my chest. "Why did you need me so bad after you saw Tyler?" she asked, her cheeks reddening.

STAIN

Brushing my thumb over her bottom lip, I leaned down and sucked it between my lips. Giving it a gentle nip, I swallowed her breath. "Fighting turns me on."

"Is that the only reason?" she panted.

"Adrenaline was coursing through me. I needed to settle it, and the only way to do that was by getting inside of you."

"You needed me that much that you couldn't control it?" Her eyes widened.

"We've been through this. Why are you so surprised?" I kissed the corner of her mouth, trailing my lips down the length of her jaw before reaching the shell of her ear.

"Because I'm not used to this." She leaned her head back, giving me full access to her slender neck.

My mouth trailed soft kisses down the length of her throat. My dick grew, itching for a taste of her sweet heat.

"Asher," she breathed, gripping my shirt in her hands.

"Mmm …" Reaching around her, I gripped her ass, pulling her flush against my body.

She moaned, her pupils dilating with need.

"Get used to it, baby. You crave me. You will always crave me. When I'm not in the room, you will feel me. My dick gets hard just from the mere thought of you. Before I see you, I'm ready for you. I'm always fucking ready." At that moment, we were enveloped in darkness, the only light coming from the neon beer sign above the bar fridge. It wasn't a lot, but it was enough. If I had to feel my way around in the dark, my hands would always find Meeka.

I silently thanked who ever turned off the lights, knowing it had been one of my brothers.

Digging my fingers into the flesh of her ass, I lifted her and dropped her onto the counter. "Spread your legs," I demanded, surprised at the roughness in my voice.

Her eyes darkened even more when she did as I said.

"Good girl." Fisting my hand in her hair, I tugged her head back, forcing her mouth open. "Don't move. Don't make a fucking sound. Your cries are for my ears only. You got me?"

She nodded. "Y-yes."

"Good." Reaching between us, I ripped open her jeans and pulled them down her legs. "Remember who you belong to. No matter what, we belong to each other." I couldn't control the urge any longer. I had to make her mine. I had to force her into the submission I knew she desired to give me.

With shaky fingers, she followed suit and undid my belt.

"What would you do if someone walked in right now?" I asked, brushing my mouth over the shell of her ear. "Would you want me to stop? Would you gasp? Would you cry out with ecstasy knowing you were being watched while having the best fucking orgasm of your life?" I pulled her to the edge of the counter, leaning her back.

"I … I would want you to keep going."

I paused. Her words made me even harder. "Fucking right you would. Your greedy little cunt can't get enough of me."

She whimpered, squeezing her eyes shut.

"Can it?" I repeated, reaching between us and inserted a finger beneath her panties.

She jumped at the contact.

The desire she felt for me coated my finger. Holding her head in my other hand, I thrust my finger hard and deep. Giving her a taste of what was to come, I nipped her chin.

Meeka moaned, her mouth parting.

"You're so fucking sweet." My dick was ready to explode, but I wanted her panting and begging. I wanted her so fucking wet, one thrust from my cock would send her over the edge. I wanted her to break.

"Oh," she panted, rocking against me.

"That's it, baby," I licked along her bottom lip. "Can you feel how much your body wants me?"

"Yes." Her tongue peeked out, sliding along mine.

"Can you feel how wet your pussy is?" Thrusting my fingers into her hard, I shivered.

She cried out.

Clapping a hand over her mouth, I leaned down to her ear. "No fucking sounds."

She nodded. "Please."

"Please, what?" I smirked.

"Fuck me."

****

(Meeka)

Asher was on fire as he stood over me, holding me against the countertop. In the multiple times we had been together already, I never wanted him so much. My body ached for him. He was shoving me over the edge just by the mere thrusts of his fingers.

My chest rose and fell. I couldn't wait. I needed him like I needed my next breath. He was the sustenance for my soul.

With one hand, Asher freed his cock and pushed the tip between the folds of my pussy. A hot shiver shot straight to my clit.

I moaned, digging my heels into his ass. Hinting. Craving. Demanding more from him. My cries of pleasure were muffled by the hand on my mouth.

"You like that, Hummingbird," he breathed in my ear.

I nodded.

Releasing me, he brought the hand from between my legs, up to my mouth. "Taste your pleasure, baby. Know how wet I make you."

Getting a sense of bravery, I licked his finger, the acidic taste of my body coating my tongue.

He growled, thrusting his cock into me in a quick move.

I gasped, my eyes rolling back into my head.

"That's it," he groaned. "Take my cock like a good little girl."

Running my hands up and under his shirt, my nails dug into his chest.

His thrusts picked up speed, his balls smacking against my ass. *"Fuck."*

He replaced his hand with his mouth, shoving his tongue deep inside me.

Pulling him closer, I tried so hard to get under his skin. I wanted to feel him everywhere. Anywhere he could fit.

Releasing my mouth with a wet smack, his eyes darkened, twinkling with a hint of mischief. He took a step back, his cock falling free from my body. "Turn around and bend over the counter."

My heart jumped, and I did as I was told.

Asher wrapped one arm around my waist and with the other, cupped my mouth again. "Spread your legs and hold on."

Squeezing my eyes shut, I braced myself. A hard thrust filled me. I cried out, my eyes popping open.

Asher didn't let up. His thrusts hardened, lifting me off the floor.

There was enough space on the counter, that he bent me over completely, holding my head against the hard surface. "Can you feel me?"

I whimpered, nodding.

"Can you feel how deep I am?" Hips slapped against me, his movements bordering on rough and violent.

"Yes," I said, my voice muffled by his hand.

His fingers moved down to my throat. "If you make another sound, I'll gag you."

My core clenched at that.

"I think someone would like that."

I smiled. "Yes. Very much."

"Do you trust me, baby?"

"With everything in me."

"Good." Lifting my arms above my head, he held my wrists with one hand. "Come for me, Hummingbird." His powerful thrusts took over, leading me to the edge of passion. And when I jumped? He was right there along with me.

CHAPTER TWENTY-FIVE

Meeka

EVERY SO OFTEN, ASHER and I would pass knowing glances at each other. My cheeks would heat. He would grin. He was quite proud of himself, I might add.

We should have gone to bed, but due to perfect timing, Jay and Angel had appeared and asked us to join them in having a drink.

Luckily, no one had caught us. But the thought of someone walking in on us set my blood on overdrive.

Asher must have caught the look on my face because he leaned over and kissed my neck, inhaling deep.

"Mmm … you still smell like me," he growled, nipping my skin.

Giggling, I hooked my arm in his, leaning my head against his shoulder. It was nice. It was perfect. I didn't want it to end but I couldn't stop the twist of anxiety that something bad was going to happen.

Instead of drudging up those feelings and worrying over something I had no control over, I reveled in the fact that Asher and I were alive. We were healthy. And strong. We had shit to deal with, and we would when we were ready.

"God, you two are worse than us," Jay teased. "You need to get a room."

My cheeks heated, but I only smiled.

Asher chuckled, kissing my forehead.

Angel scoffed. "Because that has stopped us before." He smacked a hard kiss on Jay's mouth.

She sighed, leaning against him. "I love you, baby, but even *we* have boundaries."

He raised an eyebrow.

"Hush," she huffed. "Just go with me on this."

He laughed.

It was nice seeing them so playful, but I knew something was still there. Something that wasn't taken care of quite yet.

"Is everything all right?" I asked. Instead, I wanted to scream and ask what they did to that guy. How could Jay let Brogan beat him within an inch of his life? But I didn't, because a part of me, that deep seeded darkness inside, understood.

"If you're referring to the bastard we let go, yes, everything is fine." Jay crossed her arms under her chest.

Angel stiffened, a shadow passing over his face.

"Are you pissed I didn't stay down there?" Call me a baby, but I felt safer asking that question with the guys around. Angel kept Jay in line. She was hard-headed but with him around, she was easier to deal with.

"No." Jay sighed, pinching the bridge of her nose. "I understand why you left. It's not like you could have done anything anyway. I also had Max and Creena leave as well. So you're good."

"So … *we're* good?" I asked, my voice weak.

"We will be."

I nodded. It was all I could ask for.

"Listen, Jay." Asher rubbed the back of his neck.

"What's going on?" she asked, looking between him and Angel.

Angel's brows narrowed. "Yeah, what's going on?"

"Fuck it. I'm just going to say it." He cleared his throat. "Coby and I went to see Tyler." He held up his hand, stopping her. "Charles Brian was there," he said gently.

"Okay." Jay took a breath. "What are you telling me?"

"We think Tyler is in on it," Angel told her. "Or he's undercover. Who the fuck knows? But we know something is going on."

"No." Jay shook her head. "He's a sadistic fuck, but there is no way … There isn't. Shit."

"We wanted you to know so you could be prepared." Angel leaned forward. "If he is, we will take every step to bring him down. I want you to know that."

She took a breath and another, rubbing her hands down her face. "I shouldn't be surprised. No matter what happened."

"Well, Coby and I were surprised to see him," Asher told her.

"I'll have to talk to my dad. Fuck. I do not want them here. I'm don't want to deal with their shit."

Angel leaned down to her ear, whispering something only she could hear.

She nodded, swallowing hard. "Thank you for telling me, Asher," she said a moment later.

"You're welcome." He paused. "We will put an end to this. Maybe not tomorrow. Maybe not next year. But together, we will bring them down."

Her gaze moved back and forth over his face. "I like you." She looked at Angel. "I like him." And then she looked at me. "Keep him."

I smiled.

"So," Jay waved a hand in front of her. "Is this a thing now?"

Thankful for the change in subject, I looked up at Asher. Not really sure how to respond to that question, I kept my mouth shut. We had been battling back and forth whether to make it official or not. He wanted to wait. I didn't. At first, it was because we were best friends, but now, I needed him more than I needed my next breath. Maybe for some it was too soon but Asher and I had known each other for years. It made sense for us to be together. It just worked.

"That's up to my Hummingbird," Asher said, brushing his thumb along my bottom lip.

"Hummingbird?" Jay's eyes twinkled. "That's so romantic."

"All right," Angel interrupted. "Who the hell are you, and what have you done with my girlfriend?"

"What? It's sweet. I like the pet name, and I think it's adorable." Jay playfully smacked him in the chest. "Why don't you call me something like that?"

"I call you princess."

"But I'm *not* a princess."

"And she's not a Hummingbird," Angel shook his head. "Geeze, woman."

She laughed. "I'm just saying. It's cute."

Angel wrapped an arm around her shoulders. "I think you need to go to bed."

"I'm not tired."

"I said, you need to go to bed," he repeated, slowly.

Her cheeks flushed. "Right." Turning to us, her gaze landed on me before sliding to Asher's. "Take care of her."

He nodded. "Always."

When they left, Asher and I were alone. We had been alone a lot but it was different. He had just said that it was up to me if our relationship was official or not. How could I make that decision by myself? We needed to do it together. It was the only way.

Asher cleared his throat and slid out of the booth, holding his hand out to me. "We need to head back to my place."

Placing my hand in his, I let him pull me to my feet. "Are we meeting with Charles again?"

His jaw clenched. "He's been calling my phone. I'm sure he's pissed that I punched the shit out of Tyler."

"So what are we going to do?"

"Go home. Get some sleep and meet up with him tomorrow. I'll drive my truck, and you bring your bike just in case." He kissed me softly on the mouth. "I don't want you to be stranded at my place if something comes up."

I nodded. "Okay."

We headed outside. A sense of relief washed over me at the mere sight of my bike.

She was black with pearl white flames flowing off of it like molten lava. It had been forever since I rode her. The urge to let her take me away was strong. With the wind in my hair, the sun on my face, and the rumble of the engine between my thighs. It was an addiction. Almost like sex. Except when it came to Asher, nothing was like it had been with him. He was the undoing to my suffering. Every time, he took me out of my head until we were one.

Although he had given me the choice on if we should continue or not, a part of me felt like he had already made his decision. But I wasn't sure what it was. Until he looked at me. Really looked. He had been the only one who could see into my soul. He knew my darkest dirtiest thoughts. He knew my thoughts before they formed into words on my tongue.

Asher came up behind me, placing his hands gently on my shoulders. Leaning down to my ear, a soft growl rumbled from his chest. "I plan on fucking you on that beautiful machine."

A smile tugged at my lips, a soft tingle hitting me straight in the groin. "I look forward to it."

***

(Asher)

Needing to stop to run an errand, I had Meeka meet me at my place. As much as I didn't want to let her go, I had to stop and get some food or else all of our fucking would make us wither away. She didn't know it yet, but I planned on being inside of her until we had to meet Charles the next day. It was the only way I could remain calm. The inherent need to destroy everything in my path put me on edge. I lost my footing and almost tripped several times before thoughts of Meeka forced their way into my mind. It was because of her I never went back to that dark place.

When I pulled into the local grocery store, my phone dinged.

Meeka: I'm at your place.

Me: Good girl.

Meeka: Want me to cook something for supper?

My cock hardened.

Me: No. I want you naked and spread open for me.

Meeka: Where?

Fuck me, she knew me well.
Several locations came to mind but walking into my house and her being the first thing I saw was better.

Me: On the floor in the living room. I want your skin red with my marks after I take you hard.

STAIN

When she didn't respond right away, I moved to get out of the truck just as another ding sounded from my phone.

If my dick was a fucking cannon, it would have exploded. Meeka stared up at me from the phone, all in her naked beauty. Ready. Waiting. For me.

CHAPTER TWENTY-SIX

Asher

PAIN. SO MUCH PAIN. It squeezed my soul, breaking me down until I was nothing. I didn't belong. The nightmare my step-father left me in closed in around me. Suffocating me until all I could feel was the heavy weight on my chest.

All of these women and I couldn't save one. Not a single soul left those buildings alive.

The trenches I had pounded my way through grew every few feet. My mind was spinning, the world tilting on its axis. Confusion coursed through me. Where was I?

Dark shadows zeroed in and around me. My brothers. Vice-One. Sworn to protect. Sworn to do anything we could to complete the task. But no matter what I did, I couldn't save myself.

My mind played tricks on me. Was I sleeping? Was I so far gone that the nightmare had finally taken over, swallowing me in a pit of hell.

"Asher." Meeka's sweet voice slid over me, brushing up and down my back like it had a touch of its own.

I tried calling out to her, but no words left my lips. They were dry, my throat parched as if I had swallowed broken glass.

My step-father's face appeared out of nowhere, his cold lifeless eyes staring back at me with an undying hate.

"You," I finally said.

But all he did was laugh. The sickening sound pierced my ears, forcing me to my knees. Gripping my head, I cried, trying to stop the madness from taking over.

"Asher!" Meeka's scream snapped me from my thoughts.

The breath I had been holding knocked me in the chest. My back arched, a cold sweat coating my skin. "Meeka."

"I'm here, baby." She cupped my cheeks, placing soft kisses all over my face. "It was a bad dream. I'm here. I'm always here."

"Meeka," it was the only thing I could say. The sound of her voice was enough. It soothed and calmed me. My racing heart steadied to a slow rhythm but I couldn't get the unnerving feeling that something was wrong. That I would see my step-father again. I had never worried about it. Never even fathomed that he would find me. Once I became big enough, I scared him so much that he had left town.

But he was back. Everything in me told me that he would show up again. I just didn't know when.

It was funny how a man I had looked up to had taken advantage of my innocence. But he wasn't stupid. He never touched me. He would use things to hurt me but never laid a hand on my small frail body. Not until I could fight back.

"He's here," I muttered, sitting up in bed.

"Who's here?" Meeka wrapped her arms around my shoulders, nuzzling her face into the crook of my neck.

"My …" I swallowed hard. "My step-father."

"How do you know?"

"It's a feeling." I couldn't shake it, either.

"We'll deal with it when the time comes," was all she said.

Meeka didn't tell me I was crazy. She never accused me of losing my mind. She accepted my reasoning. I realized then that everything I had done was for her. Every mistake I had made. Every fight I had been in. Every single fucking mission. It was all to lead me back to her. I had been so stupid. If I would have just confessed my feelings for her years ago, we could have been together. Life was sick and twisted at times but also had a way of bringing you closer to the one you loved. And I did love Meeka. I just prayed she felt the same way.

***

One morning I woke to Meeka sleeping peacefully beside me. My stomach rumbled and I got the idea to make her breakfast in bed. But since I had been a bachelor for years, all I had was beer and pizza. Although I knew she wouldn't mind cold leftovers, she deserved eggs and bacon. Maybe even some pancakes. Look at me being all domestic and shit.

I kissed Meeka's forehead, letting her know that I was going to grab some food for breakfast.

When she only stirred, I smiled to myself and quickly got dressed.

There was an extra bounce in my step that morning. Meeka and I were happy and I had every intention of telling her that day how I felt. My stomach somersaulted.

The only woman I had ever told that I loved her, was my mother. When she died, those words never left my lips again.

Thoughts of the last nightmare I had, travelled into my mind. A feeling of unease stabbed me in the gut. Shaking it off, I chuckled lightly to myself. "Get a grip, man."

When I arrived at the store, a dark cloud appeared over me, blanketing me in the shadows of my past. My heart jumped, picking up speed as each minute passed. It was nothing. There was no reason for me to feel this way.

Stepping out of my car, my gaze landed on an older man doing the same. He paused, his back stiffening. Peering over his shoulder, his eyes locked with mine.

Him. My step-father. Elliott Masters.

He was hunched over, his skin tanned and withered. The memories of a hard sadistic life showcased in his dark eyes.

Elliott frowned, shutting the door to his vehicle. He raised an eyebrow, sizing me up.

My feet remained glued to the ground. I couldn't move. I couldn't do anything. Seeing him took me back to years ago when I was just a boy. The acidic scent of death wafted around me, the sticky liquid of blood poured from my fingertips. I could still remember it. Every moment. Every woman. Every death.

I had promised him years ago that if he saw me again, it would be before he died but I lied. I was a scared little boy who only threatened with words.

Elliott's mouth twitched at the corners. He knew. He fucking knew I wouldn't hurt him. Not yet. But I would. If I had to die trying, Elliott Masters would beg me for his life. I would laugh, dancing on his entrails until there was nothing left.

No breath. No sound. No *soul.*

****

(Meeka)

Asher's nightmares broke my heart. They had been coming on more frequently, and I didn't know how to help him through them. So I just let them play out, and when he woke, I was there to hold him and try my best to make him feel better. It usually ended up with us having a bath. I would wash away the remnants of the dreams.

I had heard of sex helping the victim through the nightmares. They needed that close connection to the person they were comfortable with. With us, it took a couple of nightmares before Asher even considered touching me in a sexual way. I let him take the control, not wanting him to feel like I was using him.

STAIN

Sex didn't solve anything. It didn't make the shit in this fucked up world any better, but it did make *us* feel better. Even if it was just for a hot sweaty couple of minutes. Or in Asher's case, hours. It had been a couple of weeks since that night. The night he demanded for me to be spread-eagle on his carpet, ready and waiting for him. Something had happened in those minutes because he hadn't left me alone since then. I wasn't complaining, but I was concerned. It was almost as if he were saying goodbye. Like he expected me to end what we had.

We had become closer and after all of his nightmares, he had become my permanent shadow.

"You are the air I need."

Asher had been so sweet and loving. Gentle through his touch. Powerful in his thrusts. I wasn't sure what came over him, but I took it for what it was.

Things had been quiet with Charles and his band of bastards. I wasn't sure why. Asher contacted him the day we were supposed to meet up but couldn't get through to him. He told me not to worry about it, but the deep frown set on his handsome face grated at my nerves.

When Asher woke me up with a gentle kiss on the forehead, he mentioned something about running errands and grabbing me breakfast. My aching and tired body forced me back into a deep sleep, so I wasn't sure if I had been dreaming or not.

A couple hours later, I woke to a jarring sound in my head. What the hell?

I groaned, rolling over on my stomach. Shoving the pillow over my head, I ignored the sound but it only became louder and louder. That was when I realized it was my phone ringing.

Snatching my cell off the night stand, I frowned at the unknown number. "Hello?"

"You and your fucking boyfriend need to get over here or I will send out my watch dogs for you. Trust me, little girl, you don't want these men to find you."

Charles. Fucking. Brian.

Great.

"I don't know what you're talking about." Either it was my sleep-induced state or the fact that I just had enough, but I was no longer scared of him.

"Get over here," he bellowed, slamming the phone in my ear.

"Rude." Grumbling to myself, I got out of bed and was surprised to see that it was early afternoon. Asher had done a good job the night before in wearing me out. My skin burned, a small smile spreading on my face. Charles wouldn't ruin this.

Making my way down the stairs, I stopped suddenly when a loud crash vibrated from the back of the house. The sounds continued. It was like someone was trying to bring the walls to a crumbling halt.

"Asher?" I called out, my voice cracking. Clearing my throat, I yelled his name again, but no answer came. Peeking out the front window, I saw his truck in the driveway but no sign of him.

Another crash, followed by some mumbled curses. What the hell was going on?

Following the noise, I made my way to the door leading down into the basement. The sounds became louder with each step I took. I opened the door, peering down the dim stairway. "Asher?" Another crash. I jumped, instinctively reaching for my cell phone. Getting ready to call Angel even though I knew I probably should just call the police, my thumb hovered over his number. "Hey," I called out. "Are you down there?" It was a typical scene out of a horror movie. Dumb girl wakes up from a sex-induced coma only to find herself dead after searching out a noise.

"*Fuck!*"

Asher. My heart jumped. I ran down the stairs, coming to a halt when I saw him pounding his fists into the cement wall. He was cursing, yelling, mumbling. I couldn't make out anything he was saying. The darkness had taken over, his nightmares controlling his actions, forcing him to hurt himself. He kept pounding his fists into the wall until the bricks were lined with red and pieces of his skin.

"*Asher,*" I screamed, taking a step toward him. "What are you doing?"

But he didn't turn around. It was as if he didn't even hear or see me. He didn't stop. He didn't say my name. He only continued to lose himself. That piece of him that had been strong for all of these years. I grabbed a hold of him but he wouldn't let up. Punch after punch, his fists hit the wall. His knuckles bloody and bruised.

"Please stop," I cried, reaching for his hands.

He spun on me, forcing me to take a step back.

I stared up at him with wide eyes, my heart shattering into a million tiny pieces.

He looked down at me with no emotion, no hint of the man I had known for most of my life. I barely recognized him. His eyes were dark, shadowed by a past that had finally won.

He stared back at me with hate in his eyes, but I knew, with everything in me, that hate wasn't meant for me.

He didn't say anything but turned around and started throwing boxes, tools, anything he could get his hands on. He was a crazed man, a victim, fighting for the lingering hope that he could be somewhat normal again. But for the moment, he was done. And that was when I realized he had officially lost his power.

CHAPTER TWENTY-SEVEN

Meeka

WITH SHAKY HANDS, I called Angel.

"Yeah."

"Angel. Asher." The words wouldn't come out. My chest ached, tightening with anxiety. I didn't know what was going on or what to do. I had never seen Asher break before. He had only come see me after the fact but he never explained, he never told me anything. If only he would have. I could have been prepared. I could have helped him in some way. He had told me he was protecting me but after all of this time, I still believed that it was to protect himself. He hid the broken darkness from me so there was no way I would judge him. But I wouldn't. Never.

"Deep breaths, Meeka," Angel said, gently. "What's going on?"

"Something happened," I paced back and forth, my nerves jumping every time a loud sound came from the basement. "He's freaking out, and I don't know what to do. He needs you."

"No," Angel corrected. "He needs *you*."

"I tried. I don't know what to do."

"We're on our way."

The sound of Angel hanging up released some of the tension pushing on my shoulders. Asher's brothers could get him to calm down. They knew him in the field. They knew him in a different way than I did. But I knew all of him. I knew every inch, every hard muscle. Every thought. I had to go back to him. I needed to try and dig past the wall that had been built since his step-father destroyed him years ago.

Heading back down stairs, I kept a safe distance away from Asher. But I didn't want to. Every fiber of my being told me to go to him. To help him. To protect him. He had finally let the shadows of his past win.

He stopped hitting his fists against the wall, thank God, but he was still mumbling to himself and throwing things. His clothes were wrinkled from him tugging at them. His eyes were wild, never landing on me again but looking at something in the distance. It was something only he could see.

"Asher," I said gently, my throat burning. "Please, baby." All I could do was plead, beg for him to hear my voice and know that I wouldn't leave him. I wasn't going anywhere. We had our problems, but we would get out of this. We had to.

Ten minutes later, and I was surrounded by Angel, Coby, Stone, and Dale. All of whom were much larger than me and took up a lot of space. Each of them stood over six feet, weighing at least two hundred pounds. I suddenly felt very small but I was thankful for them at that very moment.

"Shit, man," Dale rubbed the back of his neck. "I've never seen him lose it like this."

Stone just nodded and grunted in agreement.

Angel and Coby only stared after their brother with worried looks in their eyes.

"What do I do?" I rang my hands together, my soul shattering at the love—a small gasp escaped me. The love of my world. My eyes welled. I loved him. God, I had been so stupid to think that I could never fall for him. One kiss and all of these emotions flooded into me, flowing through my veins until all I felt was him.

The guys huddled in front of me, shielding me from Asher. They spoke amongst themselves, watching their brother crumble before them.

"Maybe she should go to him again."

"What's that going to do? He's officially lost it."

"Have faith in the woman our brother loves."

"What if he hurts her?'

"He needs us not to judge," Coby said. "She belongs to him, so that means we protect her."

They all turned to me, piercing me with hard stares.

I swallowed hard, unsure of what to do. I wanted to go to Asher, but I had no idea how to get through to him.

"He needs you right now," Angel said. "We don't know what's going on, but together we will get him the help he needs. We'll stay back and remain quiet until you tell us otherwise."

I nodded, ringing my hands in front of me. Taking a breath, I stepped between Angel and Coby and walked to the man I loved. The man I needed. The man who had given me so much happiness when he couldn't find that happy himself. I would help him be happy. I would make him see that he deserved it. That he deserved everything. Success, love, family. Everything a man should have.

"Asher?" I reached out for him, hesitating. He had stopped throwing shit around, but he was still mumbling to himself. When I was about a foot away from him, I heard the words that threatened to destroy him. A sob escaped me.

"He can't do this to me. I won't let him. He won't win. Not anymore. I can't. I'm not a boy. I'm a man. Please don't hurt me. Not again. So much blood. God. I can't."

So long ago, he came to me at a time in his life where he needed a friend. Someone he could trust and count on to keep his shattered secrets. A friend who wouldn't judge. I was all of those things. And more. I realized then that I loved him since the first time I met him. All of those sleepless nights with him on my floor and me on my bed. Talking about the weather, celebrities, books, and more. He was the piece of me I had been missing my whole life. The part of my world I could never live without.

Reaching out, I placed a shaky hand on his strong back. His body stiffened before he slowly turned my way.

I bit back a cry.

His eyes were dark, taking on a faraway look but bright with fear.

"I'm here," I said, trying so hard to keep my voice strong and sure. "Whatever you need, I am here for you. Come back to me."

His pupils dilated, losing focus before zeroing in on me. "I saw him," he said, his voice rough.

And that was when I felt the others close in on us.

"Who did you see?" I asked, running my hand down his arm. But I knew. It was the only time he would truly lose himself.

His eyes followed the movement, his jaw clenching and unclenching. "My step-father."

"What-what did he want?"

Asher looked away, moving to pull out of my grip but I only held on.

"Tell me," I begged. "Please. I can't help you if I don't know."

"You think you can help me?" he shouted. "Do you think any of you can help me? Just let me fucking go. It's for the best. I don't deserve you," he told his brothers before looking down at me. "And I especially don't deserve you."

"You can't mean that," I stepped in front of him, gripping his shirt tight in my hands. I didn't care what he said. It wasn't true. None of it was. I loved him, and I knew he felt something in return for me.

I looked back at Angel. He nodded once. I went to turn back around when something caught my attention in Coby's gaze. It was almost a pleading for me to help his brother. They knew this was the end. Asher would have to retire or get medically discharged from the Navy. The demons from his past had snuck up on him, and I knew without a doubt that he would get diagnosed with PTSD. It would be a rough time, but I would travel the rocky road with him every step of the way.

Taking a deep cleansing breath, I turned back around and wrapped my arms around Asher's waist. I was done. I couldn't handle seeing him break anymore. Whatever happened with his step-father, I would help him get through it. We would jump over this hurdle together.

"Meeka," his voice cracked. "I can't. He didn't even talk to me, and I fucking broke."

Tears streamed down my cheeks. "I'm here. We all are." I squeezed him tight just as warm bodies stepped up behind us.

"It hurts. It hurts so fucking much." Asher ran his fingers through the hair at my nape, holding my head against his chest. It was his signature move. I had come to crave it. All this time, I thought he was doing it to comfort me, but really, he was comforting himself. All from a mere touch. The mind was a funny thing. A gentle touch could make all the nightmares disappear even if it were only for a moment.

"I love you," I confessed, my voice muffled by his shirt.

Asher pulled my head back, staring intently into my eyes. His thumbs brushed over my cheeks, wiping the tears away. "Say that again."

"I love you," I repeated with more confidence. "I've been in love with you since the first day we met. But you are so damned intense, I've never had the courage to say it."

Asher searched my face before crushing his mouth to mine.

I sighed, leaning into him, and poured all of the love I felt for the man into that kiss.

STAIN

I barely noticed the guys leaving us alone, giving us some space.

All I could focus on was the man staring down at me. My hand grazed up his chest to his heart. It beat rapidly beneath my palm but his body had finally relaxed.

When we were alone, Asher pulled me into his arms and knelt with me wrapped around him.

I sat there quietly in his arms, afraid to let him go. Afraid of losing him forever. It felt like hours since either of us spoke. The only movement came from Coby when he wrapped Asher's knuckles in bandages. He left right after, not saying a word.

"I know you don't want to, but you need to talk about what happened." I grabbed Asher's hands gently, brushing my thumbs over his damaged knuckles. "Your brothers need to know."

Leaning his head against the wall, he let out a shallow breath. "Right now all I can think about is you telling me that you love me."

My cheeks heated. Looking down between us, I played with the hem of his shirt. "What happened to you years ago scares me. As each day passes, you lose yourself. I can see the darkness that you try so hard to fight. You told me once it's why you joined the Navy. You felt it was safer for you and whoever you came across. It took you away from the man who tried so hard to destroy you. But as selfish as it is, it took you away from me too."

Asher shifted his weight so I was straddling his lap. He wiped a lonely tear that had fallen down my cheek. "I want to tell you that I'll be okay. That I won't have another episode. But seeing him triggered something. I know I need help, but I don't want to sit there and talk to a fucking shrink about my problems. I know I have shit to deal with. I'd rather talk to you and that's it. I don't need anyone else. No one else can help me through it like you can."

"You need your brothers," I said softly.

"Of course I need them, but you—" Asher pinched my chin, forcing me to look up at him. "I can't live without you. What I feel for you scares me. It terrifies me more than the fear I felt as a child. Because I know that if something happened to break us apart, I wouldn't be able to live with myself."

"Nothing will happen to us." I cupped his cheek. "I promise. Whatever happens, whatever you need; I will be there. If you go see a shrink, I'll be right there by your side. But you need to see someone."

"I know, but I don't want to take a shit load of pills for the rest of my life."

"Maybe there's another way." I shrugged. "Whatever you decide to do, I will be behind you a hundred percent."

"No," he said, his voice firm. "I want you at my side. Not behind me. We're equal, Hummingbird. Remember that."

Fresh tears welled in my eyes, threatening to escape. God, this man and how he could make my heart melt in a shitty situation.

His eyes moved back and forth over my face. "I love you, Meeka. I love you so damn much. I can't tell you how thankful I am that I broke into your bedroom that first night."

I laughed which came out more like a sob. "Well, it wasn't like you were a stranger or anything."

"I remember the first time I saw you in those sexy as hell pajamas. With your perky little tits and tight as fuck ass." He groaned. "God, the things I wanted to do to you that night."

"You could have," I whispered.

"And then what? Your dad would have fucking killed me or chopped off my dick and fed it to me."

"But you could have kissed me, at least. All this time, I thought we were just friends but then when you did finally kiss me—"

"What?"

"I knew I was done."

"Baby, I was done the first time you smiled at me." He rubbed a hand down his face, the dark mood once again taking over. "I know I need help, but I can't do this without you."

"I'll be here. Every step of the way."

He kissed my forehead, then my nose, and placed a soft peck on my lips. "I love you. Fuck, I love you so damn much." His voice wavered. "Don't ever doubt that. No matter what happens. Know that I am yours."

My heart swelled. "And I am yours."

CHAPTER TWENTY-EIGHT

Asher

"WHEN I WAS A child, I was abused by my step-father. Nothing sexual, although, what he put me through was almost as bad." I explained to my brothers what had happened in my shitty start to life. My mother dying only made my step-father worse. I told them about the blood he would make me clean up after he would destroy the pureness of the women he fucked. He was as bad as Charles, if not worse. I was a kid. There was no way I could have proved what he had done. He was a prestigious man in our small town. The only people who knew his dark and dangerous secrets were Meeka and myself. And the women he ruined.

"What happened today?" Angel asked, sitting across from me at the dining room table. He placed a bottle of water in front of me and waited. All eyes were on me, but I couldn't bring myself to look at them. Meeka sat at my side, holding my hand tight in hers, listening intently to what I had to say. Although she knew everything, I was getting to the part I hadn't told anyone. A darkness was unleashed back in the day. Charles had been right. Everyone had a darkness of their own.

"I saw him." I took a breath and another before I continued. "I went to the store to get some food. He was there. I haven't seen him in years. When I was finally big enough to defend myself, I threatened to kill him if I ever saw him again." I looked at Meeka. "But I didn't because of you. As much as I wanted to rip him apart for what he did to those women and to me, I couldn't do anything to lose you."

Tears welled in her eyes.

God, I hated making her cry but I needed her to hear what I had to say. "Because of you, I've been able to move past this. But now with Charles breathing down our necks and seeing my step-father, it triggered something." And that something was dark. It hovered over the years until finally, it brought me to my knees.

"I'm pulling you off the mission." Angel pushed to his feet, pacing back and forth. "We'll find another way. I'm not losing you to the likes of those bastards."

There was no way. I stared after him. "I can—"

"No," Angel snapped, his voice final. "There is no argument. If you stay in, we do it together." He cupped the back of my neck. "I will see to it that you still have a good career. It will fucking suck not fighting by your side, but your health is more important to me. There's no point fighting for my country when I can't fight for you."

My eyes burned, a lump forming in the back of my throat.

"Fuck, man," Dale sniffed. "You're going to make me cry."

"Asshole." Stone smacked him across the head.

"Fucktwad."

I laughed, which more came out like a sob. Dropping my head in my hands, I let it out. All of it. Every single fucking emotion I was scared to feel over the years. Love. Hate. Fear. The one I craved was the one that threatened to destroy me. Control. *God, I was never in control.*

"We're here, brother," Angel squeezed my neck. "Always."

And this coming from the guy who had no idea how to love in the beginning. Now he was telling me how to feel. The roles were reversed. I made a mental note to thank that girlfriend of his.

The calloused hand that belonged to Angel was soon replaced by a soft and gentle touch. I looked up, meeting Meeka's watery gaze.

"Hi," she whispered.

"Hi," I ground out.

Meeka had told us that Charles called her cell. The fucker wouldn't give up.

Angel and the guys left the kitchen to make some calls. Meeka and I were no longer allowed to go to Charles place alone no matter what he had threatened.

Meeka slid onto my lap, running her hands under my shirt.

My eyes fluttered closed at the love pouring from her finger tips. I always craved her touch. It calmed me. Even back in the day when it would only be a hug, it meant more to me than she'd ever begin to understand.

STAIN

Her hands trailed down to my abs, her fingers brushing over the hem of my sweatpants. It had been a couple of hours since my break down but we both knew that now was not the right time for sex.

"Let me know when you are ready, and I'll make all of your nightmares go away." She chewed her bottom lip. "Even if it's just for a moment."

***

The next day, I woke up from a nightmare to the constant ringing of my damn phone. I put it on silent and watched the screen light up every couple of minutes. Charles was adamant on speaking with me, but as per Angel's orders, I didn't answer the phone. Coby, Stone, and Dale had gone out to Charles' place last night thanks to tracking my phone weeks before. Charles wasn't stupid. He wanted my phone tracked. It was why he never took it from me when his security originally searched my pockets.

Flipping my phone, I exhaled a heavy breath and sat back in the plush chair.

Meeka stirred, sitting up in bed and frowned when she caught me staring at her. "Come back to bed." She yawned. The white sheet fell to her waist, revealing her pale skin.

My nostrils flared, a searing heat shooting straight to my groin. Her rosy nipples hardened in the cool air, the draft rolling in from the open window.

"Is everything all right?" she asked, sliding out of bed.

Rising to my feet, I charged for her and pushed her back on the bed. For the next couple of hours, I took control. I gave her what she needed and what she craved, taking what I wanted in return.

Her moans of pleasure and screams of desire were everything I craved. Everything I lived for.

"I love you, Hummingbird." I kissed her softly on the mouth while our bodies stayed connected. "More than you'll ever know."

Tears welled in her eyes. "I know. God, I know. Because I feel it too."

I made love to her for hours. Feasting on her body like it was the food for my soul, I didn't come up for breath until late that evening.

I kissed her forehead. "We have to head to the club."

She stirred, groaning, and shoved her arms under the pillow. "Just a little more."

I chuckled, pulling the covers off of her naked body. She didn't even flinch. "Come on. I'm not leaving here knowing you're naked in my bed."

"Then stay with me," she pouted.

"Angel and Jay need to meet with us. She has some information on Tyler." I wasn't sure what it was, but by the panic in Angel's voice when he called earlier, it couldn't be good.

"Fine." Meeka yawned and pulled herself from the bed.

My cock stirred at the naked beauty before me, but it would have to wait.

Charles had spent the last week trying to get a hold of me. He would be pissed if we ever came face to face again but according to Angel, that would never happen. I was confused as fuck. I was a Navy SEAL working undercover trying to bring down a sex slave ring. I needed a fucking raise.

Meeka got dressed and let out a sigh. "I'm ready."

I stared at her. She wore grey sweatpants and a black sweatshirt. Her hair was pulled up into a messy bun and those slippers that women wore as shoes were on her feet. I would never understand why someone would pay hundreds of dollars for slippers.

"Asher?"

I cleared my throat, the back of my neck heating at being caught staring at her.

"Were you staring at me?"

"Yes." I closed the distance between us and kissed her hard on the mouth. "You're so damn beautiful when you're not trying."

"Thank you." Her hands tugged at my belt.

"What are you doing?" My mouth moved down the length of her jaw.

"I'm stressed. I'm horny as fuck and I need your cock inside me."

I coughed. "Well, then." I shoved her back on the bed and flipped her onto her stomach. "I think I can accommodate your request one last time."

***

(Meeka)

He filled me. Utterly and completely. Every time I breathed, all I could feel was him. He moved above me, pinning me against the edge of the bed. Something hadn't sat well with me. I let Asher think it was because I was tired but really, I was so damn tense, I needed him to fuck it out of me.

Asher's grunts filled my ears. His hands squeezed and massaged my body. His thick length slid in and out of me in rough powerful thrusts. He was everything I needed.

We jumped over the edge together, our names melting together as one.

"I love you," his words whispered across my skin.

After we cleaned up, we headed outside and stopped in front of my bike.

He grinned. "I still need to fuck you on this."

"You will." I winked. Tilting my chin, I tapped my mouth.

His grin grew. Placing a soft kiss on my lips, he smacked my rear. "Drive safe, Hummingbird."

I giggled. "Always. With this powerful machine roaring between my legs, I have no choice but to be safe."

"Fuck." He adjusted himself, shaking his head. Walking toward his truck, he called out over his shoulder, "I will punish you for that image you put in my brain."

My heart fluttered. "I look forward to it."

***

I didn't ride my bike as often as I would like. Although it was my only way of transportation, being in a small town, most places were within walking distance. A lot of times, the bikes became a necessity to prove power. King's Harlots were still struggling trying to make a name for themselves. After the beat down Jay and Brogan gave to that guy, I had a feeling that respect would be earned. Even if it would be the hard way.

Asher's truck was a couple car lengths ahead of me. I smiled to myself, knowing he was looking at me as often as he could in the rear view mirror.

I gave him a wave, and I swore I could see him straighten a little. It felt like a lifetime since he broke down in front of us. His brothers had been supportive and Angel came through on his promise. Asher would start his new position in a month. He wasn't happy about it but his mental wellbeing was more important to me. To all of us.

Lost in my own thoughts, I missed the turn off to the street the club was on. Normally, I could drive to it blindfolded, but with everything that had been going on, I was distracted.

Turning around, I headed back to my turn off when I saw a car flipped over onto its hood. No. Another look and I realized it was a truck. A black truck. My heart started racing.

Asher. There were tons of black trucks in the area. Weren't there?

I slowed down to a stop, shut off my bike, and pulled off my helmet. Placing it on the seat, I made my way to the crash. No smoke was coming from the truck, but the gas tank was leaking. Sparks from the destruction were landing only inches away from the liquid. Where was the body?

Searching around the debris, I heard a cough and some curses. My stomach dropped to my feet. "Asher." I ran to the driver side.

"Meeka," he coughed again. "Get out of here."

"No, I'm not leaving you." I pulled at the door, attempting to get it open but it wouldn't budge.

"Get out of here," he rasped. "Please."

"The gas tank is leaking." I did everything I could to search. "I don't know what to do," I sobbed.

"Meeka," he coughed, struggling to undo the seatbelt and get to safety. But he couldn't. Blood seeped from a wound in his head. Scratches and cuts marred his skin. He was favoring his right arm, wincing every time he moved it. "I think my arm is broken. *Fuck.*"

I called Angel. No answer. I called Coby. Then Dale. Stone. My sisters. No fucking answer. Memories of Jay trying to get a hold of us months ago slid into my mind. She couldn't get through to us, either, when she needed help. We couldn't understand why. Brogan's step brother, Greyson, said someone hacked the phones. I had a moment of déjà vu.

"I can't get through to anyone." I jumped when a spark landed near my foot. So fucking close to the gas.

"Shit." He pushed against the door, grimacing and cursing out a breath when it wouldn't budge.

I didn't know what to do. I could go get help, but I didn't want to leave him. "I'm calling the police." I dialed 911 and gave the information needed to the dispatcher.

Grabbing hold of the door handle, I tugged and pulled. Using all of my strength I could muster, the door finally creaked open, but Asher was still stuck.

"Please, baby. Just leave," he said between curses.

"I am not leaving you." Reaching around him, I struggled to unlock the seatbelt, but it wouldn't budge. "Shit. Come on," I cried, sending up a silent prayer. Please let me get him out.

"The police should be here by now."

"There should be a knife in the glove box," Asher told me. "I can't reach with my arm."

A sense of relief washed over me. I crawled across him and opened the compartment, thankful when I saw the blade shining in the moonlight. "It's here." I cut the strap of the seat belt.

He fell forward, grunting when his arm hit the steering wheel. "Move back."

I left the space, helping him as much as I could to get out of the truck.

"Well, well, well. Isn't this romantic?"

We paused, staring at each other when we heard the deep voice coming from behind us. His gaze slid over my head, darkening with a hate I had never seen before in him.

"You fucking did this," he growled.

"Nah," Charles corrected. "My boys did. I'm not one to get my hands dirty."

"That's right. I forgot." Asher pushed forward, crawling out of the rubble as best he could with one good arm. "It takes a real man to do his own dirty work."

"I don't think you're in a position to talk right now." Charles crouched beside us, snapping his fingers. "Get him out of here."

"What?" I cried. "No. He needs to go to the hospital."

Charles spun on me, grabbing my arm and dug his fingers into the muscle.

I whimpered, struggling against his rough hold. "Please."

"You think after all of this, I'm going to let you go? Are you fucking stupid?" his eyes moved back and forth over my face. "You're hot, but you're not the brightest if you think I'm just going to walk away."

Two large men came up beside me as Charles rose to his feet. He pulled me with him, wrapping his arm around my waist.

The men grabbed hold of Asher, tugging him out of the truck, not caring in the least about his arm. His jaw clenched, but other than that, no sound of pain left him.

"Please, let us go." I pushed against Charles, freeing my arm and rushed to Asher's side.

He nuzzled his face into the crook of my neck. "Do as he says," he whispered. "Trust me. We will get out of this."

A sob escaped me as arms wrapped around my waist, pulling me away from Asher.

"Say goodnight, Meeka." Charles grinned.

Darkness and pain mixed as one, drowning me in a sea of black. The last thing I saw before it took over was the wide-eyed look of fear in Asher's eyes. That was when I knew—we weren't getting out of this anytime soon.

CHAPTER TWENTY-NINE

Asher

SEARING HOT AGONY COURSED through my blood, setting my skin on fire. My stomach twisted and churned, rolling over itself until acidic bile rose to my throat. I tried opening my eyes, but all I could see was black. The darkness that had threatened to destroy me over the years finally took over. I couldn't control it, and this time I let it win.

The scent of death surrounded me, but I didn't know where I was. I could only assume that Charles had taken us back to his place. I wasn't even sure if it was actually his house. Who the fuck knew anymore? Everything had happened so quickly. I couldn't even remember the final outcome of meeting with Tyler only a few weeks ago. All I knew was that he won. I left filled with rage, and all he could do was laugh. He was a sick fuck, and it still surprised me to this day that Jay had been with him.

Struggling to move, a chain clinked against the cool concrete I was lying on. I had been bound but not gagged, thank fuck. With my good arm, I tried to push myself up to a sitting position. My body felt like it weighed a ton. I couldn't move.

Replaying what had happened in my mind, a growl escaped me.

Meeka.

My Hummingbird.

I tried so hard not to think about what Charles was doing to her. He had a thing for her. I could see it in his eyes. It was the same look I had whenever she came into the room. She didn't know how beautiful she was. Her innocence made her so fucking pure, Charles wanted a taste.

"Fuck," I ground out. If he touched her … If he harmed one hair on her fucking body, I would end him. I would make it so all the shit he did to those women looked like a fucking Disney movie compared to what I would do to him. And I would make him watch while I ripped off every inch of him that touched her. As each thought crossed my mind, the rage inside of me became stronger and darker. It bordered on violent, and I embraced it.

Reaching my good arm out, I searched for anything that could help me get the chain off my ankle. The thought crossed my mind that if I had a saw, I would cut off my foot to get to Meeka. A cold maniacal laugh escaped me. It was from sheer terror and desperation. The thought of never seeing her again took my breath away but it also drove me to find an escape. From reality. From fucking life in general. Shit with Charles needed to end. If I had to go through Tyler first, I would. With everything in me, I knew he was in on it. He wasn't undercover. He was leading two fucking lives and his craving for younger girls took over.

Crawling as far as I could, I tested to see how long the chain was. I got three feet before it became taught and I couldn't move anymore. "Shit." I reached my arm out, waving it in front of me to feel for walls. My hand landed against a brick wall, a sharp pain biting into my knuckles. That pain drove me mad. "Let me the fuck out!"

Suddenly, a light turned on, blinding me. I squinted, rubbing my eyes until they were able to focus on the room I was trapped in. It was your typical room that came right out of a horror movie. Blood-stained walls. Dirt and debris lined the tile floor. Without a doubt, the room had been designed to scare. To set that fear in someone until they did everything to break free. But these guys didn't know me. They didn't know what I had done as a child to survive. So many times, I had begged my step-father to just let me go. I ran away once before he found me. I was his little bitch who kept his place clean for fear the women would run screaming to the police.

My hand clenched into a fist as thoughts traveled back to the time I first tasted the darkness. Screams. Loud and powerful screams tore at my mind until all I could focus on was ending her suffering. I didn't know who she was. I had no idea where she came from. She had fallen victim to my step-father's sadistic wrath and he left her in my fragile grip. He knew I would kill her.

He had set it up that way. She begged me, pleaded for me to let her go. But I couldn't. I was just a boy. My step-father had taught me to fight and defend myself. It was the only time he hadn't beat me.

I sighed, leaning my head against the wall and took a couple deep cleansing breaths. Regaining that control, I rose to my feet on shaky legs. My whole fucking body hurt. Everything. Even the hair on my head. I checked my damaged arm, grimacing when I noticed it hung at an odd angle. Yup. Definitely broken. "Motherfucker." I would kill him, and I couldn't wait to watch the life leave his eyes, fading before me like the piece of shit he was.

Scanning the room, I looked for anything out of the ordinary. There was a door across from me, but with the short chain I was on, I wouldn't be able to reach it. Even though I was tall, whoever locked me in there made sure they put me as far away from my escape as possible.

Everything about the room reminded me of the basement I had been forced to clean for years. Four brick walls. Concrete floor. And a door. No windows. No furniture. It was cool and damp in the air, but that was it. The door didn't even have a window in it. I was trapped. With no fucking escape at all in my near future. But I wasn't trapped. Not in the physical sense. My step-father was a bastard and knew just how to get me to break. I went to school. Hanging on by a thread. But my mental well-being was chipped apart day by day as time wore on. Every smattering of blood I cleaned, broke a piece off of my strength.

Calming my racing heart, I took another deep breath and listened. Reining in all of the training I had been given over the years, I listened for anything that could give me some sort of answer. But nothing. No fucking sounds pierced my ears. The brick silenced any noise coming from the outside. I could be in the middle of butt fuck Idaho for all I knew, and Meeka could have been in another country by then. I didn't know how long I had been knocked out for. I didn't know a damn thing. It was enough to drive a sane man mad.

"Hello?" I called out, my voice rough like I had just gargled with broken glass. "Let me the fuck out!"

A minute later, a lock clicked and the door opened slowly, revealing Charles. He stared after me, a small grin spreading on his ugly mug.

"Where the *fuck* is Meeka?" Leaning my good arm on the wall for support, I took a shallow breath.

"She's safe." He winked. "For now."

I rolled my eyes at the clichéd line. "What do you want?"

Charles walked further into the room, followed by the two large bastards who were at the crash site. They were always with him. They only spoke when spoken to or when Charles wasn't around.

My gut churned, my heart picking up speed.

"I want to know why you have been ignoring my calls," Charles said, his voice flat and even. "We had a deal. I changed the fucking rules for you. You brought in your own girl when that's not how it works. I should have listened to Tyler." He laughed, shaking his head.

"What the fuck does this have to do with Tyler?" I demanded, the drive to kill clouding my vision.

"Everything." Charles took a step toward me. "Tyler runs this part of the operation. Didn't you know that?"

"I had my suspicions," I mumbled.

"Tyler is the driving force. He's kept all of our worlds connected." Charles rolled his eyes.

"You sound like you're not happy with that."

"Why would I be? I've been in this job for years. Tyler comes waltzing in only a couple months ago, and already he's moved to the fucking top," Charles seethed, his nostrils flaring.

Ah. Someone was jealous. I could use his anger to my advantage if I played my cards right. Much like Meeka, Charles was trying to get recognition from his boss.

Charles started pacing back and forth, rubbing his chin. "I need to know how I can make him see that *I* got this. That *I* deserve the power."

"If Tyler is already at the top, your boss won't care what you do."

Charles spun on me. "Yes, he will. I'll just have to send him a care package. Maybe a body part or two."

"How the hell would that help?"

"I could send him your girl. A finger. A toe. How about her fucking tit?"

"You leave her the fuck alone!" I charged for him, stopping two feet away from him when the chain on my ankle held me back.

"And what are you going to do about it, huh?" Charles snapped. "You're stuck in here, Asher. Everything is happening because of you. If you would have just answered my fucking calls. Or better yet. You should have chosen one of my girls. But no, you brought Meeka into hell. What kind of boyfriend are you? You say you love her but your selfish fucking ass forced her into a world that eats up women like her. How does that make you feel?"

STAIN

My heart jumped in my chest. He was right, and I couldn't deny it. No matter how hard I tried, everything he said was true. I *was* selfish. I made Meeka feel guilty so she had no fucking choice but to join me. What kind of man was I? A pussy. I was a fucking pussy. My stepfather had been right. I didn't deserve anyone. And I especially didn't deserve Meeka.

"I love you."

Meeka's confession of her love for me changed things. Yes, I felt fucking guilty for what I brought her into, but I would live out my days making it up to her. I didn't deserve her, and I would never get over that, but I would love her with all of me. Nothing and no one would change that. It was the only thing I didn't control. It was all on Meeka. She loved me. She pulled feelings from me and enveloped them with her beauty.

Her face filled my mind.

"I see you don't deny anything I've said." Charles smirked. "It takes a real man to admit when he's wrong."

"Fuck you," I bit out through gritted teeth. "You don't know shit. You don't know what I've been through."

"Of course—" he threw his hands up in the air. "It's all about you, isn't it? I will have fun telling Meeka that." He snapped his fingers.

A knowing glance passed between the other two men before sauntering my way.

Charles walked to the door. "Have fun. And don't do anything I wouldn't do." He laughed, shutting me in with his goons.

I had a chained leg and a broken arm.

As I stared into the eyes of the men who closed the distance between us, I realized something.

I was fucked.

****
(Meeka)

A pounding headache pierced between my eyes. I had been awake for an hour, Charles had told me. He brought me to his bedroom which creeped me the hell out. It messed with my head when he was gentle. Even though I knew he was sick in the head, my heart told my brain to feel sorry for him. I couldn't understand why. After all of the shit he had done to these women, it didn't make sense for me to feel this way. My stomach rolled at the mere thought of him being nice. I would much rather if he yelled and screamed at me. At least then I would know where he stood.

When he brought me into his room, he refused to let his security touch me. Charles placed me on his bed and brushed a hand down my cheek. The skin still tingled from where he had touched me. I needed Asher. I needed him to wipe away every inch Charles caressed. Even though he had never crossed the line, he might as well have raped my mind. He forced his way into my thoughts much to my dismay.

Slowly pushing myself up on shaky arms, I rubbed some life back into my cheeks. A sense of relief washed over me that I was still dressed. And alone.

I tried so hard not to glance around the room. It was too personal. Too intimate. I didn't want to know Charles. I didn't want to know anything about the man. He was a sadistic bastard, and he deserved to rot in hell. I wasn't stupid, though. He brought me into his bedroom, so it messed with my head. If I could just know him a little bit, I would feel sorry for him. Well, it wouldn't work. I channeled the hatred I had for him. For what he did to the previous women. The little girls who were no more than teenagers. Some right out of puberty. He could have done something to Violet as well, but she never said. Angel and Jay had asked her if she knew the name, but she refused to talk about the missing years of her life. Even though she remembered them, she said she was lost and that those years didn't count. A part of her had died along with the other women.

As much as I didn't want to, I searched around the room for anything that could help me get out of there. The door was locked. I knew it would be, but there was still that glimmer of hope. Charles knew better. Jay had told us that Eric Vega let her leave the room. It fucked her up pretty bad so I was almost thankful that I couldn't leave. To be given that choice to either save yourself or someone else—it was not a decision I wanted to make. Unless it came down to Asher and myself. As much as he would be furious with me, I would lay my life on the line for him, and I knew he would do the same for me.

A large cabinet stood in front of me. I didn't understand why, but something about it set my nerves on edge. Maybe it would lead to my escape. Opening the doors, I gasped at the sight before me.

Whips. Chains. Floggers. *Knives.*

It was the cabinet of torture. I was all for kink but this held no hint of pleasure at all. Items I had never seen before rested on a red velvet mat at the base of the main shelf. Needles. I swallowed hard. Masks. Dildos bigger around than my fist.

Taking a deep breath, I opened the top drawer, my stomach dropping to my feet.

More knives stared up at me. All different sizes. I slammed the drawer shut and closed the cabinet doors, a cold sweat racing down my back like fingers of fear.

I didn't want to think about what Charles did with those tools or who he tortured. Looking around the room, I couldn't imagine that he did any of that here. It was clean. Too pristine to have the walls marked with the blood of his victims. Would I be one of those victims? Would he make me submit and break me until there was nothing left?

Heading to the window, I separated the curtains. The dim moon light cast an eerie glow on the field behind the house. A forest area spread a few hundred yards in front of me. It was all I could see. No people. No animals. Just trees. I didn't know how big the property was. Was Asher even there with me? Could I have been taken somewhere else?

I had to be strong. I needed to get out. No matter where I was, I refused to give up. And I damn sure wouldn't give into a man who preyed on the weak to get his dick wet.

Checking the window sill, I looked for a latch. When I couldn't find one, I attempted to lift the window, but it wouldn't budge. Paint around the edges had sealed it shut.

Not giving up, I went to the door, jiggling the doorknob. I let out a huff when it remained locked.

"Hello?" I called out, banging on the hard wood. "Is someone there? Please, let me out. What do you want?"

All of my questions went unanswered. Sliding down the wall, I curled my arms around my knees. I didn't know what Charles wanted. I didn't know what anyone wanted. *What was the point? To gain power? To be in control? Were they that desperate?*

What felt like hours later, a key sounded in the lock.

I jumped up, running around the bed to shield me from whoever was at the door.

Charles peeked his head in. "I was expecting you to have a knife in your hands."

"Why would you leave them out in the open like that?"

"Because I knew you wouldn't be able to escape. How stupid do you think I am?" He walked to the cabinet and opened the first drawer. "You could use the items on me, but you won't, will you? I'd have to get you mad enough before you would hurt me." He met my gaze. "You're too nice."

"Right now, I'm not," I mumbled, crossing my arms under my chest.

He laughed. "You wouldn't do anything to get Asher in trouble. If you hurt me in any way, one call, and I could have him ripped apart like the girls in my basement."

"What do you want?" I tried so hard to gain the control I never had but my body shook. Nerves and fear took over as this evil man stood across from me. His emotions changed, going from happy to pissed in a matter of seconds.

"I want to see how long it takes to make you scream." His brows narrowed, his eyes roaming down the length of my body.

Hugging myself, I looked away, suddenly feeling exposed. I might as well have been naked.

Charles chuckled, coming around the bed.

Before he could catch me, I jumped onto the mattress when a hot pain seared across my skull.

He gripped my hair tight in his hands, pulling me to the edge of the bed. "You think you can get away, whore? Where the hell are you going to go?"

"I just want to go home," I cried, digging my nails into his hands. "Please. Let us go."

"What? So you can run to the police?" He threw his head back and laughed. "The police are in my fucking pocket. Didn't you know that? Oh, stupid girl. Why do you think they didn't show up to the accident? I have that control. *Me!*"

"That's not possible." I shook my head. "No one has that much power."

"You're questioning my authority?" Charles pulled my hair. "I don't think you're in any position to question anything, Meeka."

"What do you want?"

"I want you." He shrugged. "Simple as that. You're pure. Untouched. Although Asher has had you, I will make it so you forget him."

"No!" I struggled against him, earning a hard slap against my cheek. My eyes welled, my lips splitting.

"As much as I love it when a woman fights me, I do not have the fucking patience for it right now."

His hand caressed the side of my cheek where he had slapped me. His touch was gentle, soft, but his gaze contradicted it. It fucked with my head. This man was supposed to be a monster. He *was* a monster. Then why was he gentle?

"You're scared of me," he said, frowning.

"Why are you surprised at that?" Even though my life was on the line and who the hell knew what was happening to Asher, I felt the need to talk to Charles. It was either that, or give in. I wouldn't. I *couldn't*. There was no way I would succumb to his wrath.

Charles released his hold on my hair and paced back and forth. "He told me not to fall. But no, I didn't listen. Why the hell would I listen?" He laughed. "It's your fault." His bright eyes snapped to mine. "You are fucking with my head. It's because of you that I've screwed up. He warned me. I told him he was wrong."

"Who? What are you talking about?" I slid off the bed, trying to get as far from him as possible but he was too quick for me.

Charles gripped my arms tight, his fingers digging into the muscles until a whimper was forced from my lips. "Tyler. *He* told me."

"Tyler?" I shook my head. "Is he here?"

"Of course." Charles sneered. "I'm sure he's getting acquainted with Asher right about now."

I knew Tyler was in on it the whole time, but hearing it leave Charles lips set my stomach tumbling.

"He's … No." Tyler was an asshole but there was no way he could be part of this.

"Why not? I know what he did to Jay. They had a fucked up relationship. I wonder if she uses that to get what she wants from Angel. Think he hits her too? Maybe she likes it rough. Vega did a number on her, but he was too gentle, if you ask me. I would have had those girls kill themselves. Not some mind fuck."

"Isn't that more effective?"

"Maybe." He tapped his chin. "The girls were weak. And they got away."

"They were saved. Jay saved them. We will save all of them. You won't get away with this."

"Oh, darling girl. I already have."

CHAPTER THIRTY

Asher

"YOU'RE A LITTLE BITCH, aren't you?" the one guy spat, digging his fingers into my cheeks. "You think you're so big and tough being in the Navy, but look at you now. You got nothing. No one is going to help you."

"I will end you," I wheezed.

"There are two of us and one of you." The other man punched me in the stomach.

I gasped, curling over myself at the new onslaught of pain. It was never ending. This shit would go on until either I died or Charles stopped it. I had no hope for the latter. I needed to fight. I needed to remain strong for Meeka.

"Where is Meeka?" I demanded, pushing to my knees.

"She's probably getting fucked."

"Or skewered like a pig. Remember that whore that wouldn't shut the fuck up? Charles warned her. It was fucking priceless."

"Yeah, her blood poured out of her like a fucking flood. It got me hard, man."

Squeezing my eyes shut, I shook my head. I didn't know who said what. I didn't care. I would praise the moment I unleashed my darkness on them.

At that moment, the door opened, revealing … Tyler.

Fuck.

"What the hell do *you* want?" the one guy snapped.

"Him," Tyler answered, his gaze locking with mine.

"He's down for the count. Boss told us to finish him." The larger man of the two security fucks, stared down at me. "What's so special about you?"

"I know his ex-girlfriend?" I shrugged, which hurt like hell.

"Unchain him and leave," Tyler demanded.

"Not gonna happen." Both men stepped up to Tyler. They were all the same height, but the two men had probably fifty pounds on the guy.

Tyler looked between them both and smirked. "Remember who I am, fuckers."

Yeah, he was a sadistic fuck. It appeared everyone was lately.

"What are you going to do?" the larger of the two shoved him. "Run to Daddy and tell on us?"

Tyler chuckled, gaining his footing. "Leave." His gaze darkened. "*Now.*"

A phone rang, the sound piercing into my skull.

Tyler reached into his pocket, smiled when he saw who it was and brought it up to his ear. "Yeah ..." He handed it to the guy who shoved him. "Boss wants to talk to you."

"Hey. No. Fine." He looked at me over his shoulder. "He is alive." He passed the phone back to Tyler and looked to his partner. "We're out." They both left the room, shutting me in with Tyler.

I wasn't sure if this was a good thing or not. I didn't know Tyler's story, but everything led to him being the ring leader of this organization whether he cared to admit it or not. Charles was jealous of the guy. Unless Tyler was setting him up as well.

"What do you want?" I slid to the ground, taking the weight off of my aching body and cradled my now shattered arm.

"I warned Jay. Back before her and Angel ever got together. She never mentioned that, did she?"

Pain was no longer an issue. I embraced it. Craved it even as hit after hit, punch after punch, marred my body. Bones cracked. Skin split. My head rang. Spots danced in front of my vision. My ribs hurt with every breath. I did everything I could to fight back but with my ankle chained and my arm broken, there wasn't much I could do.

Vice-One learned to fight. As a unit and as an individual. Channeling all of the training I had been given over the years, in the boxing ring and out, I got a couple shots in. It didn't last long as the two men powered into me. Taking the control I no longer had.

"Why would she? I'm not the one dating her." Every time I spoke, it hurt. Everything fucking hurt. A sharp stabbing pain pierced my side and I knew that my ribs were broken. Breathing through the agony, I stared up at Tyler.

"Angel talks to you." He chuckled. "My girl is still so fucking secretive."

"She's not your girl."

"Oh, Jay will always be mine. Whether she wants to admit it or not. I stole a piece of her that she'll never get back. And Angel will hold that over her."

"You're fucking crazy," I retorted. "There is no way. Those two have a powerful love." And it was something I craved. "Nothing will end them." I knew it in my heart. Angel and I didn't talk much anymore. None of us did. Not about something that personal.

"You think so, do you?" Tyler stopped pacing. "I've known Jay for years. I know what she was like before she met—" he scowled "—*him*."

"What the hell do you want? Why are we talking about Jay and Angel? Where is Meeka?" I was sick of his shit. I needed answers, and I fucking needed them now or I would drive my shitkicker so far up Tyler's ass, he'd be puking leather for the rest of his life.

"So many questions, so few answers." Tyler pressed a button on his cell phone. Voices filled the room a moment later, piercing my ears.

"What if I told you that your boyfriend was in on this?" Charles deep voice boomed from the speaker of the phone.

"I would tell you that you're a fucking liar," Meeka threw back at him.

That's my girl.

Charles chuckled. "It would make sense, wouldn't it? He had a shitty start to life so he takes out his rage on the weaker sex. One day, he just snapped. It could happen."

"No, it couldn't," Meeka argued. "He's not that type of man. He's strong. He wouldn't do that."

"No? Why not? If there is enough evidence, people will believe it whether it's true or not."

My stomach dropped. There was no way. No fucking way at all.

"What are you talking about?" Meeka's voice shook. She wasn't stupid but she needed to hear him say it. I would have asked the same questions.

"What if I told you that I could make it all go away?"

"How?"

"Why by making Asher take the fall, of course."

Tyler pressed another button and the conversation between Meeka and Charles stopped.

"What the hell?" I snapped. "Why did you shut off the phone? What's going on?"

"Because you're going to listen to me." Tyler scratched his jaw. "Charles has lost his shit, and he's going to do anything to make it to the top. And when your girlfriend is involved, he will destroy her to get his point across."

"If he fucking touches her—"

"You'll do what?" Tyler narrowed his eyes. "You're stuck. You're fucking broken. What are you going to do about it? Are you going to save her? You can barely hold yourself up."

I rose on shaky legs, my knees wobbling under my weight. Breathing through the pain, a cold sweat coated my skin but I didn't care. The agony would be worth saving Meeka in the end. "I'll save her. It's my job."

"You don't even know where she is."

"What the fuck do you want?" I bellowed.

Tyler smirked. "I want your help."

****

(Meeka)

Charles was the epitome of evil. He made the Devil himself look like a Care Bear. His demeanor was soft, gentle, but his eyes gave away everything. They say you can see into someone's soul just by looking into their gaze. With Charles, I fell. His darkness swallowed me whole, and all I could do was submit to his fists.

"The next time Asher sees you, he'll see the marks on your body," Charles licked the side of my face, his hot breath scorching my skin. "He won't want you when another man touched your innocence."

"I'm not innocent," I mumbled, licking my cracked lips.

"Oh, but you are," he pushed his hips between my legs. "You're a good girl, Meeka Cline. I could get a lot of money for you."

Tears no longer threatened to escape. All I could do was lie there. Numb and broken. Charles didn't violate my body but he sure as hell molested my mind. It was worse. I could get over the physical pain but with him towering over me, close and unwanted, I could feel the power pouring from his black soul. No. He would have to be human to have a soul.

I stared up at him, shutting off that part of myself that held true feelings. He couldn't hurt me. He couldn't damage me the way he tried to. It wasn't about rape. I learned that quickly when Charles had the power to do so. But instead, he knelt between my legs, holding me captive beneath him. He spewed off lie after lie. That was his way. That was how he broke a person. The other girls, he touched and tortured but with me, for whatever reason he didn't.

"Just sell me then. Get it over with." My voice had been strong when really, the ice cold trepidation of fear threatened to consume me.

"It doesn't work like that. You were supposed to be trained. Asher came in convincing me he was one of the best Masters out there. He paid a lot of money to get into the compound when really, he was trying to shut me down." Charles narrowed his eyes. "I will not be fucked over again."

"How did you find out?"

"How do you think? I know people on the inside. It's always like that, isn't it? You should watch more movies. Maybe you would learn something."

"We've been watching you for weeks. Asher has been watching you for a lot longer. Why now? Why didn't you reveal that you knew sooner?"

"Because it wasn't time." Charles stared at me, the small muscle in his strong jaw twitching. "When Asher came here, everything in me told me not to trust him, but when he started waving cash around, money talked." He laughed. "It's always that way, isn't it? Sex and money."

"Let me see him."

"No." Charles pulled a syringe out of the inside pocket of his jacket. "But he will see you."

My eyes widened, my heart racing and I started struggling beneath him.

"Don't fucking move, whore!" he bellowed, slamming his fist against my jaw. "Now look what you made me do. We'll just have to get that covered up with makeup."

My head rang, spots danced in my vision at the new onslaught of pain erupting in my face. "Please."

"I love it when a toy begs." Lowering the needle to my neck, he grabbed my hands so I wouldn't slap him away. "I will get good money for you."

A sharp sting poked me in the side of my neck, followed by a wave of darkness. As much as I tried to fight it, I allowed the darkness to take over, swallowing me in a blanket of terror.

CHAPTER THIRTY-ONE

Meeka

HANDS TOUCHED ME. THEY groped and prodded. Spread me open. Massaged and kneaded. My brain told them to stop, that my body wasn't meant for them. Only Asher. But I couldn't. Nothing could escape my lips.

Whatever drug Charles injected me with wouldn't allow me to move my body. I tried. I tried so hard to fight back, to move even just a toe but the exhaustion settled in and I gave up.

"Shhh … stop fighting it," a gentle voice told me. "The faster you submit, the easier it will be for you."

But I didn't want to submit. Not to them. Not to Charles. Not to anyone. I wanted my control back.

STAIN

Asher had been the only person ever to take that control and throw it back on me in blankets of pleasure and ecstasy.

"We have to prepare you," another voice said.

My eyes finally opened, scared as to what I would see but when they landed on two women, tears welled.

Why?

"We have no choice," the one woman said, reading the question in my gaze. Her eyes softened. She was beautiful, no more than twenty-five I guessed. Her long blonde hair had been pulled up into a curly messy bun. A white sheer dressed hugged her curves.

I shook my head, or tried to. I wasn't sure anymore. It didn't make sense. They looked healthy. The other woman was younger, dressed in the same attire but her hair was brown. Her eyes weren't so soft though.

"I'm Jessa," the older of the two said. "And this is Sara." Her gaze slid back to mine. "I understand this is rough, but it will get easier. I promise."

How could she be so sure? Asher. God, I prayed with everything in me that he would come to my rescue. I didn't want to be prepared. I didn't want to be sold. *Sold.* My heart started racing. No. It wouldn't happen. It couldn't.

"Master said that you're pure," Sara said. "We have to make sure you're clean."

"We need to explain to her what that means, Sara," Jessa scolded. "She won't understand."

"Sorry, Mistress," Sara looked down at her feet. "May I try again?"

"Go ahead." Jessa smiled softly.

"Master wants to put your innocence on display," Sara explained. "He said that you being pure can get him a lot of money. If that happens, it means extra treats for us."

My heart jumped. Was she fucking for real?

"Sara is in deep," Jessa explained, talking like Sara wasn't even in the same room. "They broke her, and she'll never be the same. If you listen to me, you won't get hurt."

But I wanted out. I didn't want to be here. I needed Asher. I needed my freedom.

"I know you have so many questions and you're probably thinking how you can escape," Jessa sighed. "But I'm sorry, Meeka. You're no longer in control of your life. Charles owns you. That man you were with? You can forget about him. Once he sees you on display, he won't want you anymore."

No. That wasn't true. He would always want me. It was inevitable. Licking my dry lips, I took several shall breaths before I responded. "Please," I muttered, thankful that my voice started working. But the rest of me? No matter how much I tried, nothing would move. My fingers. My toes. I was frozen, in place. Whatever drug Charles injected me with forced me immobile.

"The drugs will wear off soon," Jessa smiled.

"Why are you doing this?" I asked, my voice cracking.

"We have no choice," she explained. "They treat us well. They've given me a better life than I could have ever asked for."

"What about you?" I asked Sara.

"I had no life before here," she said, her voice firm and final.

I swallowed hard, not expecting that sort of answer.

Jessa patted my hand. Even though I couldn't move, I could still feel everything that was being done to me. The girls were gentle, but they cleaned and prepared every single inch of me. I was grateful that they were female but it still made me feel violated.

"They won't hurt you," Jessa said, her voice soft. "As long as you do everything they tell you to do."

"I want Asher." I swallowed past the lump in my throat. "Please. Just let me go." I refused to give up. Jay had been through hell when Vega blew his head off in front of her. I couldn't handle that. She had been strong and that broke her. I couldn't deal with it if something similar happened to me.

"Why does she want to leave?" Sara asked Jessa. "Doesn't she want to stay? Master won't be happy that she's being ungrateful."

"Do not worry, Sara." Jessa squeezed her shoulder gently. "Meeka is new. She has a lot of training to go through before she can truly appreciate the way of our world."

"I don't want to appreciate your world," I struggled against the drug induced paralysis. "Please. I won't tell anyone what's going on here. Just let me leave."

"I'm sorry." Jessa grabbed my hands, rubbing them between hers. "Can you move anything yet?"

A tingle formed in my toes. Looking down the length of my body, I saw my toes wiggle, followed by my feet twitching back and forth.

"Good girl." Jessa continued to massage me, her hands moving to my wrists and then to my forearms and higher.

Sara worked on my legs, her gaze piercing into mine every so often. She didn't like me. I knew that. I could feel it as her eyes burned into my soul.

"What happens after?" I needed to keep them talking. If I was being sold as they said, I wanted as much information as possible before I lost myself. It was the only way I could keep some control. I read books. I did research. I knew what could happen to the victims when their minds were stripped bare and their bodies destroyed.

"You are presented to the people of the organization. They will see every inch that isn't covered by the dressing."

"Dressing?"

Jessa held up what looked like gold chains attached to a golden triangle. "This will show off your pale skin and your dark hair." She smiled. "Don't worry. It will cover all your bits."

"I don't want to be on display." I pushed onto shaky arms, my exhausted muscles causing my head to swim.

"It needs to happen. If it doesn't, we will get in trouble. Master trusts us." Sara pushed me onto my back. "Don't fight it. Once you succumb to your destiny, it will all be worth it in the end."

"How can you say that? You're like puppets. Are there more of you?"

"Of course." Sara narrowed her eyes, grabbing hold of my hands. "But I belong to Master."

"You … belong to him?" My heart jumped.

Sara pulled me to a sitting position, holding my wrists while I gained composure. "Yes."

"Sara has been here awhile." Jessa massaged oil into my back. "As much as she wants to be Master's only pet, it doesn't work that way."

"Why not?" I didn't care, but curiosity got the better of me. The more information I had on Charles, the easier it would be to bring his organization down. Or so I hoped.

"Master, or Charles to you, doesn't want just one pet." She pointed at Sara. "She doesn't know better anymore. Each of his pets think they are the only one."

I looked at Sara, waiting for any hint of despair at Jessa's words but her face remained impassive. "Doesn't she understand what you're saying, though?"

"I wish." Jessa sighed. "She's too far gone. All of them are."

"What about you?" I met Jessa's gaze. "What makes you so different from the rest?"

"I bite." She laughed, remembering some past memory. "When they first brought me here, I bit one of the security guards. For whatever reason, Charles thought it would be a good idea to keep me in charge of the girls. Because I'm the oldest, they call me Mistress."

"Why are you happy here? These people take girls from their homes. They murder them. They're monsters." There was no way they could be okay with this.

"Those girls were in the wrong. The Masters were trying to teach them." Sara's hand tightened on my wrist.

"That's no reason to kill them," I cried, shoving from her grip.

"You'll understand eventually." Jessa gripped my shoulders. "We all do. It's a little much to take in at first, but don't worry, they won't let anything happen to you as long as you behave and do what you're told."

"No." I shook my head. "Take me to Asher." Pushing off the table, I landed hard on my feet. My knees wobbled, unable to support my weight, and forced me to the floor. The remainder of the drugs swam through my head.

"There's no way out," Sara said, her hot breath caressing my ear. "You're stuck." Her eyes twinkled. It was the only hint of emotion that truly belonged to her that I saw. The others were trained, engrained in her mind by the hands of the monsters who brought her here. Was it possible? Could a mind be manipulated into believing something completely different? Could they change me? What if I was saved and Asher didn't want me anymore because I had become a different person?

"Please," I begged, trying with everything in me to rise to my feet but the drugs weighed me down.

"It seems like the drugs are still in your system. Don't worry," Jessa said, her voice hopeful. "You'll be able to walk on your own soon. Until then, let's get you ready." She hooked her hands under my armpits and brought me to my feet.

Once the blood stopped rushing through my head, I did a quick scan of the room I was being held in. Instead of the black like Charles' room, this one was gold and red. The furniture was antique and instead of a bed, I had been placed on a table.

"Were you expecting a dungeon?" Jessa asked, a twinkle of amusement in her eyes.

"Yes, but I'm not stupid. I've been here before."

"You have?" Jessa raised an eyebrow. "When?"

"She was here with that man," Sara told her.

"That was you," I exclaimed. I thought she looked familiar. "Why? Why do you want to be here?"

"Don't even bother asking her that," Jessa interrupted. "We have to finish getting you ready." Just as those words left her mouth, there was a knock on the door before it opened.

Charles peeked his head into the large room, his gaze heating when they landed on me.

Covering myself with my hands and arms, it still didn't stop him from staring. Suddenly, I felt dirty. Like the only way to get rid of the filth of his stare was by washing myself with acid. Maybe then, I would feel better. "What the hell do you want?" I bit out.

He chuckled. "She's ready." In a matter of seconds, his demeanor switched. "Don't cover her. She wants to be a little bitch, she can crawl behind me naked."

***

(Asher)

I didn't know what I was looking at. I had been placed on a balcony overlooking a large stage concealed currently by curtains. The two security guys stood behind me, waiting, making sure I wouldn't go anywhere. I wasn't sure where I could go with several broken ribs, a limp arm hanging at my side and my blood dripping onto the ground beneath me.

Groups of people filed into the room below me. Much to my dismay, they ranged in all walks of life. The younger men sat in the front row, followed by the couples. Fuck, even women were there. What kind of world did we live in? I bit back a scoff. I was a Navy SEAL. I saw shit. I was losing my ever-loving mind if I thought the world was going to get better as the days wore on but no, they were only becoming worse.

Meeka made me realize that even though life was shitty, I could still be happy. With her. Only her. I hadn't been able to tell her that enough. If we got out of this fucking mess, I would spend the rest of my days, showing her just how much I loved her.

"Pay attention, dickhead." The larger security bastard slapped me across the head.

I had been paying attention. If they only knew just how much. People underestimated the military. No matter what rank you were, you were trained. And you were trained well. Well, Angel trained me. And having Coby at my back, I learned to be aware. Some may call it paranoid but it just meant we knew everything about our surroundings. Things most people wouldn't even notice.

Like when Charles spoke, the smaller of the two security guards, rolled his eyes every time Charles looked away. Or the fact that there were five doors leading into the staged area and that there was a camera in each corner of the high ceiling. Other things I would have noticed sooner if my body wasn't falling apart.

I grimaced, shaking my head.

When everyone was seated, the lights dimmed, but I still remained in a sea of black. Probably so no one could look up and see a bloody and broken man staring down at them. "Are either of you going to tell me what's going on and why the hell I'm here?" I asked the men standing behind me.

"Nope," the larger one said.

"After all we have been through." I shook my head. "My heart breaks."

"I'll fucking break your face if you don't shut the fuck up," the smaller one growled.

"So damn moody." I turned back around, waiting, hoping. For what I wasn't sure. I didn't know where Meeka was. I wasn't sure if we were even in the same building. No one gave me any answers.

Charles took that moment to make an appearance. He probably wanted to gloat. After Tyler got a couple hits in, he disappeared, telling me there would be a surprise waiting for me.

Charles sat beside me, crossing his ankle over the opposite knee. "These people are like vultures."

"You're complaining?" I raised an eyebrow.

"Not at all, but when they don't get the girl they want, they throw a fucking hissy fit like you wouldn't believe." He huffed. "Because *I* have that control."

"Don't you? Why else would we be here? They are paying you to get what they want so they can fulfill some sick and twisted fantasy."

"You think that's all this is?" Charles turned to me. "You think they only want girls to fuck them? Have you ever thought that they're taking them out of a bad situation and putting them in a better one?"

"Don't try and justify it," I ground out. "They are innocent and you are selling them. That right there is wrong all in itself."

"You don't understand."

"Of course I understand!" I snapped, my voice raising. "I was raised by a step-father who beat me. He kidnapped women and threw them away like trash while I cleaned up the mess. All of their blood had been on my hands while he went off and did God knows what."

"Sounds like someone who belongs here," Charles grunted. "Oh, finally. The best part." He sat forward, his eyes twinkling in the dim lighting of the room.

I followed his gaze, unprepared for what I would see. My mind understood. My heart did not. Several girls lined up on the stage, following each other until they stood in front of the ever growing audience.

Although I knew it was bound to happen, everything in me prayed it wouldn't. That she wouldn't be here. That she was safe and out of harm's way. But when Meeka walked onto the stage, my heart dropped. Bile rose to my throat, my stomach twisting with disgust and hatred for the people staring at her.

Charles spoke beside me, but I couldn't focus on what he was saying. I didn't care. I didn't fucking care one bit about anything.

Meeka wavered on her feet as she stood at the end of the lineup. Her hands were bound behind her back, exposing her naked beauty. Her bare skin forced a growl to leave my mouth. The sick fucks looking at her would regret it. I would rip them limb from fucking limb before I was done with them.

"Ah, it looks like I got a reaction from you." Charles smirked. "It's funny. When I first met you, you were quiet and straight to the point. Bring Meeka into the mix and you're a changed man."

My jaw clenched. Everything changed when I broke down and she confessed her love for me. Because of her, my strength grew. "What do you want from me?"

"I want you to see." His arm scanned out the area before him. "Look at your girlfriend. Look at all of them."

"They're teenagers." Meeka was probably the oldest one in the lineup, and even then, she was still young.

"Yes, they are, but they're prime flesh. Untouched and pure. But your Hummingbird," his eyes twinkled. "She's something else."

A growl slid to my throat. I would not react. I would not react. Fuck it. "What the hell do you want? Just say it already. I'm fucking sick of your riddles."

Charles chuckled, his face going emotionless a second later. "I want you to watch her break."

CHAPTER THIRTY-TWO

Meeka

MURMURS SOUNDED AROUND ME. Soft music, cool air, the scent of vanilla and spice— everything slid into my senses. My skin puckered with goose bumps at not being allowed to wear any clothing. I wasn't ashamed of my body. I was comfortable in my own skin but being paraded around like a prized possession forced me to try and cover myself. That was when Jessa and Sara tied my hands behind my back. They told me Master wouldn't want my beauty hidden.

Fucking please.

But I gave in. There was nothing else I could do. Sara had the pleasure of injecting me with another drug. It was all I could do not to fall at her feet, begging for more. I had heard of cases where women were taken and forced to become addicts. Maybe it was for the best. Then they wouldn't feel anything. In this case, I knew Charles wouldn't want that. He just wanted me to shut up while someone decided to buy me. When I was purchased, they wouldn't want just my body. They would want my mind and they would do everything to make it break. To make it shatter into tiny pieces until there was nothing left.

My skin burned, the back of my neck tingling. It was the same feeling whenever Asher was around. Was he here? I couldn't see over the dim shadow of the crowd. The lights were bright, casting all of us in an unearthly glow but everything in me told me that he was near.

Letting out a soft sigh, I lifted my chin. I would show whoever bought me that I would be a challenge. I would make their life hell. If I couldn't be with Asher, I would be with no one. I wasn't in a position to make any rash decisions but I refused to break.

If there is anyone up there, God, please save us.

I sent up a silent prayer to whoever would listen. I had been in some shitty situations but I would take all of them over being locked up. Held captive. Being undercover, not knowing what would happen next, my life on the line. I would take it all if I knew Asher was safe.

"The bidding starts at fifty thousand," a female voice came over a loud speaker, startling me. "Fifty thousand. Fifty thousand."

I couldn't make out who was in the crowd or how they would purchase the girl but every time the voice spoke, my heart raced a little faster.

"Fifty thousand. Number one, sold for fifty thousand."

A small gasp left me. I wavered on my feet, allowing my eyes to look to my left to see the girl who was sold for a measly fifty grand.

A man walked up onto the stage, grabbed the first girl and guided her back down the steps. The sea of darkness swallowed them whole. She would never be seen again.

"Fifty thousand. Seventy thousand. Number two for seventy thousand. One hundred thousand."

The numbers went higher for the second girl until they stopped at one-hundred and seventy thousand. Much like the first girl, she was guided down the steps and swallowed by the darkness.

There were ten of us, and I was the last. Why that was the case was beyond me. I tried to think fast but my thoughts were jumbled. Almost like death, my life flashed before my eyes. Everything I had done right or wrong. I should have called my parents more. I should have convinced Asher to search for his sisters and reach out to them. I should have told him I loved him sooner. Jay would never know what I thought of her as a president and as a sister. We had our issues to work through but now she would never know just how much I respected her. I never got to apologize to Violet, for what we put her through.

As each girl was sold, my heart beat faster and faster. This was it. This was how my life would end. I didn't want to give up but I didn't know what else to do or how to get out.

"Number eight. The bidding starts at one-hundred thousand."

My eyes widened.

STAIN

The girl being put up for auction smirked at how much the starting bid was. Most of us had been drugged to keep us calm, but instead, the next girl embraced it. She was beautiful. Her long blond hair was pulled back into a tight pony-tail. Sequins coated her body, not leaving much to the imagination. Raising her chin, she placed her hands on her hips, standing tall and proud.

"These girls had a shitty life before I took them."

Charles words banged around in my head. It didn't make sense. None of it did.

"Two-hundred thousand. Sold."

I swallowed hard. One more girl and it was my turn.

My life was officially over.

When Jessa and Sara had finished getting me ready for presentation, I had been tempted to fight them. To push them away and run for safety, but Charles was smart; he had them drug me so I was weak. I could have probably got a couple shots in, but it wouldn't have done me any good when the place was lined with security.

My mind shut off as the ninth girl sold. I didn't even hear how much someone had purchased her for.

"Number ten. Starting bid is two-hundred thousand."

A soft whimper escaped my lips, bubbling up from my chest. My bones vibrated, my heart racing in time with the rush of my blood. You couldn't put a price on someone's head. People were priceless. No amount of money could pay for them. Or so I thought. I underestimated these people. This organization. I never thought I would get stuck in their midst, assuming

Asher would keep me safe. He did what he could but they were smart.

"Two-hundred and seventy thousand." The price kept going up and up, eventually stopping at four-hundred thousand. These sick bastards had more money than brains.

"Well, it looks like we've reached a new beginning," Charles voice boomed from the speakers.

I jumped, my head whipping around when I saw him walk out onto the stage. He smirked at me, holding a microphone up to his mouth.

"Say hello to the highest paid toy in the organization. We've been open for thirty-five years and never has one been sold for four-hundred thousand."

Bile rose to my throat. My stomach churned, threatening to spew all over the stage in front of me.

"How does it feel?" he wrapped an arm around my shoulders, lowering the microphone down at his side. "Look up, Meeka. Wave to your boyfriend."

I gasped. Asher had been there this whole time?

"Please," I whispered. "Let us go."

"Why, Meeka—" he laughed, his gaze scanning over the crowd "—you will be going. Straight to your new home."

Tears burned my eyes, a lump forming in my throat. "I refuse. You'll have to kill me first."

Shouting started from the second floor.

Murmurs and gasps sounded from the crowd, the yelling becoming more pronounced. Asher's voice boomed through the large room, bouncing off the walls and hitting me straight in the heart.

"Let us go," I demanded, my voice firm. Courage and strength slid over me. Because of him, I wouldn't give up. Charles may have thought he won but I refused to go with anyone else if it wasn't Asher.

"Oh, little girl," Charles sneered, grabbing a fistful of my hair. "You're never leaving." He licked up the side of my cheek. "Guess who just bought you."

CHAPTER THIRTY-THREE

Meeka

THROWN INTO CAPTIVITY MUCH like an animal, I couldn't help but fight. With everything in me, I fought. I punched. Kicked. I took some flesh between my teeth and bit as hard as I could. Blood seeped into my mouth, skin dug under my nails. I wouldn't go easily or quietly.

Charles bought me. He actually had the nerve to purchase me. I couldn't wrap the thought of spending the rest of my life with him around my mind. There was no way. No fucking way at all it would happen. He would have to kill me.

"Let me go!" I fought and pushed.

"Fuck," someone grunted. "She's losing her shit."

"What do you expect? She was just purchased by Charles," another person countered.

"He's not even the boss." A man laughed.

I screamed, my throat going raw. "Let me go!"

"Calm your shit, girl. You're just going to make this harder on yourself." Whoever spoke, lifted me into the air, throwing me over his shoulder.

Beating my fists against his back, I continued screaming until my voice gave out. The screams turned into sobs. Everything that had happened over the past couple of weeks, weighed down on me. No one would know where we were. I never even got to say goodbye. The tears continued to fall. "Please. I won't tell anyone," I begged, my voice hoarse.

"You can beg and plead all you want," Charles voice slid into my ears. "But you belong to me now. No amount of crying will get me to let you go."

"I need to see Asher. Please." I wanted to tell him good bye. I wanted to tell him that no matter what happened, we would always be together. He was the air in my lungs and no amount of money could replace that.

"Fine." Charles snapped his fingers.

The man placed me on my feet.

Wavering, I fell back a step when Charles wrapped his hand tightly around my arm.

"If you so much as even think of running, I will gut your boyfriend, letting you watch him bleed before you," Charles snarled in my ear.

Fresh tears welled in my eyes but I refused to let them fall. I only nodded, waiting for Charles to bring me to Asher.

"Stand outside the door," Charles demanded of his men. "These two are broken enough. They won't try and escape."

The men grunted, doing as they were told.

Charles led me down the long hall, stopping once we reached a metal door. He punched a code into the security system, the door unlocking a moment later.

"Remember my warning." He pushed me forward.

I stumbled into the small room. Nothing appeared out of the ordinary. The only thing that caught me off guard was that there was no sign of Asher.

"Sit," Charles ordered, pointing at the single chair by the far wall.

Walking over on shaky legs, I did as I was told and fell onto the metal chair.

"Bring him in," Charles told his men.

And that was when I saw him. Broken. Bloody. Beaten. Asher didn't look the same. His right eye was swollen shut, his lips cracked. Dark bruises began to form on his face, his one arm hanging limp at his side.

"What the hell did you do to him?" I screamed, rushing forward and fell to my knees in front of Asher. Throwing myself around him, I held him.

He grunted, wrapping his good arm around my waist and nuzzled his face into the crook of my neck. "I'll kill them. Every single one for what they've done to you."

"And I'll do the same," I whispered.

"All right, all right." Charles hooked his arm around my middle, pulling me away from Asher. "That's enough."

"Let me go." I shoved and kicked, stomping on his feet but with mine being bare, it didn't do much damage. "I'll kill you. All of you." I continued screaming, profanities and threats leaving my mouth. It didn't do any good. It only caused Charles and his bastards to laugh. But that fueled the fire inside of me. Breaking free of his hold, I spun on him and pushed him back. Closing my hand into a tight fist, I swung, hitting him square in the jaw.

Charles stumbled back a step, his eyes wide before darkening with fury. "You little bitch."

"Come on, Charles," I yelled, shoving him again. "Show me what you want to do. Hit me. Kill me. I don't give a fuck. No matter what you do, it won't be as painful as what I do to you."

"She's a feisty one."

That voice. I had heard it before.

I glanced over my shoulder, finding Tyler standing in the doorway.

He leaned casually against the doorframe, feigning a yawn.

Charles paused, raising his eyebrows. "What the hell are you doing here?"

"I came to play, and boss wants me to watch." Tyler came into the room. "You have a soft spot for her."

I knew from what Asher had said that Tyler had been a part of the sex trafficking ring for a while, but I still never expected to see him.

"I do not." Charles crossed his arms under his chest. "What do you want?"

"Grab Jessa and Sara and have them clean Asher up," Tyler told the larger security guard. "I don't want him bleeding everywhere and dying on us. And bring Meeka a fucking housecoat."

"What the hell do you think you're doing? If you keep him alive, he'll only fight back," Charles bit out.

"You see, this is why I'm in charge, Charles." Tyler paced back and forth, scratching the scruff of his jaw. "You think with your dick first. You try and act all macho and tough but really, you get your goons to do your dirty work."

"That's so nothing can fall back on me," Charles muttered.

"Really?" Tyler scoffed. "You think they wouldn't rat you out? They are only in it for the money, and when you run out, they're gone."

"I would never run out of money." Charles waved a hand in front of him. "Leave us. This is not your place."

"Oh, but it is." Tyler glanced down at Asher. "I may be an asshole but I've learned when the right time for that is."

A light knock sounded on the door.

Tyler opened it, revealing Jessa and Sara. Jessa handed me a white terry cloth robe.

When I took it from her, our fingers touched. I caught her gaze.

She looked down at me with sympathy. She had been trained to tell me what she did, but I could see the hope that maybe I would be the one to get away.

She went back to Sara and started mending Asher's wounds.

He grunted every so often.

My heart beat hard, my body shaking with the need to go to him. But nothing I did would make it go away. His pain. His anger. Even his fear.

Sliding the robe over my skin, I tied it around my waist, thankful I was now covered.

"Please, Tyler," I begged of him. "Let us go."

Tyler glanced my way, his brows narrowing.

I had never liked him, knowing what he did to Jay but I was desperate. I would do anything to get Asher to safety.

Once Sara and Jessa were finished caring for him, they quickly left the room.

Asher's wounds were cleaned up, a bottle of water in his hand and his broken arm held by a makeshift sling. He needed the hospital but we would make do with what we had.

"Meeka," Tyler's rough voice grated over my nerves. "I suggest keeping your thoughts and demands to yourself." A silence passed between us. He was asking me to trust him. Under normal circumstances, I wouldn't have, but right then, I had no other choice.

Tyler nodded once, glancing back at Charles. "The boss wants to know where you plan on coming up with four-hundred thousand dollars. We've never sold a girl for that much but Meeka comes in here and you're willing to sell your fucking soul for her."

"Not that it's any of your fucking business, but I have the money stashed away." Charles peered at me, his gaze roaming down my body.

I shivered, hugging myself. Pulling the robe tighter around me, it would never be enough. He had already seen every inch of me.

"Jessa," Tyler snapped.

The door opened slightly. "Yes, Sir?"

"Get her some clothes. I don't need Charles making a bigger mess then he already has."

"Right away, Sir." Jessa disappeared, coming back a moment later with my sweatpants and sweatshirt.

She helped me into the clothes, using the robe as a shield from the onslaught of stares.

A sense of relief washed over me at being fully covered and not having to worry about the robe loosening. I whispered a thanks to her but she only stared straight ahead.

I handed her the robe, expecting her to glare at me but when a moment of clarity struck her, she hugged me.

Shock tore through me, but I returned the embrace.

"Get out. For us. For all of us." Releasing me, her face became impassive and she left the room.

"Better?" Tyler asked me.

I nodded, still confused as to what just happened. "Thank you."

"Why the hell are you being nice?" Charles yelled, his fists clenching at his sides. "This isn't the time to be nice. You need to show her who the fuck is the boss."

"And is that you?" Tyler shoved him and pointed a finger at him. "You have no right to tell me what to do."

"Just because you know her doesn't mean you can act all high and mighty and shit."

Tyler's body stiffened.

"You're too close to them," Charles pointed out. "You need out."

"You're only jealous because I moved up the food chain faster than you did." Tyler laughed.

"Before you two get your panties in a twist," Asher coughed, gripping his side, "why don't you tell us what the hell is going on?"

"Yeah, Tyler." Charles frowned. "Tell us."

"You'll find out in about …" He glanced at his watch. "Now."

A loud bang sounded from the hallway.

Asher pushed to his full height, leaning against the wall.

I rushed to his side, cupping his face. "I'm here." I kissed him softly, careful not to split his lip even more.

"Meeka." Reaching out, he brushed his fingers down the side of my face. "I love you, Hummingbird. More than you'll ever know."

The tears that had threatened earlier to escape, poured down my cheeks. "Let us go, please." I wasn't sure what Tyler wanted or what he was doing. I also didn't know just how deep he was in this world.

I hooked an arm around Asher's waist, allowing him to lean on me. The adrenaline surging through me didn't let me feel the added the weight. He may have been huge but my love for him was bigger.

"We need to get out of here," he grumbled in my ear, breathing through the pain.

"Tyler," I called out.

"Listen." Charles glared at me. "You are mine. Do you understand me? I paid for you. You can't leave."

"No one is worth any amount of money. You can't just buy someone." With Asher at my side, all of my fear was pushed away.

"Yes, I can." He took a step toward me. "*We* can. It's how this world works. We take you. We sell you. And you're never to be seen again by your family and friends. You are dead in their eyes, and there's nothing that they or you can do about it."

"We'll end you," Asher growled. "If I have to die doing so, I will fucking bring you down."

Charles waved a hand in front of him. "Promises, promises."

"Well, as fun as this is—" Tyler clapped his hands together "—we need to leave."

"What?" Charles shouted. "You can't just take them. It doesn't work that way. I paid for her."

"And I'm stealing her from you." Tyler stepped into Charles face, their noses millimeters apart. "There are plenty of girls out there that you can have. You seem to have quite a collection yourself."

"But they aren't *her*."

"And why do you want her?" Tyler stepped in front of me, blocking Charles' view.

"Because she's pure. Untouched."

Tyler scoffed. "Her boyfriend is Asher. I don't think she's that pure."

My cheeks heated.

"No, I'm saying she's innocent. I saw it in her eyes when—"

"When you what?" Asher snarled, his voice coating with venom.

"He didn't do anything to me, baby," I promised him.

"You told me you would do anything as long as he was safe," Charles reminded me. "Isn't that what you told me?"

"Of course! I love him. I would do anything to save him and he would do the same for me. Get that through your thick skull, Charles. You will never own me. I will die first before I let you break me." My chest rose and fell.

Tyler's head snapped around. "Leave. *Now*."

"You can't make them leave." Charles snapped his fingers. "None of you can leave."

At that moment, the room filled with several men dressed in dark outfits. Leather jackets, shit kickers and ugly as hell expressions on their faces.

"Ah, Tyler. It looks like you're stuck as well." Charles smirked.

"Touché." Tyler placed his cell phone up to his ear. "It's time. Charles is getting impatient."

"What's going on?" Charles demanded. "Tell me." He grabbed onto Tyler's arm when he went to walk away. "Now, damn it."

Tyler glared down at the hand touching him like it was offensive. "Get your hands off of me. I don't care who you are or who the hell you *think* you are."

A loud bang came from the hall way again.

"What the hell are you waiting for?" Charles snapped his fingers. "Grab her and kill them."

But the guys wouldn't move. Even the new ones who I hadn't seen before. They stood stock still, waiting for further instruction from … Tyler?

Oh, dear God. I understood a power play when I saw one.

"We can't get out, Meeka," Asher told me. "Move us to the corner. It's safer."

I nodded, tightening my hold on his waist and did as he suggested.

Charles continued shouting demands at the men but no one listened. His face turned red, his nostrils flaring. He was losing control. He wasn't even paying attention to me.

"Do you have any idea what's going on?" I asked him, making sure to keep my voice low.

"Something is going on, but I can't say." He grimaced, taking a deep breath. "All I can tell you is that I don't like the guy but if Tyler gets us out of here, I'll kiss his fucking ass."

Nodding, I sat Asher down, keeping my hold on him. We couldn't escape. We couldn't do anything but wait.

"We'll get out," he grunted. "I promise you. Just please trust me."

"Of course I trust you. I have no idea what's going on, and I don't like that but I trust you."

He grunted. "Everything that I do, is for you. Know that."

My heart started racing at his words. "What's going on?"

He opened his mouth to speak when a loud crash sounded, swinging the door open abruptly.

My eyes widened when I saw who came barging into the room.

***

(Asher)

I knew my brothers would show up. Tyler had his own reasons for being part of the organization. He was a bastard but little girls weren't his kink. He wanted to bring Charles down as much as the rest of us, maybe even more.

When I was locked in the other room, he had punched me, letting the security think he was standing with them. But after he kicked them out, he apologized to me. I must have been dreaming. Too many punches to the face, pain taking over and making me delusional.

As Meeka stared up at me, she had so many questions. I wanted to answer them but it would have to wait. We needed to get to safety first.

Tyler had told me the plan. He called Angel and my brothers showed up. As cliché as it sounded, hell had officially frozen over.

"What are they doing here?" Meeka asked, rising to her feet.

"They're saving us." I realized that as much as I didn't like asking for help, this time it was warranted. Without Tyler calling them, Meeka would end up like the girls in the basement. Everything I did was to protect her. As much as it bothered me to work with Tyler, I knew when I needed that extra help.

"Well, well, well." Charles folded his arms over his chest. "What do we have here?"

His men moved behind him.

"You think you're safe?" Charles sneered at Meeka, taking a step in her direction. "You think because you have men at your beck and call, that nothing bad will happen to you? I will fuck your mind. I will make sure you think of me every time you close your eyes."

I struggled to my full height, pulling Meeka behind me. "You touch one hair on her head, I'll skin you alive."

"Oh, Asher." He laughed. "I don't need to touch her."

"What the actual fuck?" I growled, crouching to take him on full force. No matter how broken and bloody I was, there would be no way I would let some bastard threaten my girl.

"Brother." Coby came toward me. His dark eyes held me captive. I was unable to look away. I had been a shitty friend. To him. To all of them.

"I'm sorry," I muttered.

He shook his head. "Not now." He cupped my nape, leaning his forehead against mine. "You love her."

It wasn't a question but I answered anyway. "Yes."

"You want to keep her safe."

"Yes."

"Then trust us."

"I trust you with all of me." And I did.

Coby nodded once and turned back to the crowd filling out in the small room. "It's going to get messy," he muttered.

"You can't kill me," Charles grinned, feigning a yawn. "You want to know why?"

"We need you to bring down the organization," Angel answered. "But that doesn't mean we can't hurt you a bit."

Charles' eyes widened and he took a step back. His men moved behind Angel. "What the hell do you think you're doing? You wouldn't be here if it wasn't for me."

Dale rubbed his hands together. "Can we play? Can we? Can we?"

Angel met my gaze, waiting.

I nodded once.

He smirked. "Have at it."

CHAPTER THIRTY-FOUR

Meeka

I WOULD NEVER BE able to get the sound of Charles' screams out of my mind. They pierced my ears, grating into my soul. As much as he deserved to be put away, instead, he was being tortured.

Asher and I stumbled down the hall, the sounds becoming quieter. His brothers and the men who worked for the organization were let loose on Charles. I didn't know what they did. I didn't want to know. The small smirk on Asher's face bothered me. I understood. God, did I ever understand but I was human. I wouldn't be who I was if it didn't upset me at least a little bit.

This shit wasn't done. Not by a long shot. So many questions were left unanswered. Tyler. Charles. The organization. The demand to know what the hell was going on was on the tip of my tongue but I held back. It wasn't the right time.

"Hummingbird." Asher gritted his teeth, taking deep shallow breaths. "Stop thinking about it."

He knew me well. He knew I wanted the answers. He knew I wouldn't be able to move on until I found out more.

"I'm trying," I whispered.

The house was huge. It took almost ten minutes to get out into the fresh air. Much to my surprise, the building was surrounded. Men dressed in black circled the area.

A large man walked up to us, holding his hand out. "I'm Agent Smith."

I returned the handshake.

"Is that your real name?" Asher ground out.

The man smirked, a twinkle hitting his dark gaze. "It is. For now."

So many secrets. I was getting sick of the lies.

"What's going on?" I asked, keeping a tight hold on Asher's waist.

"Thanks to you two, we're able to shut this part of the organization down," Agent Smith explained. "I understand that the operation is nowhere near being brought to an end, but it's definitely a good start."

Asher grunted. "I need to sit down."

I led him to the ambulance, sitting him on the back of the bus while Agent Smith followed behind us.

"You understand we will need to bring you in for questioning."

My head whipped around. "Asher needs to go to the hospital."

"And he will but after, we're going to get the answers we're looking for."

"What if we can't give you those answers?" I asked, sitting beside Asher while the EMS worked on him. Another ambulance pulled into the parking lot, the EMS leaving the bus abruptly to go into the house.

"You will." Agent Smith narrowed his eyes, looking between us both. "We will have to separate you two."

My heart jumped. It was inevitable. They needed to get the facts from each of us. If they questioned us together, we could feed off of everything the other said.

The EMS bandaged Asher up and took a step back. "Lay on the bed. You need to go to the hospital to get that arm taken care of and those ribs. Meeka, we will need to check you out as well."

"I'm fine." But even as those words left my mouth, my head swam. Pinching the bridge of my nose, I took a deep breath.

"Right." The EMS shone a light into both of my eyes. "Were you drugged?"

I swallowed hard, remembering Jessa and Sara. "Yes."

He nodded and looked at Agent Smith. "You can ask the questions later. These two need to go to the hospital."

I thanked the EMS and together, we helped Asher onto the gurney. "I'm going with him. You can separate us later," I told Agent Smith, not giving him a choice in the matter.

"Fine," he grunted, glancing at his watch. "I'll meet you there."

As he walked away, the rest of Vice-One appeared. They headed our way, their heads down.

Angel nodded once, motioning to Dale and Stone. He muttered something and they followed suit, heading in the opposite direction. Coby walked along side Angel, stopping once they saw me.

Coby gave a curt nod, crossing his arms under his chest and stood off to the side. Watching. Waiting. For what I couldn't be sure but I knew he was protecting his brothers.

"How are you feeling, brother?" Angel asked, rubbing his knuckles.

"Like shit," Asher nodded toward his hand. "Is it done?"

"For now." Angel frowned. "I don't like working with that fucker."

He was talking about Tyler. I couldn't imagine working with my love's ex. Especially one who destroyed a part of them and continued to cause shit.

Sliding off the back of the ambulance, I closed the distance between Angel and me. Standing a foot away from him, I had to tilt my head far back to meet his gaze.

He raised an eyebrow.

I took that as my cue and wrapped my arms around his waist, squeezing him. "Thank you. Thank you for everything. For saving us." My voice wavered. "I can't thank you enough, but please know that I appreciate everything you have done."

Angel cleared his throat several times before he returned the embrace.

I smiled. "I don't know what happened in there. I don't want to know." I released him. "I deal with enough of that darkness from Brogan."

"Really?" Angel rubbed the back of his neck.

"Yeah." I sighed, brushing it off. "That's not important. I just wanted to thank you, all of you, for what you've done tonight. For what you do. For … for fighting for our Country."

"It's our job, Meeka," Angel said, his back stiffening. His cheeks reddened.

Asher chuckled. "Come here, Hummingbird. I think you're making him uncomfortable."

"Thank you," I told Angel again as I slipped into the ambulance.

His eyes beamed but he only walked away. He met up with Coby, and they both headed toward Agent Smith.

Talking amongst themselves, Agent Smith glanced my way every so often. I wasn't sure exactly what he thought I could tell him. Asher knew more so I had hoped he would be able to give the Feds what they were looking for. If we could bring even a brick of this organization down, the rest would crumble in time.

***

(Asher)

"Tell me how Tyler Bone or T-Bone contacted you? Has he been in on this the whole time? Have you ever run into him before?"

The questions hit me over and over. Agent Smith didn't waste any time. I was holed up in the hospital with Meeka at my side, trying with everything in me not to drive my fist through the man's face.

"Can you wait to ask questions?" Meeka placed her hands on her hips.

"No," he gave her a once-over, lifted his chin, and focused back on me.

Dick.

"Tyler didn't contact me." I told the Agent how Tyler showed up at the mansion. I also mentioned the fight between him and Angel and how Coby and I went to his place to force him to drop his shit. And that was when Charles was there.

"So you had no idea that Tyler was working with Charles?" Agent Smith raised an eyebrow.

"No. I told you that," I huffed, sitting forward and winced through the onslaught of agony in my side. "I don't know shit. I'm tired. Hungry as hell. And I would like to spend these last couple of minutes with my girlfriend before we're separated for questioning." And I wanted to fuck her. God, did I ever want to. I wanted to hold her and never let her go. The urge to mark her, to make every man aware that she belonged to me, was intense. Charles touched her. He laid his hands on her. My girl is strong but I can see the fear in her beautiful eyes. I needed to erase what Charles tried to take from her. I needed to bring my Meeka back to me.

"I'll give you five," the Agent mumbled and left the room.

"Asher."

"Meeka."

We spoke at the same time.

I laughed but a sharp pain shot up my back. *Fuck.*

Meeka only smiled, cupping my cheek. "I love you. I love you more than anything. Don't worry about me."

"I have to worry about you. Charles touched you. You were fucking—" I swallowed hard. "You were sold. He bought you." I didn't know where he was. Everything in me prayed that this was over. That we would be left alone. But I wasn't stupid. It took more than us being kidnapped for—God, who knew how long we were gone—to bring him down.

"Asher?" Meeka's forehead creased in the middle, a dark set of worry shadowing her gaze.

I didn't know how to express my fear into words. Charles bought and paid for her. Fair and square in his eyes. But I knew my brothers. They had beat it into him that if he so much as breathed the same air as her, he would be skewered like a pig.

"I don't know how long they will need to question us," I grabbed her hand, pulling her down onto the bed beside me. "And I have no fucking idea how long they will keep us separated. The only thing I can ask is for you to tell them everything."

She nodded. "I will."

I had to ask. Something had been eating at me since we were taken. Just the mere thought of it, made the beast within raging with fury. "Meeka," I growled, my voice harsher than I had intended.

Her eyes widened. "What's wrong?"

Taking several deep breaths, I closed my eyes. It didn't happen. It didn't. It couldn't have. Meeka was strong but even that would have broken her. "Did Charles …" I couldn't say it, but that one word was on the tip of my tongue.

"Did Charles …" Her mouth formed a silent o.

"No." She shook her head. "God, no." She kissed me softly. "He didn't hurt me. Not like that."

A breath left me on a whoosh. It had been a fear I had been holding onto since her and I were taken a couple days before. I had come to learn that Charles had no intentions of keeping me alive. If I were him, I would have done the same thing. He didn't need me.

He only needed me to make Meeka break. Fortunately, it never came to that.

"What else happened?" I asked her, needing to know every single detail.

"I woke up in his room. He threatened me and had his girls clean me up." She shivered. "It didn't make sense. It still doesn't. Why was Tyler there? What does he get out of it? Does he think Jay will take him back?"

"I don't know," I grumbled. "I don't know anything. All I know is that there was a reason Tyler was there. He may have saved us but there is an underlying reason behind it. He's not the type of man who gives without taking."

Meeka scoffed. "Jay can vouch for that."

As if she heard her name, Jay and the rest of the King's Harlots made their way into the room. Much to Agent Smith's dismay, his questions would have to wait.

Brogan came up to Meeka, wrapping her in a tight hug.

"Angel told us what happened," Jay said, shifting her weight from foot to foot. "I'm so sorry."

"For what?" I asked. It wasn't her fault we were in the wrong place at the wrong time. Because Charles wanted Meeka, I didn't think it would matter where we were. He would get her no matter what. And I would kill him. I made that promise to myself as soon as I found out he had touched her.

Meeka touched me gently on the arm. "You're growling."

"Sorry," I cleared my throat. "I can't stop thinking about Charles buying you."

Max gasped, shaking her head.

Brogan swore.

Jay stayed silent and immobile.

STAIN

A soft knock sounded on the door. "Boss, that Agent is heading here to speak with Asher and Meeka," Creena stated.

Jay nodded once. "We'll meet you back at the clubhouse. I'm just glad you two are okay." Much to Meeka's surprise, Jay hugged her, not letting go for a couple of minutes. Soft whispers passed between them before Jay pulled back. "Let's go."

"Take care of each other," Max said, her gaze sliding between us.

"We will," we replied in unison.

And we would.

CHAPTER THIRTY-FIVE

Asher

I SAW HIM ONE last time before things ended.

Leaving my step-father alone in the alleyway, surrounded by boxes and garbage, the scene was made to believe that he was homeless. That someone had murdered him in his sleep and stolen what little property he had left.

A part of me stayed with him. The darkness that simmered inside of me since I was a small boy. Growing up, every shadow I saw reminded me of Elliott. The man who destroyed my innocence. Made me see things a young child shouldn't see. Do things no human should be held accountable for.

STAIN

Relief flooded through me. I should have felt guilty. I committed murder. Smiling to myself, I scratched the scruff on my jaw. But it was self-defence. He came at me with a knife. I would never say anything to get under his skin. In all of the years of training I had, one thing would stick with me forever. Get them to make the first move. And I did.

Pulling my phone out of my jacket pocket, I dialed the one person who could make anyone disappear. "It's done."

As soon as the words left my mouth, I knew right then and there that I could spend the rest of my life being happy.

It was time to move on.

***

(Meeka)

It had been a week since I saw Asher. One-hundred-and-sixty-eight hours since I felt his touch and heard his deep voice. After everything went down at Charles' mansion, I for sure thought he would make an appearance again. I didn't know what happened when Vice-One left their mark on the guy. The screams of agony still haunted my nightmares. I was just thankful that we were okay and taken out of that hell. It could have been so much worse.

But I didn't want to think about that. For whatever reason, Charles had been quiet. We still didn't know who the front runner of the organization was. I had always assumed it was Charles but Asher made it clear that he was too much of a pussy to put something so powerful together.

"Meeka." Brogan snapped her fingers in front of my face.

I blinked. "What?"

"I asked you when the last time you saw Asher was?"

"Oh." I frowned, looking down at my folded hands in my lap. "Sorry. It's been a week." Way too damn long if you asked me. But Agent Smith refused for us to be together while he got all of his questions answered. I had only been holed up in that interrogation room for a couple of hours. With Asher, the agent was shoving his weight around and tried to intimidate him. But I knew it wouldn't work.

"When are they releasing him?" Brogan asked, spinning on the stool and took a chug of her beer.

I shrugged. "I don't know."

"You would think with him being innocent and a victim, he would have been released days ago." She shook her head. "The system fucking sucks."

Yeah. It did.

As much as I missed Asher, at least I knew he was safe. But I wished we would find out what was going on with Charles. The guy just disappeared. He was needed to bring down the main hub of the sex crimes but how could that happen if we didn't know where he was? A thought crossed my mind. Maybe I wasn't told where he was to keep me safe. The less I knew, the better.

Squeezing the bridge of my nose, I breathed through the impending headache. The hairs on the back of my neck tingled. My body stiffened, sitting up straighter.

Before looking behind me, I met Brogan's gaze.

She winked, smiling and jumped off the stool.

STAIN

Turning around, I caught sight of the person who made every nerve ending on my body come alive.

Asher stood at the door, one arm in a cast and the other reaching out for me.

He didn't even have to ask. I ran toward him, jumping into his arms.

He grunted, wrapping his good arm around my waist.

"Sorry," I reigned kisses on his face, careful not to hurt his damaged arm again. "I missed you."

He chuckled, kissing me back. "I missed *you*. A week is too fucking long."

At that point, we were surrounded by everyone.

"I know you two just became reunited." Angel clapped a hand on Asher's shoulder. "But we need to sit down and talk."

Asher nodded, grabbing hold of my hand, and led me to the largest booth in the club.

He sat, pulling me down beside him and waited.

My sisters, his brothers, everyone, joined us. Max and Dale, although they had their issues, were civil enough to focus on the main issue at hand. Angel and Jay had their own problems, but the past couple of weeks allowed them to work through whatever they had going on as well.

As I looked around the table, it was funny to me. There were five men and five women. We were being paired off. Life was unpredictable at times and this was one of those moments where I wished I knew what the outcome of our growing family would be.

***

(Asher)

"I told the Feds everything I know. I also told them that I will be medically discharged because of my mental health problems." I took a deep breath, squeezing Meeka's hand in mine. "I didn't tell them about my step-father. They don't need to know that shit." My brothers had helped me clean up that mess anyway. And I knew Charles wouldn't rat. He had too much riding on the line for him to say anything. If he did? I would deny it all. I killed my step-father. It was self-defense. I smirked to myself, pushing down that darkness that enjoyed watching the life leave his eyes.

"No one needs to know what happened," Angel said, rapping his knuckles on the table top.

"We are your family, and we'll keep that secret to our grave." Stone's words came out firm. "You can trust us." Meaning I could trust him. We didn't talk much. Hell, I hardly talked to any of them anymore. With being undercover for weeks, I wasn't allowed on any missions. I met the new Colonel once. "I'm a shitty friend," I blurted, the back of my neck heating.

"What are you talking about?" Dale asked, leaning forward in his chair.

"I don't talk to you anymore. God, I sound like a fucking pussy," I grumbled, scrubbing a hand down my face. "What I'm saying is, I haven't been there when you needed me. You're my family. The only family I have. After everything—" I swallowed hard. "I can't thank you all enough for taking me in." It had been a long time coming. I never thanked Angel for taking me under his wing. For showing me the ways of the Navy life. For giving me the chance no one else would. These guys were my brothers. And Meeka was my life.

"We're family," Angel reiterated, motioning his hand around the table. "All of us are family. Yes, we're having our own issues, but no matter what, we are here for each other. These women have taken us into their lives when they didn't have to."

"It's not like you gave us a choice," Jay teased, poking him in the ribs.

He grinned, kissing her forehead.

"Listen." Jay clapped her hands together, leaning her head from side to side before zeroing her gaze in on Meeka. "I love you. We could talk in private, but I'd rather say this in front of everyone. I love all of you. Yes, I'm still hurt that you kept my sister's return a secret from me, but I understand why you did it. And I'm glad you two have found each other.

Meeka squeezed my hand, her lips curling up into a small smile. "I'm-I'm sorry about everything." Her gaze moved around the table. "I am. Please tell Violet that as well."

"You can tell her yourself," Jay placed her phone in the center of the table. "Go ahead."

"Meeka?" a soft voice came over the speaker.

"Hi, Violet." Meeka's chin trembled. "I'm sorry. I'm so fucking sorry." She snatched the phone off the table, turned off the speaker, and placed it to her ear. "I'm sorry. I know." Tears rolled down her cheeks. "Thank you. Yes, I would like that. Next week? Sure. I'll get the Harlots to come with me, and we can get drunk and watch girly movies." Meeka laughed. "Yes. Just like old times. I love you too." And with that, she hung up the phone. "Thank you," she whispered, her gaze locking with Jay's.

"You're welcome." Jay smiled. "I haven't heard us being referred to as the Harlots in a long time. Thank you. I'm sorry I've been a bitch. There are some—" she glanced at Angel "—things we're working through."

Angel glanced down at her, his eyes heating with a powerful love. He kissed her softly on the mouth, leaning down to her ear.

Her smile widened, her cheeks reddening.

He grinned, kissed her again and looked my way. "I'm going to make you manager of Rod's Construction. If you want to be, of course. I know you will need something to do to keep you occupied, and I'll pay you just as much as the Navy would. With everything that is going on, I need a strong minded person to take over my business. I'll miss you out on the field but we have to look out for you first."

"I would like that. I … When I was at the hospital, I was put on meds." Several weeks ago, I would have been ashamed to admit that. Mental health problems may have become the norm nowadays but I was a Navy SEAL. I survived more shit then most could even dream of. But admitting that I had a problem lifted a weight that had been bringing me down since I was a boy.

"Good," Angel said. "I know I can speak for all of us when I say this. We want you to be happy. Yes, it fucking sucks you won't be a SEAL anymore but—" Angel winked "—doesn't mean you won't overhear things or just happen to walk in on classified conversations."

"Yeah, because that would never happen," Dale said, fighting back a grin.

"Or maybe you just happen to be in the wrong place at the wrong time." Stone shrugged. "It happens, you know."

"And one of us could just get drunk and spill everything." Coby clapped a hand on my nape. "We're not perfect."

"What?" Dale gasped, gripping his chest. "I'm not?"

I chuckled. "Thank you. All of you."

"We love you, brother." Coby squeezed my neck.

"And I love you," Meeka whispered, kissing my cheek.

"I love you." I pinched her chin, placing a soft peck on her forehead before I turned to my brothers. "All of you."

EPILOGUE

Meeka

One month later...

I'M STILL TIRED. I'M still sore. And I'm still fucking hungry," Asher growled, coming toward me.

My body burned from just his words but I ran behind my bike, the machine shielding me from my boyfriend. My best friend. The man I loved more than I could ever say.

A wicked grin spread on his handsome face. "I'm coming for you, Meeka, and when I catch you, I'm going to fuck you on your bike. I will remind you that the only powerful thing between your thighs, is me."

Oh, dear God.

Asher had been insatiable, not leaving me alone since the whole incident with Charles. He didn't say, but I knew it had been because Charles touched me. Asher wanted to erase those memories and sear himself into my skin. And he had. Over and over again until I was begging him to stop and let me sleep. He rather enjoyed the fact that he fucked me into exhaustion.

When he caught me, he gripped my hair in his large hand, forcing my head back to meet his mouth. All thoughts were lost as he took over my soul. His tongue slid between my lips, his hands roamed over my body. His love poured into my being. I loved this man. Every broken inch. Every aching bone. Every dark desire.

With him, it was enough. Our love was strong. It had been for years even though it took a nightmare to bring it to light. His darkness had laid dormant, but I could still sense it at times. It would be a long while before he regained control of his thoughts. I knew he had killed his step-father and that he had help. I wasn't sure by whom. A knowing glance passed between Coby and Asher every so often. I couldn't be sure if Coby was the one who helped get rid of Elliott. They saved me the gory details. He knew I could handle it, but he didn't want to relive it when he had to replay it over and over in his mind. What could he have done different? Was death the only way? Did it make him feel better? It would be a long while before he was able to answer those questions but as time wore on and our love only grew, he would be able to look back with surety. Knowing it was the only way, he wouldn't get over it, but he would be able to deal with it. With everyone at his side, he would battle those impending thoughts.

"I love you, Hummingbird," Asher whispered against my mouth. "With you, I am strong enough to battle the war inside of my head. And because of that, I will forever be grateful."

Tears welled in my eyes at his sweet words, and I could only kiss him. Pouring my feelings into that small touch, I embraced the love he gave me and returned it with everything in me.

Asher Donovan was everything I needed.

It never crossed my mind that I could fall in love with my best friend, but I thanked God every day that I had. And because of that, my world became complete.

THE END

Grab Grim (King's Harlots, #3):
https://www.aboutjmwalker.com/grim

ABOUT

J.M. Walker is an Amazon bestselling author who also hit USA Today with Wanted: An Outlaw Anthology. She loves all things books, pigs and lip gloss. She is happily married to the man who inspires all of her Heroes and continues to make her weak in the knees every single day.

"Above all, be the HEROINE of your own life..." ~ Nora Ephron

Website: http://www.aboutjmwalker.com/
Facebook: https://www.facebook.com/jm.walker.author
Reader Group: https://www.facebook.com/groups/JMsJems/
Twitter: https://twitter.com/jmwlkr
Instagram: https://www.instagram.com/jmwlkr/
Goodreads: https://www.goodreads.com/author/show/51 32169.J_M_Walker
BookBub: https://www.bookbub.com/authors/j-m-walker
Amazon: https://tinyurl.com/y7dpjkud
Newsletter: https://tinyurl.com/ya9hycak

Want more? Head on over to my website for my

complete backlist!

https://www.aboutjmwalker.com/books